Feeling That Way

Kat Ryan

To Taylor Swift -

Thanks for reminding me to dance through the lightning
strikes.

From one eldest daughter to another.

Chapter 1

Small-Town Living

Jules

My eyes blurred as I scanned another spreadsheet. How much longer was I going to do this to myself? Don't get me wrong, this office was light-years better than the one I'd been killing myself at in Chicago. And if my lifelong dream was to be an accountant, this would be a great job. However, that wasn't the dream anymore. It was something I was good at and did enjoy, but the schedule wasn't sustainable. Or it hadn't been. As a result, for now I was going to kick ass as the best new accountant in Sue's small firm here in Highland Falls and attempt to figure out my life.

"Jules, you doing okay?"

I turned to see Sue, my new boss. Sue was in her late sixties and a friend of my aunt Lou. I would have been concerned that she'd given me this job as a favor to Lou, but I knew my own worth and it was tax season. Sue needed help, though they were far more caught up here than I would have thought when she told me I'd be doing her a favor...

I rubbed my eyes and tried to look more alert than I was. "I'm good, thanks."

She made a disapproving sound and pulled out a chair at my table. "Sweetheart, I don't know how things ran at that place you were at up north, but I know your aunt shared the toll it took on your health. I'm not speaking bullshit when I tell you I want the people who work here to look after themselves. I know it's tax season, but there is also a reason I brought you on staff—none of us are working ourselves to an early grave on my watch. If you aren't doing well—mentally *and* physically—then you aren't any good to me. No use martyring yourself on our behalf—the returns will get done and without you running yourself ragged, you hear me?" She looked at me over the top of her funky reading glasses. "This is important work, don't get me wrong, but it is not more important than your life." She stood up, pushing her chair in as she gave me another no-bullshit look. "Remember that."

And with that mic drop, Sue trotted down the hall without a backward glance. She might be in her late sixties, but she didn't look like it. Today her long gray hair was pulled into a low ponytail, and she wore a yoga outfit that said she'd been to Nomad Yoga at some point this morning. The woman lived the message she spoke—work-life balance. Maybe I'd figure it out by her age? I could only hope.

I shook my head to re-center and sat up straight in my office chair, stretching my back from side to side and trying to work out a kink. Unsuccessful, I reached for my coffee cup and took a swig. Cold. When did that happen? I thought about heading to the staff room to get a warm-up, but Sue's disapproving look appeared in my mind. Maybe it was time to get out of here for a bit.

With a glance at my watch, I did a double take. It was

already just before three in the afternoon. I hadn't had lunch—hell, I hadn't moved from this desk since nine this morning. No wonder the coffee was cold and my back was irritated. Welp, that settled that. Time to go.

Within a few minutes, I was packed up and out the door. If necessary, I'd get another hour in from home, which was another benefit to working for Sue, though I'd clocked enough hours last week that I knew I was good. Hell, Sue would probably be irritated if I put in more time, but I could make that call in a bit. I could swing by the Sanctuary Café and then head home. Some more coffee, something to eat, and a leisurely walk on this early-April day sounded like perfection.

Sue's accounting firm was just off the square in downtown Highland Falls, my new community. Moving here from Chicago had been a shock to the system at first, but after almost two weeks, I was starting to adjust. I'd lived in a Chicago neighborhood called Lakeview since I graduated from college, and even though it was part of a huge city, there was still the feel of community. Everywhere you went, there were great walkable areas with shops and restaurants. I'd say it was like its own small town, but in such a different way. I'd loved it but was starting to appreciate living in a smaller town too. The pace seemed more relaxed, which was something my nervous system welcomed.

As I crossed one street and headed up Main, I marveled at the lack of traffic. Heck, my older-than-dirt car hadn't left the driveway since I got here, which worked for me. I was babying that thing as long as I could because the idea of buying a new car seemed like a waste of money. Here I could get anywhere I needed within minutes by walking from my place, same as in Chicago, thus the reason I was still driving my car from high school.

Moving from one of the largest cities in America to one of roughly ten thousand people with two traffic lights was a bit of adjustment but one I'd needed, though I hadn't seen that when the idea was first shoved upon me.

See, my mom had sounded the alarm a month ago when she visited me as she and Dad were passing through Illinois. According to her big sister Lou, she'd called in distress and stated that my eyes were "lifeless" and I seemed to be at the end of my rope. Now, Lou and I were both well aware that my mom was prone to dramatics. My dad knew it too. Mom's motto was that everything was better with a touch of her flair, but she had a point, as much as I hated to admit it. I had been simply burned out and wasn't taking care of myself.

Was it the huge accounting firm that I worked for that was sucking me dry? That was what Mom and Lou decided, and I guess it was partly true. Mostly true. Unlike Sue, the firm didn't give the first shit about work-life balance, just that you got the work done even though everyone there was working so much overtime they were drowning. They cared so little that quitting was a matter of filling out a form online and packing up my stuff. Safe to say there were no heartfelt goodbyes or thanks for a job well done. I'd be replaced by another cog in their wheel and forgotten in a matter of days. Frankly, it said little about how I'd spent the past almost eight years. But they weren't completely to blame for my current state of exhaustion. In reality, there was also the little, or maybe not so little, secret I'd been keeping for the past five years, and most people would never guess. Shy, introverted Jules Maxwell was also a steamy-romance author named Jules Jenkins.

You might ask why that was a secret, why I wouldn't tell anyone that I wrote romance books? Well, at first it was because I thought it was just something for me. One day, after four years at my firm, I'd come home and thought I might scream if I looked at another spreadsheet. And as awesome as Lakeview was, I didn't know very many people when I first got there and wasn't close to a whole lot of them even when I left. That might have something to do with my introverted nature, but I digress.

I had been at home and mindlessly started to open another romance book on the app on my phone when *poof,* I thought of a character and she popped into my head, fully formed. That wasn't terribly surprising—stories had always comforted me. They were my go-to when I needed a break from the world, but I hadn't written for myself since I was in middle school.

That day, however, my imagination went wild as I brainstormed a backstory for my heroine, then a love inter-est. Thinking *what the hell did I have to lose*, I started typing. What I found in the months that followed was that writing that story gave me the clear mind I needed to go back to work and look at those numbers. For a while it provided a balance of sorts between work and home. Writing allowed creativity that my job didn't. It allowed me to create a world I wished I could inhabit with characters who felt like friends. It continued to be just that as I finished a few books, learned how to indie publish them and put them online, thinking maybe they'd bring joy to some-one, and went on to dream up new stories. To me it was still just a way to find a reset in my life. Well, that was until my third book gained traction on social media. Then the shit hit the proverbial fan.

My royalties from my books were trending to outpace my salary as an accountant. Hell, it likely already happened with my move down here considering the cost of living—

and my salary—was drastically lower. Yet I was hesitant to give up the security of a nine-to-five job, much less the benefits. Health insurance was a big deal and all.

So why not just keep doing both jobs? That would be possible if it was just setting aside time to write. However, writing didn't only involve creating a story. There was social media, newsletters, advertising, and so much more. Add that to a job as an accountant and in tax season no less, and I was wondering how I was going to make it even at my new firm with much more doable hours. God forbid I ever decided I wanted a life outside of work and writing—there wouldn't be time.

I came to a stop in front of the coffee shop, marveling that I'd already reached it and apparently just in time. The gray sky had been ominous my entire walk here, and I felt the first drop as I opened the door.

Lou had been after me to stop by this café and get to know the owners since I arrived in town, but I hadn't made it a priority. It felt too much like she was trying to set me up on a playdate. There were a handful of women my age in town that Lou was convinced I'd be friends with, and one of them owned this place. Another owned the bookstore. Several worked at the library. I couldn't keep track, but I got a text daily from her, encouraging me to stop in a variety of places and say hello from her. She meant well, but I struggled to put myself out there. I did much better on my own in my small comfort zone. O'Malley, my cat, was enough for me.

But this café was familiar even if much of my new home wasn't. Lou had opened this place decades ago and ran it successfully until selling just three or so years ago. Whenever my parents decided to visit, we'd always stop at the café even if it was just on our way out of town. I wasn't sure what it would be like now that it wasn't Lou's.

Still, my rumbling stomach told me that it could do with a snack of some substance, and I was not in the mood for anything I had in my kitchen, so in I went. Stepping through the doors onto the worn wood floors, I scanned the room. Not much had changed. Looking around, you could still see the ghost of the church this once was. Now there was an eclectic vibe with mismatched tables and chairs, some low tables with couches, and large comfy armchairs strewn about for you to curl up in. Even though it was three in the afternoon, there were people scattered all over—some working, some reading, some visiting. Music flowed from speakers around the space, and I smiled at hearing the latest Taylor Swift song's refrain. Well, if the owner liked Taylor, we already had something in common. Point in Lou's favor in setting up my friendships. And kudos to the new owners. This place felt as great as ever.

As I moved over to the counter to order, I paused at seeing a six-foot-tall cardboard cutout of Jason Momoa standing to the side. I was still lost in confusion when a voice broke through.

"Hey there, Jules, I've got a bone to pick with you."

I turned and saw that a woman had appeared behind the counter. She had piled her long blond hair on top of her head in a knot, and her graphic T-shirt said IT's ME. HI. I'M THE PROBLEM IT'S ME.

I snorted, took her in, and realized she was familiar. Before I had to think too long, I remembered her from when I'd gotten to town and gone to dinner at the brewery with Lou and her friends.

I paused, trying to pull up her name. Hmm. Something with an *M*. Mae? No. Maeve, if I remembered correctly. I shuffled through the bios Lou had been peppering me with over the past two weeks in her effort to give me a social life. If I had the right person, Maeve's sister owned the café, and I thought I remembered Lou saying Maeve was new to town and was going to be a part owner here.

Moving toward her with a few butterflies in my stomach that always appeared when I wasn't certain about something, I reached out a hand. "Maeve, right? And before you get into this bone you'd like to pick, what's up with the two-dimensional Momoa?"

Maeve nodded toward the cardboard cutout. "That's Flat Max, a nod to our Momoa-look-alike friend who works at Highland Woods and is married to Emma from the library. He gives Allyson good advice whether it's the cutout or the in-the-flesh version." Maeve clasped my hand in both of hers, moving on like what she'd just said made any sense. "I'd hug you if this counter wasn't in the way. But back to my bone—why haven't you called?"

My face heated, and I was certain the flush would spread to my neck. So that was her issue. I chose to play ignorant. "For what?"

She shook her head at me. "I gave you my number, remember? At the Homestead? We need to have dinner, and I'll introduce you to the ladies in town. Getting to know folks in a small town isn't always easy—I can help."

It was true. I thought back to my exhausted arrival; Maeve had given me her number when I first met her. However, I'd assumed she was doing it to be polite more than actually wanting to get together.

"Oh, sorry." I bit my lip. The stupid insecurity that had plagued me since childhood rose up. I always felt like others were better at social interactions than I was. I never seemed to read people correctly. That was why fictional stories were easier.

Maeve studied me for a minute, then kindly changed the topic and gestured at the case in front of her. "What can I get you today?"

Relaxing at the easier direction of conversation, I looked at the case and my mouth watered.

"Sorry." Maeve pulled me out of my thoughts, and I looked back up at her, confused as to why she would apologize. "We usually have more offerings, but we close in an hour, so we're down to these choices."

This was a smaller assortment than normal? I mean, I'd take any of it. I pointed out a ham-and-cheese croissant and ordered a vanilla latte. Maeve sent me on my way after I paid, saying she'd bring it over and I could pick a seat.

I scanned the place and selected a deep leather armchair near a window with a low table between it and another chair. They both faced the windows, and I liked the idea of shutting out the folks in here that I didn't know and just watching the dreary April sky.

My current work in progress was at a tricky spot, and some daydreaming might be just what I needed. Contrary to what so many people seemed to believe, my characters weren't people from my real life and the sex scenes certainly weren't a documentary. Hell, if that were the case, a barren desert would be a more apt metaphor. What *was* real in my books was music I listened to, places I'd been, conversations I'd overheard, bits and pieces of people I'd seen. I stole it all, mixed it in a blender, and out popped a romance. If I was lucky. Sometimes it was more akin to trying to build a house in the middle of a tornado.

And this story was one of those being constructed in the midst of a storm. I wasn't sure if it was the fault of the story or my new awareness of readers, but the pressure was getting to me. I'd already had my fourth book ready for publication when book three took off, so I'd had no issue there. But writing book five was far harder than it should have been.

As I lost myself looking out the window, I felt someone next to me and looked to my left. Maeve gave me a smile as she placed my order on the table between us before curling up in the other armchair with her own coffee. She looked over her mug with light in her eyes, almost a mischievous glint. The hum of conversation from the café's patrons surrounded us as a soft rain drizzled down the window. I felt cocooned for the moment. Safe.

"Maeve." I acknowledged her as I picked up my coffee and gave her the room to say whatever it was she needed to get out. The first sip hit me with surprise—it was far and away one of the best vanilla lattes I'd had. Considering Dark Matter in Chicago had spoiled me for excellent coffee, that was saying something.

"Jules." She took another sip, then said in a gentle voice, "I get the feeling that you and I are opposites in terms of personality."

"Oh?" My heart sank. Was she trying to say she didn't want me to call her after all? While I was nervous about having a new friend, if I was honest, I also truly wanted one. It was a conundrum that I didn't understand myself.

Maeve gave me a gentle smile. "I just mean that you seem a bit more reserved than I am, and I don't want to force you into a social gathering if you aren't interested." She wrinkled her nose. "I haven't lived here—officially— very long, just a few weeks, but I've visited often. Your aunt can be a force of nature, but I don't want you to feel oblig- ated to hang out with us."

I covered my face as a snort escaped. "Lou, a force of nature? Yeah, that's an apt description." Taking a breath, I worked to calm my nerves. "And thanks. Honestly, I'm jealous of your ease at talking to strangers, but I'd love to meet you and your friends for dinner sometime. I promise to work on coming out of my shell because I'd rather fast-track some friendships if possible. It took several years to find a few people I was comfortable around in Chicago." Come to think of it, I hadn't heard from any of them other than Kylie since I left, so not sure how strong those friendships were to begin with. I guess I'd call most of them acquaintances and doubted I'd see them again.

Maeve's smile widened. "Excellent. How do you feel about an early dinner in a couple of hours? Homestead? Some of the women I'm friends with are open, and we're meeting there at five."

I swallowed down the strong inclination to say no and race home to hibernate instead. "Sounds good. Guess this croissant will be my appetizer?"

Maeve held up her coffee cup to click it with mine. "We'll see you at five, chickie."

Chapter 2

Dinner Plans

N*oah*

I stood outside the local elementary, scanning the kids as they exited the building. The long line of cars for pickup made me grateful, once again, for my home just off the downtown area. It was less than a half mile from my place to Addie's school, and I didn't have to deal with the hell of waiting in that line. The light rain had let up, but the gray skies made me worry more might be on the way.

"Daddy!"

Addie's screech from across the playground brought me back to the present, as I'm sure it did for anyone within earshot. My girl tore out of the line and ran at me, ignoring anything that was in her path. I crouched down with my arms outstretched and worked to brace against her eventual force. She might be small, but she was mighty.

When she hit my chest, I wrapped my arms around her and stood up, marveling once again that I'd had a hand in creating this perfection.

"I missed you so much," Addie whispered against my neck.

My smile couldn't be contained. "I missed you too, sweetheart. It's been a long two days." I also had to admit that I missed her calling me Daddy One, which she had for a bit when Jake and her mom got engaged. He was Daddy Two; I was Daddy One. At some point she asked if I cared if we were both Daddy, which was—of course—fine. I just loved hearing the way she'd draw out the "one" as she ran at me.

"I know," Addie said mournfully, ignorant of my stroll down memory lane, as she kicked her legs and slid down my body until her sparkly purple rain boots hit the ground. "Why did you have to go out of town?"

I knew time worked differently when you were almost six, though two days seemed like a long time for me too now that I was used to seeing Addie regularly. Her mom and my childhood friend, Ivy, lived only a few blocks from me. Addie was used to going between our houses since I moved to Highland Falls a year and a half ago.

Heck, I lived in the house Ivy and Addie had when they first moved to Highland Falls. Once she and Jake had gotten engaged, they moved out and Ivy had asked me to move in. I knew that to many, our family dynamic was odd, but I thought it was perfect. Ivy and I had started dating in college after a long friendship, but we'd never considered it a long-term thing since I had planned to head to Africa to help with water access once I saved up enough funds. When she got pregnant shortly after graduation, we acknowledged that we both felt we were far better off as friends. After all, we'd started that way in childhood, commiserating over parents who were more concerned about their social status than being decent parental figures.

Our romantic relationship was more of convenience than any romantic chemistry, and I was grateful every day for the loyalty I had in Ivy, even when I didn't always feel deserving of it.

See, the thing was, I wasn't sure I'd ever forgive myself for continuing with my plans to go to Africa after graduation once I found out I was going to be a dad. It had been important work, but it meant I missed much of Addie's first four years. Ivy swore she hadn't resented me for being gone, but I couldn't say the same for myself. One night in Kenya, I had looked at a picture of Addie that I carried around and decided I was never getting this time back. Within weeks, I'd convinced the company to get me a stateside job that was heavy on remote work, and I'd headed to a small town in Illinois to try to make up for lost time with my daughter.

Arriving in Highland Falls almost a year and a half ago, I hadn't known how receptive Ivy would be for me to change things up and become an actual part of Addie's life. True to her nature, she'd been more than generous. She and Jake had shifted to a shared parenting structure without hesitation as I reminded her along the way that I wanted to make Ivy's life easier and not harder.

Our changes had been gradual. We'd started with me picking up Addie from school a few days a week and tried for dinner together one night. Now we alternated where Addie lived every other week, depending on my work schedule. It wasn't unusual for all of us to get together for a family meal no matter where Addie was staying.

Part of me felt like I'd asked for too much, but both Jake and Ivy had worked to assure me that wasn't the case. With their new baby Lorelai arriving this past December, I knew it helped them when Addie was with me, but I still felt like I hadn't earned it.

Looking down at Addie with her hand in a tight grip in my own, I marveled at her curious nature. We were walking toward my place and her gaze was all over the place, but she was silent.

Since she typically spoke a mile a minute, I figured I should ask. "What are you thinking about, Ads?"

Her blond head turned toward me, and I noted her eyes were open wide. "Plants are magical."

I smiled, thinking of her mom, who strongly identified as a green witch. "Agreed, Sunshine. But what has that on your brain?"

She dropped my hand to gesture at the tall oaks and hackberries standing sentinel on Main Street as we headed to my block. "Look at the trees. Bare. But in just a few weeks..." She mimed an explosion with her hands. "Magic."

I laughed at the gravity in her voice as I took in our surroundings. "Yep, there should be some green appearing by the end of the month for sure."

"And..." Addie paused, tugging my hand till I crouched down by her. Her voice lowered to a whisper, like she was sharing some big secret. "Momma planted so many tulips at Daddy's house last fall. Any day now... Bam." Another hand explosion crossed with jazz hands.

I gave her a serious look. "Do you remember planting tulips up my front walk with me last fall?"

Addie's mouth made a perfect O. "I forgot." Her voice was hushed. "Oh, Daddy, that's going to look so good."

I nodded in agreement and stood up to continue our walk home. Addie swung our hands as I mulled over what we needed to accomplish tonight. I'd gotten my work done before picking her up today so I could be present. The never-ending guilt over the time missed with Addie drove me. I briefly wondered if that would ever go away before I began thinking of more practical matters of the night ahead. "All right, Sunshine, dinner tonight is salad and English muffin pizzas. Sound good?"

"Yep." She tried her hand at skipping for a minute, which was not smooth, but she was getting there. "Can I use American cheese and make it like a jack-o'-lantern?"

"You bet." I thought over the typical homework she had in kindergarten. "Then we'll read. Do you have anything else for school?"

She dropped my hand to nod and then do a few twirls, making the sparkly tutu she still loved wearing over leggings fly up around her. "I have a story I need to cut apart and glue down in order." She paused to pass me her backpack for easier twirling.

"Sounds good. Want to play when we get home, or do you want to get the work done first?" Ivy had taught me that Ads was a relatively easy kid when you presented her with options. Parenting win if either option was fine with you but gave her some control.

She spun in place and looked up at me with big eyes. I knew a big ask was coming. "Daddy, can I go play with Chief and *then* go home and do my work?"

I bit back an internal groan. Chief was Jake's dog, or now Jake and Ivy's pup. The bond between Addie and that animal was strong. Heck, the dog had raced in front of a car to shove Addie out of the way a year and a half ago, getting struck by the car for his trouble. It happened right when I was moving to Highland and was by far one of the worst experiences I'd ever been through. Luckily Addie was fine and Chief had fully recovered, but I'd pretty much do anything for that dog, including interrupt my plans for a quiet afternoon.

With a look at the time on my cell, I opened my group text with Ivy and Jake, which Ivy had named Fam Jam.

Me: *Ms. Addie has a burning desire to play with Chief. Anyone home?*

Ivy: *At bookstore. Will be in thirty.*

Jake: *I'll be home at the same. Come on by. Chief will be excited.*

I looked down at Addie, who was watching with a hopeful gaze. "Sunshine, we can go over in thirty and they'll be home. How does work first and then Chief time sound?"

"Thank you, Daddy!" Addie squealed as she wrapped her arms around my legs and rocked back and forth on her rain-booted feet. With that, she grabbed my hand and began marching down the street toward home.

A little over half an hour later, we were headed back toward the downtown of Highland Falls as Addie told me her latest version of the Little People stories. Jake had started them when he and Ivy began dating. Apparently they were stories his parents had told him and his siblings. Addie loved to create her own and share them with me. I adored her imagination; it was something to behold. Sometimes I thought of my own parents and how little they'd seemed to care about what I was thinking or dreaming up as a kid. After having Addie, I recognized there was something wrong with them, not me. How they didn't appreciate the beauty of parenting would never cease to astound me.

Addie walked down the sidewalk, singing the sound of the Little People's drums. "Da da dum dum du, da da dum dum dum... And you know what they were, Daddy?"

I knew my part here after a year and a half of stories. "They were bug-eyed?"

"Yes!" Addie squealed. "I saw them walking into the basement through the missing brick, with their music instruments and everything." Jazz hands accompanied that last bit.

"Interesting. What were they doing in our house?" I asked, curious where she was going to take this.

"Daddy." Addie gave me a serious look and waved me closer. "They were checking out if you would be a good home for a doggy."

Well, shit. It had been several months since Addie had been on her last kick of telling me I needed a pup. I'd thought she might have forgotten about it.

"Sweetheart, we've talked about this. I travel one weekend every month and then to Africa at least once a year. I'm not sure my house is the best for a puppy." My inner eight-year-old was shouting at me that Addie was right. Lord knows I was never allowed to have a pet when I was young.

"Well, Daddy, the Little People told me they thought you were ready." And before I could put forth a counterargument, she saw the man of the hour. "Chief!"

I laughed and watched the back of her head as she ran up the drive to Jake and Ivy's backyard. She was through the gate and racing the lab around the fenced-in perimeter within seconds. I shook my head and headed in the back door.

Jake Spencer looked up from his spot in front of the open fridge. "Hey man, beer?"

I nodded, and he passed over one of his brewery's cans, Black Hole Sun, which was a great IPA.

"Glad you texted." Jake pulled out a chair and sat at the farmhouse table in their kitchen. "Chief will be thrilled, and God knows we can always use Addie to wear the old guy out and give him an earlier bedtime. Sometimes that crazy pup wants to go on a walk at eleven p.m. But when he and Addie hang, he's ready to head to dreamland by ten at the latest."

I gave him a second glance and took note of the shadows under his eyes. I did some mental calculations as to Lorelai's age and the little I knew about babies as I moved to sit down with him. "Lorelai not sleeping through the night yet for you?" I cracked open the beer and took a sip.

He shook his head.

"Is that typical?" I felt like a colossal idiot for not knowing the answer to that question when I had an almost-six-year-old daughter, but that was my reality and Jake was well aware of it.

"Ivy says the average baby doesn't sleep through the night until six months, which isn't till June, so time will tell." A noise caught his attention, and he looked toward the front of the house. "Speaking of..."

I followed his smile and saw Ivy walking in with their baby in a sling strapped to her chest. Baby Lorelai's dark hair just poked out, but she was clearly snoozing.

Jake quickly moved to Ivy and kissed her cheek, then ran his hand over Lorelai's head and back before the two of them headed back to the table. I was struck by the connection between them, just as I had been the first time I'd met Jake a year and a half ago.

Others struggled to understand how I could be around my ex and her husband and not be jealous. What Ivy and I knew and couldn't seem to explain was that we were friends first, and even though that dynamic changed for a bit, our friendship was what felt right. It was like our brief romance was trying on a pair of pants that didn't fit. They might look good, but you knew you didn't want to wear them often.

I wanted Ivy in my life as a friend—she was my oldest one at this point and for sure my most loyal. I'd never regret our relationship, and I knew she felt the same because Addie came out of it. And I was damn grateful that Jake understood and had become someone I could turn to as well.

"Hey Noah." Ivy turned toward me and kissed my cheek before sliding into the chair next to me. "Ads just had to see Chief, did she?"

I shook my head and gave her a rueful smile. "You know our girl. And now she's on me to get a dog of my own. Says the Little People have spoken."

"Oops, sorry," Jake murmured. "Not that I told her to hit you up for a pup, just introduced the stories."

"Not your fault, man." I looked over my friend, who had matching shadows under her eyes. "You all want me to take Lorelai for a bit tonight when Addie and I go? She was fine last month at my place. Well, at least she was for a few hours." Man alive. I remembered when the baby realized Ivy wasn't there. She sure did have a set of lungs for a tiny one, but I'd been happy to babysit for them.

Ivy gave me a tired smile. "You are too kind. And no, we'll make it. Last night was just a rough one—she's teething and pissed about it. However, we've had a brainstorm and were just talking about having dinner at the brewery because she sleeps better when we're in noisy spaces before bed. Harder for her to snooze through dinner, you know? You and Ads want to join us?"

Hmm, the brewery hadn't been my plan for dinner, but some time out with friends sounded great. "Let me ask her, and we'll go from there. She planned on English muffin pizzas."

"With American cheese for jack-o'-lanterns?" Jake was aware of Addie's favorites. Hell, once I'd come back, he'd taught me everything he learned about my own kid. Seeing her less than ten times by the age of four hadn't allowed me to really gain any knowledge of my own. Now, though, I'd become an expert.

"You know it." I headed to the back door and opened it, sticking my head out to yell at Addie. She and Chief were having a conversation over by a swing set that Drew, Jake, and I had spent hours, and I do mean hours, putting together last fall. "Ads, how about we switch to Homestead for dinner with Momma, Daddy, and me?"

Addie's blond head swiveled in my direction, and her arms shot up. "Yeah!" Immediately she stood up and shimmied in place. Chief watched, used to the antics.

With a laugh, I turned from her back to the kitchen. Ivy looked over at me with twinkling eyes. "So you're in."

"Yep." A chill night at the Homestead with those I loved. Sounded good to me.

Chapter 3

Mortification, Party of One

J*ules*

I scanned the table I was sitting at in awe. We were in the brewery, at a low table near the bar. So far I still had all the names down pat. It was a lot easier to keep track of all these people Aunt Lou had told me about once I'd met them because, spoiler alert, these were the folks she had thought I'd enjoy spending time with. I was still debating whether I was going to admit to her that she had been right or not. Lou didn't need any more validation of her "rightness" in the world—she had that in spades.

But these women? I was tentatively excited about the possibilities of so many friends so quickly in a new town. At this table tonight, let's see, there was the library crew: Grace, Emma, and Elle. The café sisters: Allyson and Maeve. The yoga contingent: Kristine and Kate. Maggie worked at the school but was best friends with Emma from the aforementioned library. My mind positively whirled. They were so welcoming but seemed to accept that I liked to sit back and observe more than stand up on the table and dance. Not that anyone had done that, but I had a feeling that Maggie would be open to it. And maybe Maeve. Not sure where the rest of the crew would fall yet.

Speaking of, I'd left Maeve at the café and raced home after getting coffee with her. That gave me just enough time to feed O'Malley and have some quality conversation with him about how maybe I should just stay home, to which he'd promptly turned his back on me and stalked off. Oh well, point taken.

I'd looked at my clothes, debating if what I was wearing was okay or not. Finally, I decided to go with the outfit I was wearing. Sue's firm was a blessed change from my Chicago one. A dress code was nonexistent, as was evident in my boyfriend jeans and baggy white hoodie. Heck, even my shoes wouldn't have passed the test a few weeks ago. Sneakers, trendy or not, were a no-go at my old firm. I loved my Nikes and was thrilled I got to wear something daily that I was comfortable with. If only I could create more hours in the day and continue to do both my jobs.

Before I could spiral into anxiety about my current to-do list coming from both jobs, a text from Maeve told me to march my happy ass down the street and hit the brewery or she was coming to find me. A glance at the clock on my phone told me I wasn't late, but she was sending a preemptive strike. That was fair.

I arrived at the brewery and headed in, my stomach tied up in knots. This was nothing new; I'd been this way my whole life. Meeting new people, going places for the first time, having to figure out how to get somewhere or where to park—all surefire experiences that would make my anxiety bubble up. I wouldn't say it had gotten better as I'd gotten older, just that I knew to expect it and that it would eventually go away.

Fortunately, I was only a handful of steps into the brewery and talking to Laurie, the hostess, when I heard my name. We both turned to see Maeve waving from the bar area. I felt the smile on my face grow as I said goodbye to Laurie and headed over. Seeing Maeve's welcoming expression helped. So did the flurry of introductions accompanied by hugs and explanations of the connections between the women gathered. I felt like I was being ushered into a group where I wanted to belong.

Turned out all the ladies knew Lou, and many had stories on her. That was okay—I did too. I knew my aunt, and she was happiest when being her busybody self. She'd known all the gossip in town when she ran the coffee shop. I didn't know where she got her info now, but it was still part of her currency.

"Jules, you've got to tell us what it was like growing up with Lou as your aunt," Maggie said as she sat down after grabbing drinks at the bar. She handed seltzers to Emma and Allyson, both of whom were visibly pregnant.

I could feel the eyes all turn in my direction and marveled for a moment that it didn't make me feel as queasy as it normally would. I'd have to think on that reaction later. Still, I slid forward and decided how to explain my family. "My mom and Lou are fourteen years apart, my mom being the younger sister."

"Fourteen." Grace nodded. "I thought Lou might have been your great-aunt. Are there loads of siblings between them?"

"Nope." I shrugged a little, thinking about Mom's family. "I'm not sure if Mom was a surprise or if they just couldn't get pregnant for a while after Lou. I was young when my grandparents passed. Lou has always been there for me though. My mom's pretty dramatic..."

"Compared to Lou?" Maeve interrupted, her tone saying that Lou was no straitlaced woman.

I paused, thinking of how to compare the two. "I mean, I think Lou looked out for my mom. I'd imagine their relationship wasn't the normal sibling one when there was such an age gap. And yes, Lou's always been... well, who she is. But my mom has a flair of her own." I thought of how best to describe my mom who, though she drove me mad, was one of my favorite people. "What I'm saying is that she could be on a stage with the way she reacts to everything. Does that make sense? My dad just rolls with it, always has. The two of them are funny, love the heck out of me, but I look to Lou for any sense of stability..." I thought of my mom's lack of concern about things like bills or groceries. Unfortunately, Dad did not help there either—they lived life thinking things would just "work out." Not that we were ever destitute, just that sometimes as a kid, I'd wondered if we were going to be okay.

"That must have been so hard." Emma reached over and squeezed my hand.

"Yeah." Maggie gave me a compassionate look from across the table. "I understand tight times when you're young. They have a lasting impact."

I sat at the table, looking around, fascinated at how different these women were but how they were clearly almost like a family to each other. And the level of kindness, even early stages of friendship, they were showing me wasn't something I was familiar with. I did casual friends where we talked about vacation plans, work frustrations. Talking about relationships with families, our own insecurities—that brought a level of vulnerability I wasn't familiar with. This was more aligned with the characters in my books than anything I'd experienced in real life.

Someone clearing their throat brought my attention back to the present. I looked up into the twinkling eyes of Lou. It was like we had conjured her from thin air.

"Excuse me, ladies. You causing all sorts of trouble tonight?" Lou asked.

"You know it, Lou," Allyson said as she put a hand on her pregnant belly. "Really out of control over here."

"For sure," Emma said, mirroring Allyson's actions with her own belly. From what Maeve had told me, Emma was due in May and Allyson in June. This group was doing their part to help grow the population of Highland Falls, that was for sure.

"Well, I'm glad to see you out tonight, Ms. Jules." Lou's warm eyes met mine. She was a meddling busybody, but her heart was in the right place.

"Thanks, Lou. Is Verdell here?" I asked, scanning behind her for my very understanding uncle.

"Nope, it's girls' night out. Jeanie and Hattie are with me." She nodded back to the dining room where I could see her two friends.

Maggie gave out a hoot. "And you were worried about us causing trouble? The three of you are surely plotting to take on some overlord tonight."

Lou scoffed. "As if one would dare mess with us."

I laughed as I looked from Jeanie and Hattie, who were singing along to the Chris Stapleton music that was playing, to Lou. Just then, my attention was snagged by a gorgeous man walking into the brewery. *Hello.* He could've literally walked right out of one of my romance books. Tousled honey-brown hair and, when he looked my way, piercing blue-gray eyes. He had stubble that indicated he didn't shave daily but did often enough that he wasn't sporting a full beard. And ignore my exploding ovaries—he was holding the hand of an adorable little girl. Why were competent dads such a turn-on? Do men get hot and bothered by decent moms? Fucking patriarchy. Bring on the matriarchy.

The little girl looked to be somewhere around five and had a style that was clearly all her own. Her leggings were striped, her outfit complete with sparkly rain boots, a tutu, and a purple hoodie. A blond woman was walking ahead of him, and I couldn't help but feel disappointed. Like this guy would be interested in me. Clearly I needed to get over myself.

Just then, another guy joined them. He also had dark hair but was a few inches taller and had a baby strapped to his chest. Hot guy number two leaned over and kissed the blonde before putting his hand on her lower back and leading her to another couch-and-armchair grouping in the corner of the bar. Smart man. I noted that the little girl let go of hot guy numero uno's hand and immediately went to the floor in the corner and began to spread out her coloring supplies.

I was drawn to the little family and, I had to admit, a little captivated by them. Maybe it was because I was in the midst of character development for my fifth book, but I couldn't help but draft a narrative for them in my head. In my dream world, the second guy and the woman were together. The baby was theirs. But the five-year-old looked enough like the woman that she had to be her mom. So who was that first guy? An uncle? Or could I dream up a friendship between the adults, leaving mystery man number one available for accountants who moonlight as romance authors?

"Earth to Jules..."

I looked over to Maggie to see that she was watching me

expectantly. Scratch that, so was the whole table, including Lou. Crap. Crap. Crappity crap. This wasn't good. If Lou got any ideas...

"See something that interests you?" Lou asked with a waggle of her eyebrows.

Damn, too late. One did not covet the focus of Lou Williams. Nope. It was far preferable to fly under the radar with my aunt.

"Hmm?" I worked to play ignorant. "Sorry, I didn't hear you. Tired, you know. Tax season." There. That was an acceptable excuse this time of year.

Lou watched me with an assessing glance. Then her smile became what could only be described as wicked. "Noah," she called at a volume that spoke to football games, not standing inside a brewery.

Shit. Hot guy number one looked over from his spot in the corner and smiled warmly at Lou. He tilted his head as if to ask why she was bellowing across the room at him.

Lou simply waved him over. The man turned to say something to his dinner companions as well as the little girl, then headed in our direction as the blonde waved in our table's general direction and the women I was sitting with waved back to her.

Mortification, party of one. Your table is now ready. I felt heat racing up my neck to my face. Redness commencing in three... two... one...

"Hey ladies," Mystery Man, now known as Noah, said when he reached our table. His name was familiar to me, though I wasn't sure why. Then he looked to Lou. "Causing trouble again, Ms. Lou?"

"Don't you know it." Her eyes sparkled. That was the only way to describe them, and after knowing the woman all my life, I knew what it meant. She was scheming.

My brain chose that moment as the time to hit me with a memory. Really just a flash of one. My stomach sank as it came rushing back. Two weeks ago, when I first arrived in Highland Falls, I'd come to the brewery with Lou and her friends. That was the night I'd briefly met Maeve, who'd made a comment to Levi about introducing me to her friends and given me her number. And then my ever-interfering aunt had said something about making sure a Noah was on the guest list. Wild guess that this was the Noah she'd referred to.

I had no words. Illinois was not known for chasms opening and swallowing people, but a girl could dream. I felt like not only had Lou been trying to arrange friendships for me, but now she clearly wanted to fix me up. I mean, bravo on the guy—he was my dream man come to life—but how pathetic did that make me?

"Noah, I believe you know what time of year it is," Lou began.

Oh, sweet Lord, I had a feeling I knew where this was going.

"Lou..." I warned in a severe tone hoping she'd get the message. Shots fired across the bow, but the woman gave zero fucks. I could feel the eyes of everyone on the table pinballing from Noah to Lou, to me, back to Noah.

Noah gave Lou a quizzical look, then scanned the faces of the women I was with before coming to stop on me. His expression was warm with something else there, but he looked back to Lou before I could think on it more. I was too busy cataloging the man's eyes as stormy sea blue and debating how I'd describe his hair in a novel. It helped me ignore the nausea welling up at Lou's match-making games. Tousled? Artfully messed up? Dark blond or honey brown? Long enough to hold on to. Damn, down girl. The correct description didn't exist, but I'd workshop it.

"Springtime?" Noah answered Lou's question about the time of year. Bless his innocent soul. Would he make a good cinnamon-roll hero? I felt certain of it.

"True, it is spring..." Lou replied. Then, with a sly glance in my direction, she asked the question I'd known was coming. "However, I was thinking about something else. Who does your tax preparation?"

Someone at the table let out a snort of laughter. Okay, a few someones, but not me.

Yeah, that was a normal, everyday kind of conversation and not out of the blue at all. I slid my head down on the table as I felt Maeve pat my back in commiseration.

"You can't be surprised," she whispered.

True, I really couldn't be. Didn't change the desire to hide, but I'd work though that as soon as Noah fled our table.

Chapter 4

Here's to New Friendships

N*oah*

I tried to focus on what Lou Williams was saying, but I had to be honest—my attention was grabbed by the gorgeous stranger sitting at the table. I knew most of the women in town, of course, because Ivy knew no stranger and constantly introduced me to her ever-growing group of friends. But the woman sitting between Maggie and Maeve, looking at Lou with an expression of ever-growing horror—I was certain I hadn't seen her before. I tuned back in to Lou.

"...who does your tax preparation?" Lou gave me a raised brow and then nodded her head toward the dark-haired beauty. I'm not sure how tall Lou was, a hair over five feet maybe, with silver hair and an expression that said she knew what you were thinking, so watch your step. I noticed the woman Lou was indicating had lowered her head to the table while Maeve patted her back and whispered something in her ear. Maggie just grinned at me. What had I gotten myself into?

Um, tax prep? Odd Monday-evening conversation even for Lou. "Uh, I typically do it myself."

Lou shook her head, giving me a tsk-tsk-tsk sound of disappointment. "Don't you think you could benefit from a quality accountant? Perhaps one who is new to the area?"

I studied Lou as her eyes darted from me to the woman. She wagged her gray brows at me like I should be getting on board a lot faster than I was. I considered Lou and all the nonverbal communication she was sending. I honestly wasn't sure where this was going, but what the hell. It couldn't hurt and would likely be entertaining at the least. I'd learned the fastest way to deal with Lou was to just go along with her.

"Sure, who doesn't need an accountant at tax time?" I said, noting that Maggie's and Maeve's smiles became roughly two times larger than they had been. That alone indicated trouble because those two, from what I could tell, were kindred spirits with Lou, which meant we should all be on alert.

Still, being friendly to someone new to town was always good. And if it had something to do with the dark-haired woman, I was game. I wasn't looking to date anyone, but nothing said I couldn't help out when she'd been put on the spot by Lou. Might as well let Lou do her thing and make a new friend in the process. A drop-dead gorgeous one, but that was neither here nor there.

"Lou," the dark-haired woman groaned as she picked her head up and looked at her nemesis in this situation, also known as the town gossip. Lou was usually flanked by her two cohorts, Jeanie and Hattie, or her calming presence of a husband, Verdell. I scanned the restaurant and didn't see Verdell—the man was several inches over six feet and a tall, bald Black man at that, so he wasn't someone you would miss. However, I did see Jeanie's and Hattie's gray heads bent together, eyes on us. So there was no one to reel her in tonight, only to encourage her brand of whatever. Good to know.

"What?" Lou asked, trying for an innocent appearance it seemed. Of course, that looked completely wrong on her face.

"Please don't force me on anyone," the mystery woman murmured, her cheeks heating up with clear embarrassment.

"Noah, am I forcing Jules on you?" Lou sounded indignant.

I noted that Maggie coughed as Emma laughed. Maeve gave a sound that was akin to a cackle, which made Allyson snort. The rest of the ladies looked on like they were wishing they had popcorn to make a night of it. I was floored Ivy hadn't butted in to have a front-row seat but knew I'd be grilled about all this when I got back to our table.

Also noted, the mystery woman's name was Jules. That fit her somehow, which was crazy since I knew next to nothing about her. I reached across the table and held out my hand, deciding to put her out of her misery. "Hello, Jules. I'm Noah. How do you know this troublemaker?" I nodded toward Lou.

Jules's small hand slid into my grip, and there was... something. My stomach was suddenly unstable. The excitement I felt before a big game in high school was present, but that was a new one to come from a handshake. Something to think more about later.

Jules's voice was a whisper, so I stepped closer to the table even as I dropped her palm, the rest of the brewery fading from my attention.

"Lou is my aunt," she said.

Oh man. I mean, I had no family beyond Addie and our crew here in Highland to speak of because life was better for me when I didn't try to insert myself into the lives of my parents. I'd written them off after college, and they didn't seem to be too broken up about it. Probably because they'd turned their backs first. What would it be like to have an aunt like Lou? I guessed she'd be supportive but also a whole lot to deal with. Likely a riot at family gatherings. And Jules seemed to be someone who would prefer being able to fly under the radar if I was reading her right. Unfortunately for her, I don't think Lou knew the concept of living her life in the shadows.

I tried to lighten the mood. "Well, welcome to Highland Falls, Jules. Are you here visiting your aunt so she can get you clients for your accounting business? That's a new marketing strategy, I suppose." I gave her a small smile, trying to indicate that I knew what a cluster this was and didn't hold her responsible for one bit of it.

Jules's own expression appeared a little strained, but she shook her head like she was trying to clear her mind and take back control. Good luck with that. "I just moved to town two weeks ago and started working at Sue's firm. Do you know it?"

I wanted to high-five the woman for the backbone I could see growing before my very eyes. Go, Jules. "I do and, in a strange way here, Lou might have done us a favor. I'm sure I could use an accountant this year, though the big deadline is approaching and I don't want to cause you a headache."

"It's totally fine," she murmured.

"Okay. In that case, do you have a card or just want me to call the office tomorrow?"

I watched her fair skin flush again, the freckles across her nose and over her cheeks standing out in stark relief. She was wearing a white hoodie, which only made the flush more evident. And her long brown hair was swept on top of her head in some type of messy bun, allowing me to see the blazing trail of red up her neck. A foreign instinct rose inside me, wanting to reassure her, to take her out of the spotlight, but I held myself back. Jules didn't need me fighting her fights for her. If I even tried, Ivy would come over here and lose her mind. So there was that.

Jules bit her lower lip, worrying it between her teeth before speaking. "Um, since I just started down here a couple of weeks ago, I don't have any cards yet, but you can call the office." She hesitated before proceeding. "Or not. I mean, please don't feel like you have to."

I could see how uncomfortable she was, and I badly wanted to excuse myself so I wouldn't stress her anymore. I locked eyes with her, trying to convey the truth behind my words. "I absolutely don't feel like I have to, Jules. You're doing me a favor, so expect a call tomorrow." Her eyes widened, but she didn't look away, so I considered that a success. I glanced at the other women at the table and nodded at them all. "Ladies." I started to walk away but then thought better of it and turned to Lou. With a squeeze to her hand, I whispered, "Behave, Ms. Lou."

She squeezed back, and I noted that while her hands betrayed her seventy plus years on this earth, she was stronger than she appeared. Her eyes twinkled at me as she said, "Now Noah, where would the fun be in that?"

I shook my head at her and waved to the table so I could head back over to my own group. As I walked to where Jake, Ivy, and Addie sat—which was only twenty or so steps—I fought the urge to turn around and see if Jules was watching me. It felt like she was, but surely my mind was messing with me. Finally I reached our group and a leather armchair, my mind a mess.

Sliding into my chair, I looked to see Addie happily spinning in the corner, lost in the music that was pumping out the speakers, having a dance party of one. Her coloring supplies decorated the low table already, so she had made herself at home. Considering Jake was a part owner, she did spend a fair amount of time here, so that wasn't shocking. This was our normal table because it easily contained her free spirit with room to dance and color, but there was no concern about her wandering off. Tonight her blond hair had escaped her ponytail, and her tutu was flaring out as she spun. I loved that she was so comfortable in her own skin. Ivy had done so much right with our daughter. I hoped one day to see my impact on her too and prayed it was as positive.

Ivy and Jake had already ordered some appetizers. This was far from our first dinner together here, so they knew what I liked. It looked like they'd ordered up the usual: fried pickles, mac and cheese bites, and a beer for me plus their own drinks. I took a sip and relaxed, something I hadn't been able to do fully since we arrived.

I found my gaze drifting to the table I'd just left only to find Lou had gone back to her friends and Jules and Maeve were whispering, heads close together. As I watched them, lost in thought, suddenly Jules looked up and her eyes found mine. Heat filled my gut as I watched her cheeks redden again.

"Interesting, very interesting. Don't you think so, Jake?" Ivy said as she picked up a pickle and popped it in her mouth.

Jake had an arm around her shoulders and glanced over

from their spot across from me on the couch. "Babe, I'm assuming you are alluding to the fact that our friend Noah here can't seem to take his eyes off Lou's niece."

"What?" I began to protest, but Ivy held her hand up like she was waving away a bug.

"Oh no, my friend. Don't even start with fibs over here. I've known you since we were young, and you, sweet Noah, have the signs of attraction." Ivy leaned forward over the low table between us and beckoned me to come forward as well. Begrudgingly, I did so because I knew it would become a whole thing if I didn't. "And I, my dear Noah, am going to nurture this little flame until it grows because it has been forever and a day since I've seen this look on your face."

Fuck. That thought was internal because my daughter was here, of course, but it might bear repeating. Fuck. Ivy was a determined woman. Was I drawn to Jules? Of course. You'd have to be dead or, like Jake, in a perfect relationship not to be. Did I want to pursue those feelings? In another lifetime, sure. In this one I had one goal—making up lost time with Addie. I was a dad. Period. End of story. Maybe one day in the future I could find someone. But right now friendship was all I had time for. So I could be friends with Jules, and she'd get my taxes done for me. Here's to new friendships, right? It was a win-win scenario. No big deal.

I met Jake's gaze once I settled that in my mind.

"You're screwed, my friend," he said before taking a swig of beer.

Truth.

Chapter 5

Just Being Neighborly

J*ules*

I was a chicken. A coward. Yellow-bellied, what-ever that was. A fraidy-cat, a scaredy-cat, or both. Why? Because I was working from home so I wouldn't be at the office if Noah called.

I was disgusted even with myself. And yet no part of me could get out of bed and go to work. I simply couldn't. The mere thought of it had me wanting to upchuck. I would see the man again, I knew. This was a temporary, yet completely necessary, reprieve. Highland Falls was a small town, and that came with pros as well as cons. My rationale, however, was that if I wasn't there when he called, I was giving him the out the only way I knew how in case he truly didn't want an accountant. I felt horrid that Lou, in all of her conniving ways, had put the man on the spot the night before.

Maeve and Maggie had been sitting on either side of me, and they both told me I was overreacting, but it felt like Lou was setting me up with the guy. I mean, I know she'd said she just wanted to get my name out there as an accountant, but I wasn't born yesterday. She could have worked to find me more clients with her friends, with the women I met last night, with any random person she knew at the brewery because it felt like she knew the whole town. But had she? Nope. The *only* person she suggested I help with their taxes was Noah, and that was mortifying. And hell, we were in tax season—it wasn't like Sue *needed* more clients right now. One of the reasons I'd been hired so quickly was to help alleviate the workload of others.

I woke up this morning at six, and my mind immediately began to spiral. Before it could get too out of control, I thought of a former therapist's advice—*you can only control what you can control.* The fact of the matter was that I couldn't control Lou. Hell, beyond Verdell, I doubted anyone could, and I didn't know if even he was able to claim that ability.

Another thing that wasn't changing? My overall nature. I was who I was and, frankly, at thirty years old, I was good with that. Did I wish I didn't immediately become fire engine red when I was embarrassed? Sure. Was that also a bit of an overexaggeration? Yes, it was, but it felt true when my face was burning.

At any rate, when I woke up mired in some anxiety spiral about seeing and/or talking to Noah, I decided I had an out and I was going to use it. This was what I *could* control, so that's what I'd do. Sue had been after me to look after myself, and that was what I was doing. One call to her and I had her permission, no, her blessing, to stay home and work from here for the day.

She really was an amazing boss. I wondered once again how I could possibly keep two full-time jobs, because the more I worked for the lady, the more I wanted to. It was clear why her employees were so loyal. She created an amazing environment for her staff.

In the next five hours, my productivity soared. I tided the house, which likely hadn't needed it, and watered the plants, which absolutely had. I managed to get a half day's work done in three of those hours because I had zero interruptions like I might have had at the office. Then I spent the last hour folding myself into pose after pose, using yoga to try to find my center. Unfortunately for me, none of it was distracting me from the cowardly decision that had me stuck at home.

"Ahhhhhhhhhh," I growled to myself, coming out of downward dog. I moved to a seated position and put my hands on my knees, trying to let go and find some semblance of peace.

"Mwah?" O'Malley sat on the window seat, cleaning his long hair while he watched me with what amounted to not a small bit of disdain.

"I know, I know," I muttered. With a glance at my phone, I debated what to do next. I could get some more work done, though I was pretty caught up, or I could make some lunch. I also considered moving my afternoon work to my back deck since it was in the sixties and in Illinois, you took advantage of the weather when you could. Maybe a change of location would do the trick?

Standing up, I reached for the doorjamb that framed the bump-out window seat my cat liked to lounge in. I'd never seen anything like it—it was as if the former owners had decided to build a hiding spot off the kitchen that was the best lounging nook ever. Frankly, if the house had a bathroom, kitchen, and the window seat, I could live happy. There were steps up to the raised platform with a thick cushion—kind of like a built-in bed, bookshelves around the perimeter above your head, a wall I had propped a pillow against to lean back on, and windows overlooking the backyard. So far it was my favorite spot in the house.

As I held on to the opening for balance and grabbed my right foot to stretch my quads since they were perennially tight, I caught a movement from my neighbor's yard that had me diving back down to the floor.

Holy shit. Was that... I lifted back up and peered over the window seat and back out the window, looking at the man who had just walked into the yard behind my house.

Yep. That was Noah from the brewery because of course it is. Ahhhhh. Was he just visiting next door? I had met my neighbors on either side of me, but no one from behind my house yet. I took another glance. Yep, that was Noah pulling a mower out of a small shed. He lived there, right? That would make the most sense because unless he was just the kindest human ever, I doubted he'd just start randomly mowing yards.

Staying as far back from the window as I could—not that the man could see in, but still—I reached for my phone and texted the first person I could think of.

Me: *Umm, Maeve, do you know if Noah lives behind me?*

It took less than a minute to get a reply.

Maeve: *Hold on.*

Sure. No worries. Not freaking out over here or anything. Before I could panic too much, Maeve texted back, but this time it was in a group text with... One, two, four... Oh my god...Nine numbers plus mine. What the hell?

Maeve: *Ladies, we've got a Highland Falls hottie 911. Please reply with your name before I go on so Jules here can know who is weighing in.*

There were dots indicating people were typing as I contemplated moving back to Chicago. Was this what you could expect in a small town? Before I could pull up Zillow, names flooded in. Grace, Emma, Elle, Allyson, Kristine, Kate, Maggie, and—holy shit—Ivy. Ivy hadn't even been with us last night, but Maeve had pointed her out. And hell, Ivy was Noah's ex, though everyone telling me about the connections between Noah, Ivy, and Jake seemed to think they were the kind of exes who were good friends and also co-parented a child. Sweet Lord, I didn't know what to do, but I knew I wanted to flee. One thing was for certain, I was never leaving this house again.

Before I could put that plan into action, the group chat started flooding with more than their names and hellos to me. I quickly added all their contact info so I could follow the chat.

Maeve: *So, here's the situation. Our girl Jules just realized who her backyard neighbor is. Thoughts?*

Well, thanks Maeve. You could have just responded to my original text with a *yes, Noah lives behind you.* But now I was in some kind of group-text horror show, and I couldn't look away. It was like a car wreck on the side of the highway and getting worse by the minute. Seemed healthy.

Maggie: *I'm invested. What's he wearing, Jules? Can you see him right now?*

Emma: *Girl, behave.*

Maggie: *You should know this is me behaving.*

Grace: *This is true.*

Ivy: **Squeal* Maeve, thanks for adding me to this chat. Jules, hi! We didn't get to visit last night. Sorry. Now, important stuff, do you like said neighbor? Want me to put in a good word for you?*

Was I banging my head against my window seat? Yep.

Sure was. But there was a cushion, so it was more symbolic than anything.

Kate: *it might be important to remind you all at this juncture that not everyone is used to talking about all the intimate details of their lives like many of you.*

Kristine: *Kate, you're no fun.*

Kate: *you know I speak the truth.*

Allyson: *Sweet Lord, Maeve, talk about overwhelming a person new to town.*

Elle: *Jules, I'm here for support, but I'm one of those people Kate's referring to. No pressure from me.*

Elle's message had heart icons on it appear from Emma, Kate, and Allyson. I had a feeling I'd found my fellow introverts.

Maggie: *Are you insinuating that I'm pressuring anyone?*

Processing this chat in real time was something. These ladies must be voice texting, because the messages were coming fast and furious. I wasn't even sure where to interject.

Maeve: *No pressure, Jules. Just want you to know you have a team of women at your back and here for any conversations you want.*

Ivy: *I just realized my inclusion here might make you uncomfortable. Please know that I love Noah as my childhood friend and daughter's dad, but nothing said here would be shared with him. That being said, happy to hop out of this chat if that helps.*

Damn, the woman was kind as well as gorgeous? Of course she was. I couldn't let her think my hesitation had to do with her. I fired off a message.

Jules: *Hey all, I'm here. Ivy, no need to leave. Not sure what to say because there isn't much to say. Just wanted to* *know if I was seeing things correctly and Noah is my neighbor.*

There. That sounded nonchalant, right? Several folks "liked" my message, but then I saw someone was typing. Maggie's text came in.

Maggie: *Sure, babe. Whatever you need to tell yourself. Just know we're here for you if you want a different conversation. But yes, Noah lives in Ivy's old house, which is behind yours.*

Oh, I hadn't realized that. But then again, my entire interaction with Ivy had been a wave when Maeve and Maggie were filling me in last night. And now I was in a group text with her. Make it make sense.

Jules: *Good to know. Might take me a while to get used to the small-town vibes here. Thanks for the chat.*

I read, then reread, my text. I worried that I sounded bitchy or like I didn't appreciate the inclusive nature of this group. But that was all I had the bandwidth for right now, so I was going to let it go.

My phone lit up with another text. I glanced down and saw that it was Maeve.

Maeve: *Sorry, chickie. Was that too much? Wanted you to know you have a support system here. No woman left behind and all.*

Maeve was a lot, but I knew she meant well, so I put a heart on her message. I glanced out to see Noah still mowing his backyard. It would be okay, but that didn't mean I wanted to go out and say hey.

Instead, I headed to the kitchen to grab something that could be considered lunch. With a scan of my fridge and the cabinets, I settled on egg tacos. It was what I often ate when I wanted some protein but didn't want to think too much. Eggs scrambled up and placed in corn tortillas drizzled with olive oil and topped with cheddar, I slid them in the oven to do their thing while I cleaned up and worked to get my mind off my neighbor.

This place was perfect for me. A little Goldilocks-esque, it wasn't too big, and it wasn't too small. Lou had found it for me. For all I knew, she'd kicked out the former resident when I needed a place. I jest, but I bet she'd be tempted. It was a cottage with a stone chimney on the front. You walked into a giant open room—the front half of the house was a living room, the back half a kitchen with a ton of windows—and a farmhouse table split the two spaces, a bathroom to the side with the laundry. My favorite spot, the aforementioned window seat, jutted out in the back corner. I'd claimed it as my writing spot.

Upstairs were two small bedrooms and a bathroom. Clearly whoever built this place either loved plants or just really enjoyed natural light. I was a fan of both, so I was in heaven except for now when I walked around the lower level, wondering if Noah was able to see into the place from his backyard. Likely not, but...

Holy moly, did he already know I lived here? Had he been thinking I was stalking him yesterday? Would he just come over instead of calling Sue's today?

I began to spiral again, fully aware of it but unable to slow my mind. Of course the man didn't know I was his neighbor. I was reminded of my mom's advice when I was in middle school, that I was the center of my own story but a side character in every else's. Other people didn't think about me as much as I thought they did. When you're a nervous introvert, that's hard to remember.

Movement from outside caught my eye, and I watched as Noah finished up mowing the back and headed toward the front. I let out a breath I didn't realize I had been holding. Phew.

The timer rang on the oven, and I pulled out my tacos, stacking them on a plate and heading to my window nook. Once I settled myself on the seat, I inched my way back to the pillow I'd propped against a wall. I stretched out my legs and tugged the thick cream throw over my legs. While I let my lunch cool, I opened my laptop and pulled up book five.

I had my heroine for this book fleshed out. She'd been fun to dream up because she was the opposite of me—an extrovert who loved small talk and spending time with people. Now I had Maggie and Maeve in mind whenever I thought of her as well as Kylie, my closest friend in Chicago.

Kylie was one of the first people I'd met at work. She'd been at the accounting firm four years longer than I had but did a much better job at keeping a work-life balance. She also retained the honor of the only person who knew of my secret side job and had been absolutely fascinated about where my ideas came from. I tried to explain that I might take, in the case of my new heroine, the personality of two friends, the hair of a woman I saw in a restaurant in Chicago, my own body type, the job of one of my college roommates, the speech pattern of an actress in my favorite movie, and the style of my neighbors and voilà! I had a character.

Kylie had just shaken her head but then whispered, "But the sex scenes, those are real, right?" It was then I reminded her of the sexual drought I was currently residing in and that I owed all my current satisfaction to LELO, the company that made my vibrator.

"You're ruining my fantasy world," she'd said with a laugh, then ordered me another glass of Shacksbury's rosé cider, our favorite after-work drink.

When I moved down here, Kylie had been in Ireland on a once-in-a-lifetime trip with her family that she'd saved up vacation time for years to take, so I hadn't heard much from her in the past two weeks beyond a text or two, but knew I would get a call once she hit stateside again, any day now. She'd been disappointed when I shared my mom's concerns and told her I was making the change, but she'd also understood.

"Babe, my car knows how to drive three hours south just as my feet know how to take me to the nearest shoe store. You take care of you, and I'll come visit and see what life is like 'down south.'"

I tried to tell her that south of I-80 didn't constitute the South, but she was hearing none of it. No matter what her opinions were about our geographical region, I was ready for her to be back so that she could resume her most important job of beta reading my books. I sent her chapters as I wrote because the encouragement was vital for my confidence in continuing a story. My nasty impostor syndrome was a feeling strong enough to make me stop writing. Kylie's quiet, and sometime not so quiet, encouragement was exactly what I needed.

And right now it was needed to get over this writer's block. My heroine felt great. My hero, not so much.

My phone's vibrations pulled me out of my doom and gloom. Looking at the notification, the clouds cleared. Speak of the devil—looked like Kylie was home.

"Hey," I said in greeting.

"Girl, you will not believe what that country is like." No preamble, straight to the point. That was Kylie all right. "People are unbelievably nice, and the guys... Damn, I could spend the rest of my life staring at some of those faces."

"Am I to take it that you've decided to move to the Emerald Isle and have found a man to settle down with?" I smoothed out the blanket on my legs while I waited for her response.

"Do you know me or not?" she fired back. "Lots of nice dates between family stuff. A few that led to more, but no one that I want to change my citizenship status for." She paused, then said in a softer voice, "And how are you?"

Kylie liked to keep things real, so I considered her question before answering. "Better." I thought of how to describe my past two weeks. "Lou had a place for me to rent before I came down here. I love it and have an option to buy. Of course, my rent here is a fraction of what it was in Chicago."

"And the firm you're at? I'm guessing you're on a lunch break like me right now, so at least you're taking your lunch again instead of working through it." Her tone of voice told me what she thought of my previous habits.

I smiled, thinking of Sue and her worry for her employees. "My boss is Sue, and she is adamant that we all have a healthy work-life balance."

"Well, that is something our boss could work on, but we all know he won't."

I snorted. "Yeah." That was a colossal understatement.

"So you're at lunch?"

"Well, working from home today." I hesitated, not sure how much to reveal. Apparently my tone of voice gave it all away, because Kylie called me out.

"Spill, Jules. What's up?"

Noah chose that moment to bring some deck furniture out, placing it on his back patio. I watched him for a moment as he carefully moved items around. The temperature must have warmed up, because his threadbare shirt clung to his back.

"So there's this guy who lives behind me…"

"Yesssssss." I could practically hear Kylie rubbing her hands together in glee. "I can't wait to hear how you're just being neighborly with this guy or whatever excuse you're getting ready to spill. Jules, put your expertise as a romance writer to work and let's go."

My heart felt a tug as I thought of all the times we'd sat curled up on a couch, sharing the minutiae that made up our lives. "I miss you. When will we see each other again?"

Kylie let out a laugh combined with a sigh. "Well… considering I just got back from vacation, it will have to be a quick weekend trip, but soon. I'll come down and check out your neighbor."

I shook my head, thinking that was the last thing I needed. Kylie would be only too happy to join forces with Lou, and God forbid she meet Maeve or Maggie. "Well, in that case I better find a spot around here that has our rosé cider."

"Hell yeah, you better. I expect nothing but the best," Kylie said. "Now chickie, let's chat about this neighbor of yours."

Chapter 6

———————

Best-Laid Plans

Noah

Tuesday was not shaping up as I'd envisioned. I had three meetings online to deal with some gaps in fundraising we had for this year. Those went according to plan. I talked to our local office out of Springfield to debrief about my last trip to Chicago. Addie was with me until Friday, and I'd dropped her off at school that morning and would race through the day to get as much done as possible before it was time to pick her up at three. My daily goal when I had Addie was that by the time she was at home with me, I was all hers and my work was done. All that was going like clockwork. So what wasn't? A certain brunette accountant I'd expected to see this morning, or at the very least, talk to.

I'd figured I'd call Jules's firm bright and early, find out what her hours were, and drop off my paperwork. Would I want to linger and talk to her for a bit? Maybe, but just to be friendly.

However, upon calling I had been told she was out of the office for the day. Weird, right? She hadn't mentioned anything the night before. Even stranger was the text I had from Lou right after lunch. Hell, I hadn't known it was even Lou at first—it wasn't like she and I were texting on the regular. But unless someone was punking me, it was indeed the one and only Lou.

Unknown Number: *Noah, this is Lou Williams. Sue told me you were looking for Jules. Heads up that she's working from home today and lives directly behind you. Pop over and drop off your tax documents to her directly and she can get to work.*

I'd replied after debating for a few minutes what to say.

Me: *Hey Lou. Thanks for the text. Nice to know you are keeping your finger on the pulse of the town as always.*

Her reply had been a wink emoji.

Ivy had told me what a meddling, if well-meaning, busybody Lou was. The text was clearly evidence of that. I should just ignore her suggestion and move on with life. So why was I considering it? Would it help Jules if I got her what she needed for my tax return? Would she even want to see me?

More importantly, why did anything involving this woman make me feel like a confused teen?

I sighed and decided to take care of some organizational items on my to-do list before making the call on whether to pop by Jules's place or not. The day was unseasonably warm. I'd already mowed that morning, which seemed early for April but made sense due to the unseasonable weather we'd been having. I then got the spring beds ready for planting and moved some deck furniture to my back patio. Now for some tasks that didn't involve manual labor. Laptop in hand, I grabbed a water bottle, some folders, and sunglasses before heading outdoors.

Settling in on the corner of an outdoor sectional, I took

in a deep breath. Sometimes it was hard to believe I was back in the US, much less in this small town. It was so far from the life I'd known for the majority of the past decade. Well, twelve months in the familiar hell known as my childhood home had been a necessary evil because it allowed me to save enough money after college to continue with my goals. But from there, nothing had been the same. My time in Malawi and Tanzania in Southeastern Africa had been the norm for the next five plus years of my life. When I decided to make my way back home eighteen months ago, I wasn't sure if it was the right call.

I grew up privileged in that I had food, water, a roof over my head. From what I knew of Maslow's hierarchy, I had the first level down pat. Well, except for you know—the love and support of my parents. Not sure why they decided to procreate and I supposed I should be grateful for it or I wouldn't be here, but for the majority of my life it was apparent I was a nuisance. To say they weren't present in Addie's life would also be an understatement. I tried not to think about them much, they brought up too many bad memories.

Shaking myself from the trip down memory lane, I opened my laptop and looked at my list for this week. Cross-referencing that with Addie's schedule, I began thinking through meals and outings we could do before Friday. Maybe someday I would feel like what I did with her was enough to make up for years of things I'd missed. Today, however, would not be that day.

The sound of a throat clearing caught my attention. Looking up, I saw Jules standing there, clearly feeling uncomfortable. I fought to keep my gaze neutral because the visual of her in leggings, some type of crop top or sports bra, and an unzipped hoodie had caught my attention, and I was having a series of more than friendly visions pop into my mind.

Jules is in my backyard, standing on my deck. The words whirled through my brain as I tried to imagine what had gotten her over here. Did Lou text her too? There was only one way to find out.

"Hey, Jules." Did my voice sound too raspy? She didn't know me well; maybe she wouldn't notice. The flush working its way up her neck, however, was something I clocked. Had to admit, I loved that she made it easy to read her.

She cleared her throat again, shifting from side to side. "Hi, um, Noah." She paused, worrying her lip between her teeth before continuing. "Sue let me know that you called this morning. I, um, well, I decided to come over because I wanted to make sure you really wanted me to do your taxes and weren't just appeasing my aunt Lou."

I gave her what I thought was a reassuring smile. "So is that why you're working at home today?" I nodded toward what I now knew was her house. "Avoiding any unsuspecting clients your aunt might send your way?"

Whoa. At my words, her flush deepened. Holy shit, was she avoiding *me* by working from home? Had she known we were neighbors? When did she figure that out? And was she avoiding me because she didn't like me or because she was embarrassed by her aunt? So many questions.

"Um, it seems that you're the only person Lou has strong-armed to get to agree to being a client for me..."

"So far," I pointed out.

She considered that, shrugging her shoulders. "I guess you're right. Give her time." She looked down, then back up as her warm brown eyes met mine. "Did you know last night that you lived behind me?" Her voice had an air of vulnerability that I had a strong desire to protect. "I promise I didn't then, but I did find out this morning." I could tell she was worried about it, which I wanted to think more about, but first wanted to reassure her.

"No, I didn't know last night." I pulled my phone out of my pocket. "In the spirit of total honestly, I did get this text from your aunt about an hour ago and that's when I found out." I passed her my cell.

Jules took it, her brow furrowed as she looked down to see Lou's text, then my reply. Her eyes shot up to mine with an expression of horror on her face.

"Oh my goodness, Noah, I'm so sorry." She sank down on the couch a cushion away from me, placing my phone between us. "I wish I could say I was surprised, but that would be a lie."

I smiled, quite frankly charmed by the woman. There was something about her that made me want to reassure her, shield her. From whom? The world? No idea. Lou was a lot, but she was harmless. Jules felt younger than me and the same age at once. I couldn't puzzle it out, but I knew I'd like to be around her more. *As a friend*, I reminded myself.

"Jules, it's okay. While I don't know Lou well, her reputation proceeds her. And I'd love you to file my taxes for me. I'm sure I could do them as I have in the past, but I've left it to the last minute. And I'll be honest, mine aren't terribly complicated, but the time of year snuck up on me and I'm currently swamped at work. You getting it squared away would be a relief." I watched her face as I spoke and noted how her forehead smoothed out. "However, I also recognize that it is nine days until tax day, so am I putting you in a bind?"

The relief was evident on Jules's face. "Oh no, that's

fine. You said yours would be pretty standard, correct? I have time to get that done, no problem."

Without another word, I grabbed the stack of folders I had on the cushion next to me, flipped through them until I found the documents, then passed it to Jules. "I think this is everything you'll need."

Jules accepted the folder, then opened it to look over the contents. I could practically see her making checkboxes in her head. Hmm, I wasn't aware I had a thing for competency, or was it just that this woman was attractive to me in all ways? If I was being real, the fact that it was so easy to read her—that what you saw was what you got—that was the most attractive. I abhorred the games that some women played. That was probably why I didn't have many relationships in college. And when it came down to it, that's how Ivy and I ended up together. I *knew* her, had known her for years. Ivy was not one to bullshit either.

"Be honest," I began, making Jules look from the papers to me. "Are you sure I haven't earned a spot on your shit list by handing off my taxes this late? I don't typically live my life trying to make more work for others."

To my absolute delight, she let out a gorgeous, unfettered laugh. "No worries, Noah. I wouldn't have said yes if I didn't have time. Starting here two weeks ago gave me the benefit that I'm picking up the slack in the office for others but have no actual clients of my own. I can easily finish this for you in time." She returned to flipping through my papers.

I cleared my throat, getting those brown eyes aimed at me again. "In that case, are you just being neighborly and coming to take care of me and my tax needs, or do you want to stay for a minute?"

Jules tipped her head like she was considering my words. "Stay and do what?"

Oh, Jules. I watched as her skin flamed again. Yep, I saw how that could be taken in the wrong way, but I was keeping this PG and getting us back in a comfortable zone for her. "Let's just get to know each other better. You know, as neighbors?"

"Okay." Jules still looked hesitant, but she scooted back on the couch and folded her legs pretzel-style.

"So how are you liking Highland Falls?" Softball question there—hopefully that would be helpful.

"Oh, um, I really like it." She paused, clearly trying to decide whether to keep her thoughts short and close to the vest or just to spill. I was voting for letting it all out, so I stayed silent, giving her the time she needed. "I loved Chicago. I lived in Lakeview, and it was a fabulous neighborhood, but I like the slower pace here." She brushed her hands down her leggings. "So far my life is more balanced."

I nodded. Ivy and I grew up in Madison, which wasn't near the size of Chicago, but the pulse of a city just made you want to speed up. "I hear you. I think you know I was in Africa before landing here?"

She gave me a nod to let me know the gossip in town had at least given her that.

"Living there wasn't like being surrounded by eight million or more of my closest friends, but it was a job that never seemed to be done. You know? Like I was never off the clock."

"That would be hard," Jules murmured. "I hope Highland Falls is helping you find that balance too."

Before I could get my next get-to-know-Jules question out or follow up on that comment, a noise from her yard had us both turning.

"Oh, there you two are! Don't let me disturb you." Lou stood in Jules's backyard, twenty feet or so from us, with a cat-that-ate-the-canary expression on her face.

"Oh, I should go check in with Lou." Jules scrambled up, my folder in hand. "Thanks so much for this, Noah. Talk soon."

I couldn't even get one word out to slow her down—the woman was off my porch and hotfooting her way through my yard to hers and through her back door, pulling Lou along with her.

Hmm. My plan for getting to know Jules would have to resume later.

Chapter 7

Bird-Watching Era

Jules

My gaze was unfocused as I looked out the sitting area windows into my backyard. There were still several hours until dusk, but the April skies were gray. I was not someone who struggled with seasonal affective disorder, but even I had to admit I was ready for more blue skies. And sun. Loads of sun.

It was funny—I didn't notice the sun as much in the city. Was it because I was surrounded by tall buildings wherever I walked? I wasn't sure. I mean, a gorgeous summer day was great, and no urban landscape could take away from that, but I somehow didn't notice the changing of the seasons like I felt I'd already become attuned to down here. Maybe that was the fact that I had about a mile walk to work each day. That gave me the chance to notice small changes around me. I also was headed there and back during daylight hours. Sadly, working overtime had been my norm for years as I tried to keep up. Possibly I hadn't noticed seasons while in Chicago from a standpoint of sheer exhaustion. Whatever the reason, I liked the new rhythm.

Right now I was staring at a bird feeder. Yep. I was thirty years old and had my own bird feeder. To be fair, Maeve had shown up with it yesterday and told me it would help me on this journey of appreciating the small things. I wasn't aware I had delineated a goal for any life journey for myself, but it couldn't hurt.

Then Maeve shared that Lou had been in the Sanctuary that morning. She'd apparently spilled the details that she'd interrupted a "moment" with Noah and me on Tuesday. I tried to argue with Maeve that there had been no moment, but no luck—she was taking Lou's words as the gospel truth. She'd muttered something about maybe I wasn't in the best place to see what was in front of me due to the "Chicago meltdown," as Lou was calling it.

Apparently Maeve and Lou then held what Maeve referred to as a meeting of the minds, and the result was that I now had a metal pole complete with a squirrel baffle that had two tube bird feeders hanging from it. Maeve even brought a bag of black-oil sunflower seed because she said Max recommended it and the other stuff sold is crap.

Had to admit, it took me a hot minute to even remember who Max was. I needed a tree diagram to keep up with these people.

Maeve stuck the pole in the ground outside my sitting area windows, so I had a view of the feeder while I was lounging in my cozy spot or writing. Her recommendation was to download an app called Merlin Bird ID, and then she was off like a real live Santa that had come in and dumped gifts for no reason and left.

And while I can't say I had "buy a bird feeder" on any to-do list of mine, all my free time for the past twenty-four hours found me watching the feeder. Who knew there were so many varieties of birds? So far that afternoon, I'd seen cardinals—males and females—robins, blue jays, and a black-capped chickadee.

Looking back to my laptop, I pulled up my story bible for my book. It was sadly lackluster, which was one of the reasons I was stuck. I had been struggling to visualize my hero; he had been stubbornly silent while my heroine had whispered in my ear. Even then, I went to the column where I wrote down hobbies for my characters and added bird-watching to the heroine's row because I felt sure my Maeve/ Maggie/ Kylie mash-up would enjoy the ridiculous names I'd been learning for some of the birds in the region. I mean, dickcissel? Come on.

Staring at the row on my story bible I had for my hero's qualities, I started typing as a vague image began to come to mind. Hmm, age around thirty seemed right. Height? I thought of my heroine, whom I'd named Collette. She was taller than me with curves for days. If I had to write some-one, why not write what I'd love to have? Although her five foot five wasn't much taller than me, but four inches was nothing to sneeze at. I'd certainly take it.

I thought about the guys I'd met down here. All were six feet or taller. Let's start there. Six two seemed good. Hmm, a name. I wanted something a bit pretentious. Collette wasn't a typical name. What went with that? I looked out the window as I racked my brain. Maybe Julian?

Yes. Julian. Okay, so he was six foot two, dark hair, piercing blue eyes. No, blue eyes weren't common with dark hair. But as I pictured Collette in my head, closing my eyes to visualize a partner for her, he definitely had blue eyes, though they were dark, almost a blue gray. Okay, and maybe a sandy blond/brown hair.

My fingers flew across the keyboard, filling out my story bible and finding inspiration for my hero for the first time since I'd opened a doc for this book. I added qualities for him as they popped into my mind, then opened a new tab and created a secret Pinterest board, adding inspiration pictures fast and furious. Then came the fun stuff.

I grabbed my large notebook and just let my mind wander, thinking through three story arcs—the arc for each of the main characters and what they overcome, then the arc for the romance and the obstacles for each.

As I thought of Julian and Collette, I pictured people who had money. Where did they live? Maybe the Gold Cost in Chicago? Or... what if Julian was a billionaire and Collette was his long-suffering assistant? She'd had feelings for him forever but hadn't acted because of their different lifestyles. Maybe mid-book she would quit? I tried to let that story play out in my mind. No, that wouldn't work—they needed to get together far earlier than that. She could quit at the start.

I put a giant X through my paper. Living on the Gold Cost and working as an assistant didn't match what I'd already brainstormed. Starting over, I thought of Highland Woods. The park outside town was gorgeous, but I hadn't visited it since moving here. I had, however, checked it out on earlier trips.

Julian could still be a billionaire, but maybe he and Collette didn't know each other. She'd be out at the park to participate in one of the bird hikes I'd heard mentioned, and they run into each other on the trail. Or maybe they're both on the hike?

The movie in my mind was rolling the scene that was unfolding. Did it feel right? As I watched Collette and Julian bump into each other, Collette fell to the ground. Julian turned to offer her a hand and...

Damn, he had Noah's face. I shook my head. I'd already

planned on borrowing some inspiration from Noah, but the man wasn't a billionaire, so it was fine.

Speaking of Noah, I glanced to my phone. I'd texted him in the morning that his taxes were done. He wasn't kidding—his were straightforward, and I'd been able to quickly get them done the previous day at work. I'd said he could pick them up at the office during the day or I'd have them with me if he wanted to drop by my place. Did I want him to pick the second option? Yep, sure did. And I was refusing to examine that too closely.

Oh, my lock screen had several texts. I must have been deep into my fictional world to not hear the alerts when they came in. I looked at Noah's first.

Noah: *I was in Springfield this morning and just dropped Addie off with Jake and Ivy. Want to come to my place for dinner?*

Um, yep, sure did. But then I thought of my kitchen. I'd already started dinner. Shit.

Me: *That would be awesome, but I already have chicken in the Crock-Pot. I mean, if you haven't started anything, you could come here?*

Did I want to cross my fingers? Sure did. But instead, I worked on a centering breath as I watched the dots that indicated he was typing. Finally, the text came through.

Noah: *Sounds good. What can I bring?*

A squeal came out of me that I hadn't been aware was something I did. Super mature. Fighting the urge to let another one fly, I thought through my kitchen situation. I had everything for my version of burrito bowls. I had some cookie dough in the freezer if he wanted dessert. Beer. Umm, there wasn't a lot of variety.

Me: *How about you bring whatever you want to drink. Seven?*

Noah: *Seven it is. See you in a few hours, Jules.*

I could hear the way he said my name as I read that. Gracious. It really had been a while. *Friends*, I told myself.

The other text notifications were for the group chat. Looked like someone had named it the Coven. Nice. They had just started and were rolling in.

Ivy: *Ladies, Emma, Grace, and I have been debating the May romance book club book, and we have a selection!*

Maeve: *Ooohhh, I'm excited to hear this, but I also forgot what April's is and we meet next week, right? Someone help a girl out.*

Allyson: *It's Pippa Grant's newest book. You could have just asked me. I'm across the café from you.*

Maeve: *Now where would the fun be in that? And what if someone else forgot? Problem solved. Ohh, Jules, you're invited next week even if you can't read the book that fast. We don't shame nonreaders. We host it at the library, one of our houses, or the bookstore. Sometimes at the brewery if a lot of people RSVP. We even have outings as a club when the occasion arises.*

It took me a hot minute to place the sensation in my chest, but I got there. Happiness. A sense of belonging. My eyes welled up with tears in gratitude that my mom and Lou had seen what I couldn't and helped me to do something about it. I should be able to meet with them next week as long as it was after work. Sue was understanding and all, but I needed to give her my full attention during working hours. Hell, I knew that next year my tax season would likely not feel as chill as this one—I was soaking it up while I could. And Lord knew I loved Pippa's books. I hadn't read her newest release; I'd even missed that she had one out. Was it in Copper Valley? Either way, this was a social gathering I could get behind.

Me: *I'm in. Tell me where and when for this month.*

Ivy: *Now can I share our May title? We'll text you about it again in three weeks so some people can read it last minute, per usual. Not naming names or anything.*

Maeve: *I resemble this text.*

Grace: *Good Lord, ladies, let Ivy get this out.*

Emma, Allyson, and Ivy liked that message.

Ivy: *Thanks, Grace. We're going with book two in Jules Jenkins's small-town romance series, Sleepy Valley. We read the first one last fall. Jules, have you read her first book? Or does that give you enough time? Though like Maeve said, we don't shame if you just want to show up and chat.*

Maeve: *Unless it's me.*

I stared at the texts in horror. They'd read my first book and were going to read my second in May? It was one thing to leave out that I wrote romance when it didn't come up— was I going to outright lie to them? But if I didn't, was I telling Lou? My mom?

Shit. Shitty shit shit. Part of me wanted to fire off a text that said, *guess what...* The other part of me knew immediately that I wasn't ready. I closed my eyes and took a centering breath. Then another one.

Nope, I couldn't do it. These ladies would just have to forgive me later, but this was not the day. I sent out a prayer to the universe that they'd understand and promised to work toward a time where I would own up to my books, being a giant chicken, and fired off a reply.

Me: *Sounds good. I'll get Pippa's newest. Just let me know when we're meeting.*

Someone was texting immediately, and then Emma's whooshed in.

Emma: *We meet the second Sunday of the month most of the time. Locations rotate like Ivy said, but this month is at*

Allyson's. Again, that's only a few days away, so no worries if you can't read the book by then.

Me: *I love Pippa, and reading obsessively is my superpower. I should finish no problem.*

Sliding my phone to the side, I ignored the other messages I could see popping up. I hated how guilty I felt about holding back. I knew they'd be understanding, but I wasn't ready to tell my family. And honestly, part of me didn't want to hear how they felt about the first book of mine that they'd read or the one next month. Maybe I could skip May's meeting and rejoin for June? My stomach turned.

Noah would be here in a couple of hours. I glanced around my writing space and noted a stack of my books, notebooks full of ideas, and a few writing resources scattered over the cushion. Yep. All this needed to go.

Outside the window, a male cardinal watched me with what I took to be a knowing look.

"I know, Red. I'm an idiot."

The bird gave me a nod and flew off, surely to tell his friends that I didn't know what I was doing. I shrugged—what was a girl to do? With that, I started clearing my writing nook so I could get ready for dinner with Noah. That was sure to settle my nerves.

Chapter 8

Secrets Revealed

N*oah*

I glanced at my phone once again to double-check the time before I knocked on the door. Seven on the dot. My parents had instilled in me the absolute fact that neither lateness nor being early were socially acceptable. Frankly, I was floored that my mom abhorred lateness—the woman did like to make an entrance—but I stopped trying to analyze them ages ago. I hated that so many of their lessons were still internalized, but it was what it was.

I rang the doorbell, trying to clock the feeling shooting through me. It wasn't fear, not nerves, but... maybe... antici-pation? Was that it? I looked up at Jules as she opened the door. Her brown hair was up in a messy pile on the top of her head with a few pieces escaping down her neck. She looked cozy—that was the best way I could describe her. She wasn't dressed up and shouldn't be for an impromptu meal at home. Her loose cream sweatpants were topped with a matching sweatshirt. She had on fuzzy socks, and I had a strong desire to curl up on a couch and pull her into my lap. Like that was an appropriate thought. I worked to clear my mind.

"Hey," Jules said, a flush working its way up her neck already. She stepped back, allowing me to come in. "Thanks for coming."

"I feel like I invited myself," I admitted as I stepped in, then followed her through her open living room into her kitchen, noting that I could see my place through her back windows. I was surprised I hadn't noticed her sometime over the past few weeks. She said she'd moved to Highland Falls two weeks ago. The Wilsons had lived in this house since I'd moved to town, but they'd headed to Florida four weeks ago to be closer to their son, who'd moved to somewhere on the Gulf. It hadn't even occurred to me to wonder who was now in their place.

"You absolutely did not," Jules said as she opened the top of her Crock-Pot and stirred something inside.

Had she said it was chicken? Smelled awesome regardless. My mouth watered.

"I told you that you could stop by for your taxes, and you messaged to invite me to dinner. Not your fault I'd already started dinner."

Something winding its way around my legs drew my attention. I looked down to see a gorgeous long-haired cat. He, or she, was mostly white with a touch of gray. When he looked up at me to vocalize his need for some attention, I was mesmerized by his blue eyes.

"Who is this?" I asked, bending to run my hand down his back.

Jules laughed from her spot in the kitchen. "O'Malley. He can't handle not being doted on by all."

"As he should be, gorgeous boy." I placed the bag of drinks on the counter. "At any rate, back to whether or not I was too pushy I'll just say I'm grateful for the invite anyway." I paused, wondering if I should say anything or not. Fuck it. "I felt like we got off on the wrong foot and wanted to make it up to you."

Her head shot up from the Crock-Pot to meet my eyes. "What?"

O'Malley took off to hop up on the raised platform or couch thing off the kitchen. I turned back to Jules and shrugged as I pulled cans out of the bag. "I felt like you were pressured by Lou to do my taxes, and I know you felt bad about that even though it wasn't on you. Wanted you to know that I was happy to get to know you without her interference."

"Oh," she said, her eyes going back to the contents of the Crock-Pot. "So you wanted to make sure we could be friends without my aunt setting up a playdate?"

Playdate. I coughed back a laugh at that comment while working to ignore the word *friends* and how it felt wrong somehow. It was all I had time for right now, so it would have to be fine. "Umm, sure."

Jules's eyes met mine, then looked to the cans I'd put on the counter, and she let out a small gasp of surprise. "You brought Shacksbury's rosé cider? How did you know?"

I looked from the cans to her growing smile, the lightness in her eyes. I could get addicted to making her react this way. "I wish I could take credit for whatever I did here, but honestly, Ivy loves this stuff. I stock it at my place because it's hard to find locally and I've grown to like it too. Wanted to see what you thought of it."

Jules beamed at me as she gestured to the drinks with a relaxed vibe that I definitely hadn't seen from her yet. Was it because she was in her home? Because we'd met a few times? "My best friend in Chicago is Kylie. We were just talking about when she could come down and she joked that I'd have to find this cider. Once we found it last fall, we became obsessed with it, and I didn't know if it was available here."

I shot her a wink. "I'll have to let you know the secrets spots to buy it."

A flush reached her cheeks, but she nodded. "Please do."

I passed her a can as she grabbed two glasses for us. She poured the rosé in hers as I grabbed a beer, leaving her more of the rosé while making a mental note to pick up some for her when I restocked for Ivy. "Tell me about the goodness that is in your Crock-Pot, Jules."

She took a sip and closed her eyes for a moment, savoring. I took her in, thinking this was only the third time I'd seen her—the brewery, my backyard, now here. The vibe that poured off her was welcoming and open, giving me a strong desire to get to know her better. Yeah, friends would work. Something about her made me want to ensure she felt at ease when she was around me.

Jules put her glass down and then grabbed a spoon and turned to the pot I hadn't noticed on the stove. "Nothing too exciting, I promise," she said as she lifted a lid and stirred. "I love to make burrito bowls, you know, like Chipotle. I don't know what they do, but for my version I make what I call salsa chicken in the Crock-Pot. It's just chicken, my mix of taco seasoning, a jar of salsa verde, and the juice of a lemon. That does its thing all day, then you shred. I put it on top of cilantro lime rice"—she pointed with her spoon at the pot she'd just stirred, then her spoon moved to point at another small pot—"and pinto beans. Top with guac." Another gesture to a bowl on the counter near her fridge. "Cheese and sour cream if you want." She paused, biting her lip as she did some kind of mental inventory before she added, "I think I have lettuce too if you like."

I watched as she moved around her kitchen, pointing out all the food like it was nothing, but to me it was more. I knew she hadn't made this with me in mind, but it wasn't as if my parents ever cooked a meal for me. Hell, they often couldn't even be bothered to be home for dinner. Luckily, for most of my childhood they'd employed Mary. She'd made up where they lacked. But having Jules make me a meal felt nice even if it hadn't been planned. "This is awesome, Jules."

She moved from one thing to another, light on her feet as O'Malley wound around her legs in a dance they were clearly practiced in. "Oh, it's nothing," she murmured as she met my gaze.

"It is to me. Let's just say my parents weren't the type to nurture through food or otherwise, so besides the staff my parents paid while I was growing up and Ivy once we were in college, no one has made a meal for me."

I grew up lonely, eating on my own while they were at one function or another, feeling fine to leave me with the staff as they went about their lives, unburdened by their only child. I'm sure if I thought about it for any time, I could point to that as to why I wanted to spend every moment with Addie that I could because I hadn't had that. Hell, a good therapist could absolutely point a clear connection to my rushed decision to upend my life and head back here to be with Addie when I realized she was going to grow up without me as a support system much like I had with my parents. I'd been born to privilege but had missed out on a lot and couldn't have my own child experience the same. I didn't think that desire was all that unique though. Doesn't everyone want to do better than what had been done to them?

I realized Jules hadn't said anything as my brain had taken me down memory lane. Too deep for our third time meeting? Maybe. I wasn't a big fan of small talk, preferring to actually get into deep conversations, but I knew not everyone was the same. Maybe I needed to steer us back to some lightness? "At any rate, the bowls sound delicious. How can I help?"

She was watching me with an expression I couldn't read. "Don't think you're getting off that easy, Noah. I want to know more about these parents that didn't cook for you, but I'm currently starving. Bowl assembly and then get into it?"

I nodded. "Sounds good."

An hour later, after we'd eaten an amazing dinner with O'Malley visiting us on his own timetable, then heading off on his own once again, we'd shared the bare bones of our childhoods. Jules knew that I didn't have contact with my parents, and I could never measure up to their beliefs in what I should have been. I knew her parents were kind but absent-minded and that her mom had a flair for the dramatic.

I was wandering her living room while she got her kitchen in order just behind me. I'd tried to help, but she'd insisted she wanted to box up lunches for the week and then was going to let the rest of the dishes soak. The past two hours had flown by as I found that we had a startling number of similarities, from the little TV we did watch, to music, to a fondness of concerts at small venues, to the fact that we both loved nonfancy food: tacos, pizza, burgers being the favorites. And while I couldn't lie and say I wasn't attracted to the woman, I could easily see a friendship developing. For now that was more important.

Browsing her bookshelves on a far wall, I noted that she had a mixture of what looked like cozy fiction, some mysteries, a lot of romance, and a plethora of what appeared to be books about writing. Interesting. I wondered if she wanted to write something or if they were left over from some class she'd taken in undergrad.

I picked up a book with a green cover that was book one in a series called Sleepy Valley. Checking out the shelf, it seemed Jules had several in this series by an author named Jules Jenkins. I flipped over the book to read the description on the back. Something dropping pulled my attention back to the present, and I looked up see Jules standing a few feet away, her phone at her feet.

"Hey, you okay?" I asked, looking from her phone to her face, which wasn't flushed at all but paler than looked normal. She seemed frozen. "Jules?"

She looked at the book in my hand, then back to me. "Umm." She cleared her throat and seemed to sway on her feet.

I took a few steps toward her, then gently tugged her toward her couch, pushing her to sit before she fell. I scanned the area for her water, saw it on the island and headed across the small space to grab it, then moved back to her before she could speak. I sat down on the opposite corner of the couch from her and turned to face her.

"Jules, you good? Feeling off?" She'd been fine moments ago; I wasn't sure what changed. Then I noted that her horrified expression seemed to be focused on the book in my hands. I looked at it again, then back to her. "Is there something wrong with this book?" I asked quietly, not wanting to spook her but at a loss as to what was going on.

Jules looked up from the book to meet my eyes, her own watery. Well, this was a hell of a way to end what had been a great evening, making the woman cry. I put the book down between us, wondering what I had done but not wanting to do anything more to hurt her.

She took a deep breath and seemed to gather strength from some internal well before reaching out to take the novel in her hands, gripping it tightly. "Noah, I know we don't know each other well, but I need to tell you something because the universe is clearly giving me some signs today that this secret needs to come out." Her gaze drifted away from me to the windows as she spoke, as if whatever she had to say was too much if she was looking at me.

I noted internally that Ivy would be a big fan of Jules listening to the universe but didn't speak so she could have her space to figure out what she wanted to say. She took her time, relaxing her grip to allow her finger to almost reverently run over the author's name on the cover. When she did it again, I took a second glance at it. Jules Jenkins. I met Jules's gaze once more and then snagged on the author's first name. Jules.

I met her anxious but determined expression. "Um, do you know this author?" I asked as gently as I could, my gut telling me the answer before she could speak.

She took a deep breath, then gave me a slow nod before whispering, "You could say that. She's me."

Chapter 9

The Weight of Lies

*J****ules***

I lay in bed, unable to sleep. Dinner had been excellent, surprisingly. My friend groups over the years had typically been small but leaned toward female. And sure, I'd had relationships with guys over the years, but none of them had ever been my friend first. In hindsight, that might be telling as well.

The evening with Noah, had been... unexpected. I was still attracted to the man. I would have to be dead not to be. But as much as I'd like to find out what the man's lips felt like on my own, I'd also enjoyed just getting to know him.

That was rare for me—with men or women. I just felt like I was missing the ability to get to know people easily. It took quite a bit of time before I was comfortable with someone, which was why I'd disappeared into novels since I was a kid. Fictional friends were far easier. Noah, however, was proving to be an anomaly, as were the women of Highland Falls. Here I felt freer to be myself than I ever had. And Noah? He was easy to talk to and made me feel comfortable... Well, that had been true until he found my books.

Shit. Shit. Shitty shit shit. Turning to see the man standing with my baby—the first book I'd ever written—had been mind-blowing as my world threatened to turn on its head. My stomach seized up; my hands stopped working as I dropped my damn phone. I'd thought I'd faint until he'd luckily clocked my panicked state and pulled me over to the couch.

I'd briefly debated staying quiet and denying that anything was going on, but after an evening where I felt like we were building a foundation of friendship, that didn't sit right. I wasn't a liar. I knew that sounded like a load of crap considering most people didn't know I *was* Jules Jenkins, but I'd never been confronted with anyone talking about my books to *me* in person. So it was a lie of omission I'd been okay with until earlier.

I'd known I needed to tell my family for a while, but since the publication of my first book, I'd created an ever-changing set of benchmarks and swore I'd spill the beans once I reached them. At first I'd thought I'd tell them when I earned out on my book. Once that happened, I'd thought I would when I had a certain number of reviews. Then was the benchmark of when cracked the top sellers on Amazon upon a release. After meeting that, I'd reasoned with myself that I would when my income from writing was higher than my actual income. Now I was approaching that threshold, so I needed another goal or I needed to bite the bullet and find the guts to tell my parents and Lou. Would they be fine with the news? Likely. But the idea that they wouldn't be...

Earlier in the day, I'd felt so conflicted not speaking up in the group-text thread about the book club that when presented with Noah in front of me, not even knowing the quandary he was unwittingly throwing me into, I was just done. I hadn't had it in me to continue the subterfuge. I don't know that he'd understood why I had been so freaked out. Hell, I don't know if anyone would get it, and I hadn't really had time to explain. It was a combination of impostor syndrome—no matter the sales, I still felt like I didn't know what I was doing—and the way people treated romance books as well as their authors. Would I still be *me* once they knew about my side job that was on the way to eclipsing my real one?

My admission had just left my mouth when Noah's phone rang. He'd glanced at it, seen that it was Ivy, and immediately answered. She'd been at his house because Addie had left her current prized stuffed animal at his place and sworn she couldn't sleep without it. He'd apologized to me and taken off to meet her and locate the important stuffie.

Fast-forward to me in bed, staring at the ceiling, questioning the life choices that had landed me there.

"Mrow?" O'Malley was making biscuits on my stomach as he stared into my eyes by the light of the moon. His judgment was strong, damn cat. I swore he could somehow read my mind. The misogynists of the late 1600s thought cat ownership was a sign that a woman was a witch, but I think they missed the real power in that relationship. Surely the cats were the ones that knew all. And fuck them for persecuting women anyway.

"I know, I know," I said, rubbing a hand over my face. It was not the time to spiral on women's place in humanity. Not now. There were two people in this world who knew my secret identity—Noah and Kylie. I had a frightening premonition involving Kylie meeting Noah. She'd have a lot of things to say; mainly I could envision her telling me to "hit that." Yeah, subtlety was not her strong suit.

Mental note—pray they never met when Kylie came to visit.

My phone vibrating on my bedside table pulled me out of my spiral. I picked it up, nerves flooded my belly when I saw Noah's name.

Noah: *Crisis averted. We found Addie's elephant, and Ivy has headed home. Do you want me to come over to finish our conversation?*

I glanced at the time. He'd left thirty minutes ago—that was a hell of a search for a stuffie.

Me: *No, O'Malley and I have already made it to bed. We can talk more later. Glad you found the elephant; it must have been well-hidden.*

I reread my text because I liked to second-guess myself like that. Did that sound like I was giving him grief for not getting back to me sooner? Or was that a breezy text that indicated I was good with whatever. Ahhhhh, why did my mind read into everything? So frustrating.

A reply pulled me out of my pain-in-the-ass brain.

Noah: *Ellie, that's the elephant, "decided" to take a bath in the washing machine. Or so Addie told us when we called Jake to have him ask her where it was since we couldn't find it. At any rate, I do want to talk more, Jules. I get the vibe that what you shared with me was a big deal, and I don't take that lightly. Breakfast tomorrow at the Sanctuary?*

My stomach did another roller coaster ride. Breakfast? To talk more about it? That sounded mildly terrifying. I dug deep and laid down some more truth.

Me: *In the spirit of continuing to share, I half want to say hell no and go curl up in a ball somewhere. However, I'm working on being open here. Just an FYI—the only other* *person in the world who knows I'm a writer is my friend Kylie.*

The dots telling me that Noah was typing tormented me until his text finally came through.

Noah: *I'm honored to be part of that selective group and promise no one will learn about this from me. You're my accountant now, right? We can call this client confidentiality. That's a thing, right? So, breakfast? I'll make sure you don't need to take the fetal position.*

I snorted at the "client confidentiality" comment before taking a few deep breaths, thinking that would help my skittering heart rate. No luck. Maybe I needed to see a doctor.

I shook my head. One step at a time.

Me: *Breakfast works. Nine sound good?*

Noah: *It's a date. I'll see you there.*

Date? Sure, sleep was going to be easy to come after that text. I put my phone down and settled on my side, O'Malley curled up behind my knees. "Everything will look better in the morning, won't it, boy?"

"Mrow?" He rubbed his head on my legs, bringing me comfort from the familiarity.

"I've got to believe it will," I whispered.

Saturday morning dawned, and I hurried down Main Street toward the Sanctuary. It was a bit cool with bits of fog lifting off gardening beds on either side of me, the sun shining through them. Gorgeous.

I had been correct—sleep hadn't come easily, and I'd tossed and turned until the early-morning hours. All that was to say I'd overslept because I'd finally found the shut-eye that eluded me until far too late in the night, or early in the morning to be more precise. Luckily it was only a few blocks to hit the Sanctuary, and the weather was gorgeous—

blue skies, light breeze, warm sun. It all worked together to help me wake up as I rushed to meet Noah.

Stepping into the coffee shop, I was hit with the delicious aroma of the magic elixir I knew would fix my exhausted state. Add the amazing smell of baked goods, and I wondered if I could just move in.

"Hey, Jules!"

I looked over to the counter in the front of what would have been the altar in the former life of this building when it was a church. Allyson offered me a wave before waiting on a customer. Her belly was like a small beachball under her fitted shirt. I looked around for Maeve, but there was no sign of the more outspoken sister. Noah, however, waved at me from the leather armchairs by the window I'd sat in just a week ago. I pointed at the counter, indicating I was going to order, to which he nodded and raised a book he had open in his lap in response.

"Hey, Allyson," I said as I reached the counter.

She tapped the steamed-milk pitcher on the counter, then proceeded to pour the milk in the coffee before passing it off to the guy in front of me. "Medium latte," she said, then turned my way, gesturing to the stools on my side of the counter. "Want to order and grab a seat? We can visit while I make drinks."

"Um." I bit my lip and looked over to Noah, who was reading with an armchair ready for me.

Allyson followed my gaze, then looked back to me. "Ahh, meeting someone?"

I felt the heat warm my neck and cheeks as I nodded my head, mumbling out a reply. "Yeah, it's just, we had dinner last night and..."

Allyson interrupted, her eyes twinkling. "Dinner? You

are holding out on us, Jules. You're lucky that Maeve and/or Maggie isn't here right now."

I laughed, knowing that was the truth. "We're just friends," I said, rolling my eyes. I had to admit, after having a small group of friends in Chicago, it was going to take some time to get used to knowing people wherever you went in this town. Jury was still out as to whether this fishbowl feeling would get old or not. For now it was somewhat comforting.

"Okay, friends it is," Allyson said reassuringly. "What can I get you?"

I scanned the menu board. "Umm, how about a vanilla latte and an egg sandwich?"

"Bacon?" she asked, immediately typing in my order.

"Absolutely."

"Put this on my order." My aunt's voice came from behind me.

Good Lord. As if my morning breakfast date wasn't already stressing me out, Lou was going to be the witness to this? Oh no. Nope. Not ready for this in any way, shape, or form.

That being said, I did love her completely, so I turned to find her standing behind me with Verdell, that saint of a man, and was immediately engulfed in her arms. The floral perfume she'd always worn immediately settled my nervous system.

You might not realize how affectionate Lou was if you didn't know her well. Her quick wit and sarcastic nature, coupled with her salty language, were the first things I'd bet most people thought of when she came to mind. However, I knew her as one of the best huggers and most steady people in my life. She was an oasis of calm for me growing up. Especially with my mom's flighty, if well-meaning, nature.

Lou's hugs were a reset for me, and the fact that she and Verdell lived here was the number one factor in agreeing to move when my mom suggested it. Lou was in her seventies, and while I felt like she could potentially outlive us all, I knew in reality that I needed to soak up time with her and Verdell while I could. They were active and healthy, so I hoped moving here would give me many more years with them.

"Lou," I mumbled into her shoulder.

Her arms squeezed me, and all the while she gave me shit. "You moved down here, and I still don't see you enough, girl."

I peeked over her shoulder. "Hey, Verdell."

"Looking good, Jules," he said, his eyes twinkling. "No more shadows under your eyes."

Verdell was a tell-it-like-it-is kind of person. He didn't have room in his life for bullshit, which is likely why he got along well with Lou. You never questioned where you stood with her. Even so, I was a touch mortified that it took my mom doing her elaborate freak-out to realize how run down I'd gotten. I mean, for Pete's sake, I was thirty years old. You would assume I'd know when I wasn't doing well.

You would be wrong. Or maybe denial was just my friend. Jury was still out.

At any rate, Verdell spoke the truth—I *was* doing better.

I stepped back from Verdell and looked from him to Lou. "It's good to see you both, but you don't need to get my breakfast..."

"Of course we do—that's the benefit to moving near family," Lou said, giving me a look. "Besides, you can sit with us and we can catch up."

"No need," an alarmingly attractive and familiar male

voice joined the party, coming from behind me. "I've already got her."

I turned to see Noah stepping back from the counter behind me, credit card sliding into his wallet as he gave me a grin combined with a raised eyebrow. What in the world? How did he get from the spot by the window to the register all while I soaked in Lou with a hug? And what in the world was he thinking? No way Lou was going to let this slide without commentary. Did he know what he was getting into?

Lou's sharp gaze pinged from Noah to me and back again. "What do we have here?" she asked with barely concealed glee lacing her tone.

"Lou..." Verdell's tone betrayed his own warning.

Didn't matter, I could see that she was positively vibrating with excitement. The train was out of the station, and we were the passengers. Dang.

"Morning, Lou," Noah said, wading into the disaster with no heed for his own safety. "Jules and I had our dinner interrupted last night by the crisis of Addie's missing stuffie..."

"Oh no, Ellie's lost?" Lou asked, clearly able to switch from Queen of Gossip to caring grandma-like figure in a heartbeat.

"*Was* lost," Noah said. "At any rate, we're continuing our conversation from last night over breakfast since I had to race off to find said elephant."

Oh, innocent Noah. Did you think simply telling Lou facts was the way to go? You sweet summer child. I wanted to groan and bury my head in my hands, but I worked to stand strong.

Lou's gaze moved from Noah to me. "Hmm, Jules.

Seems like we have more to catch up on than I thought. Did the girls invite you to Sunday's book club?"

I looked at her in abject horror as my mind began to connect some dots. "You're in Ivy's book club?"

Verdell snorted. *Snorted!* I'd never heard that from the man. "In it? What's your title, Lou? Smut Instigator? Queen Smut Leader?"

I was in danger of hyperventilating. Noah was watching me in fascination, but I was a moment from expiring. Lou needed to speak, to set this all to rights. Unfortunately, that was not in the cards.

"In it? I help pick all the books. The dirtier, the better," she said with a cat-eating-the-canary grin and, *shiver*, a suggestive wink to Verdell.

Yep, I was going to pass out. Did that mean Lou had read my books? At least the first one? Holy bejesus. There was no coming back from this. Wave a white flag, I was done.

Chapter 10

Damn Magnetic Pull

*N**oah***

Did I know what a hornet's nest I had just inadvertently stepped into? I absolutely did. It couldn't be helped, however. I'd seen Lou and Verdell talking to Jules and went up to say hello and, as I overheard Lou wanting to get Jules's breakfast, I'd stepped around to do that instead. Why? Excellent question that I had no answer for. Something in my gut had said *I* needed to. I was no caveman and strongly believed in women's rights. Ivy would kick my ass if I didn't. So why did it matter who paid?

A tiny voice that I was working to ignore told me that in buying Jules's breakfast, this was in fact the date I was trying to tell myself it wasn't. So everything was going along swimmingly. My brain was a mess. Maybe I could convince Jules I'd like to start dating in twelve years when Addie was an adult? I'm sure that's a completely normal request that women everywhere want to hear.

To make matters worse, I went ahead and put out there in front of Lou that I'd been at Jules's place last night and had dinner with her. I've lived in this town for over a year and wasn't oblivious. I knew *exactly* who I was talking to and what she was capable of. Still didn't stop me as I laid it all out there for public consumption. I wouldn't blame Jules if she wanted to ditch our breakfast date—no part of the woman I'd started to get to know said *please make me the focus of town gossip.*

However, as Lou talked about her steamy-romance club, one I knew all about because Ivy was a member, I could see Jules was quickly looking as uncomfortable as she had last night when I'd found her book, but this time I didn't think it had anything to do with me. A quick exit was in order.

I nodded at our audience and placed a hand on Jules's back to move her toward my chair. "Sorry to break up this party, but I need to borrow Jules for a bit. Have a great Saturday, all." With that, I passed Jules her coffee from an amused-looking Allyson and took a decisive step toward where I'd been sitting. Jules, thankfully, moved with me.

"We'll talk more later, Jules." Lou's voice followed our rapid retreat and indicated that none of this would be forgotten.

"And I'll bring your breakfast in a bit," Allyson called.

"Ughhhhhh." The noise coming from Jules was a combination of a moan and a gurgle. I looked at her in amusement as I led her to the comfortable armchair and away from prying eyes.

"Sorry?" I murmured as we both sank into our respective chairs. I mean, I might as well have pissed in a circle around her. One didn't "claim" their friends, but I figured I could just continue on my path of denial. It was working so well and all.

"Are you?" Jules's voice was laced with a combination

of amusement and what sounded like nerves. "Are you aware of what you have set in motion?"

"This isn't my first day in Highland Falls." I lifted my coffee and raised it in her direction. "Let them talk." I sounded far more confident than my thudding heart felt.

She shook her head and mumbled something that sounded like *he doesn't know what he's in for*. Time would tell.

I settled back to get comfortable in my deep leather chair. It was perfectly worn and ridiculously comfortable. I had a brief thought of wishing I could convince Allyson to sell it to me.

"So, shall we pick up where we left off last night?" A flush worked its way up Jules's neck to her cheeks as she bit the corner of her lower lip. I worked to keep myself from prying it free as I thought of how I could possibly set her at ease. "Sorry, if you don't want to share, that's fine too."

Jules held back on replying as she moved to find the perfect spot in her chair, drawing her legs up to sit cross-legged with her back resting on the far arm before looking over to me.

I took the moment she needed to situate herself to soak the woman in without being obvious. Her hair was up in a messy bun with strands escaping all over. She had on some loose jeans, rolled up at the bottom, and a too-big long-sleeved T-shirt. While none of her clothes were fitted, they were somehow even more alluring than if they had been. Like I desperately wanted to see her without them.

Jesus, man. Get yourself together.

Whatever Jules wanted to say had to wait during a momentary reprieve from Allyson as she dropped off Jules's breakfast sandwich and an almond croissant for me.

"Enjoy," she said as she gave me a knowing look. Yep, I'd be hearing from Ivy later.

"Okay." Jules's voice pulled me back to the present, thankfully. "So I mentioned last night that the only other person who knows I write is my friend Kylie." She looked over her shoulder as she spoke those words, as if to ensure herself no one was eavesdropping.

I gave her my full attention. I could tell this was a big deal. "Why haven't you told anyone?"

She stared at her coffee, running a finger over the rim of the cup repeatedly. "Honestly, I don't know if I can fully verbalize why. When I first started writing several years ago, I wrote for stress relief and to do something just for me. I never thought anything I wrote would see the light of day." She took a sip of coffee, still not meeting my eyes. "Then, once I decided to try to publish it, I still thought it was for me to be able to say I did it—even just to myself. I figured no one would ever read it."

I nodded, not wanting to interrupt her. Seemed like this was something she might be processing as she spoke.

"Once my books started selling and I got over the shock of it, I realized I needed to share with my family, but I didn't want to. My friend, Kylie, found out because she stopped by my apartment one day when I was writing and saw my computer before I could stop her. She tried reassuring me, built up my confidence, but it was hard to even have her read my books. The idea of my mom or Lou—" She shuddered with obvious discomfort before shaking it off. "I tried to make rules for myself, like I'd tell them once I reached a certain level." She looked abashed. "But then I kept moving the level."

"So you wouldn't have to say anything." I nodded, attempting to offer her support even from my seat. I didn't know what it was about Jules, but there was a part of me that wanted to protect her, to offer her comfort. I felt that on some level with my long friendship with Ivy, with being a dad to Ivy, but this was different and something I reminded myself I couldn't have, not yet.

"Exactly," she whispered.

"And now?" I prodded.

She grimaced. "And now I just learned that my aunt has potentially already read my first book."

I had to laugh at her horrified look. "And this is terrible because..."

Jules leaned toward my chair. "Noah, my books are *steamy*."

Interesting. "By steamy, I'm taking it that there are descriptions of characters having sex?"

There went her lower lip again as she worried it between her teeth before giving me a slow nod. Mental note, add reading Jules's books to my immediate to-do list.

"Are you embarrassed or ashamed of that?"

Her head tilted as she thought for a moment. "No, not ashamed. But as a culture, people are weird about it, you know? Like I've had people ask me on my writing accounts on social media if those scenes are based on my own life. One, that's strange. And two, the answer is no, of course not." She paused, looking lost in thought for a moment. "I don't know if that's why I get so freaked out by my family reading them—maybe I'm scared they'll assume the same? Or..." She looked out the window as she mulled it over. "Maybe I'm afraid they'll think the book is just bad overall."

I thought about that. "Well, I don't know many people who write books, only Elle who lives in town. She's a historical fiction author. But Jules"—I made sure she met my gaze —"I think that it's incredible that you are able to take something that exists in your imagination and put it in a form for others to enjoy. I have a feeling that anyone you share this news with will think similarly. *Especially* people who are related to you."

Jules looked down again as she mumbled a reply. "Yeah, confidence in myself isn't something I have in droves. Heck" —she rubbed her thumb over the handle on her mug—"the struggle to even write my current book is real. Just the knowledge that people were reading it made writing harder. The idea of being open with everyone..." She shuddered.

I reached over and tapped her knee to get her to look up. "Jules, it's not for me to decide if or when you share your writing life with others, so I am not judging what you've done so far. And I don't know your parents, but trust me when I say that Lou would likely be your biggest cheerleader if she knew."

Her eyes welled up, which made my heart clench, and I wished I could scoop her into my lap and hold her.

"Thanks, Noah. It's nice to talk to someone about this even if it's not easy."

I kept my seat and tried for reassurance. "You've got this, Jules. Maybe you need to work on imagining what it would feel like no longer carrying it around as a secret."

At that comment, she nodded and picked up her sandwich and began to eat while gazing out the window, clearly processing my words. I took a moment and sat back, sipped my coffee, took a bite of my croissant, and gave her some space to think.

A glance around the café found that they were busy today, like always. There were tables of folks by themselves working on laptops, a group that appeared to have come from one of Kate and Kristine's yoga classes judging by their attire and a few rolled-up mats, and clusters of two or three folks spread out around the space. Allyson had small sections of seats situated in the café so that even when most spots were taken, you still felt like you had some privacy.

That being said, my eyes found Lou's across the room where she was sitting with Verdell and a few of her friends, though her gaze was fixed on us. She raised her eyebrows at me as if to remind me that she was keeping tabs. I gave her a nod to tell her I had this.

I hoped I did.

"Noah." Jules soft voice brought me back to her.

"Yeah?"

"What if knowing that people who *know* me read my books takes away the magic? What if I can't escape into my fictional world anymore because I'm thinking of their reactions as I write? What if my current writer's block is permanent? What then?" The only way to describe Jules's expression was sad. Like she was worried about something she'd lost before she even had.

But I was stuck on something she'd said at the beginning. "Um, Jules, what are you trying to escape?"

She blinked rapidly in my direction. "When did I say that?"

"Just now." This woman. Everything in me was telling me to comfort her, reassure her it would all be okay. I was holding strong because we were in public and Lou would certainty have something to say. And oh yeah, I wasn't dating. Anyone. And yet...

"I guess." Jules looked at the ceiling for more than a few beats before turning back to me. "I guess escaping my reality?"

"Want to elaborate on that?" I looked around, and the space I'd felt we had seemed to be evaporating. "And want to go on a walk as you share?"

"What?" Jules looked around, behind our chairs, seeming to see how many people now filled the café. "Sure. Want to walk back toward our houses?"

I nodded and scooped up our now-empty plates while she grabbed our mugs. We dropped them in the black tub by the door and left without a glance toward Lou, or at least I did—I couldn't speak for Jules. I just felt certain the older woman would have a lot to say if I looked her way.

Stepping outside, I enjoyed the warmth of the sun as I fell into step with Jules. "So why were you escaping your reality?"

Jules was looking down at her feet as she walked; the feeling I got from even seeing her profile was one of being lost. *Fuck it*, I thought, grabbing her hand. Friends held hands when needed, right?

Sure.

Jules looked at me in surprise but then squeezed my hand and laced her fingers with mine as she reassumed our trek, apparently on board with the friends-who-hold-hands idea. "I think when I started writing, I was stressed about work." She gave a slight shake to her head. "No, I know that was it. Writing was this thing to do for fun and just for me. The company I worked for in Chicago isn't known for caring about work-life balance but how much you can do for them. And, well..."

I gave her a squeeze, trying to send her the confidence I felt certain she had buried deep.

We crossed a street, and I took in the trees that were showing off the beginning of their spring leaves. Tulips were coming up in the front yards we passed, the sky was a brilliant blue, birds were singing their songs, and we were the only people on the street.

Jules squeezed my hand again as she cleared her throat. "It's probably obvious that I'm a bit introverted—"

I gasped for dramatic effect.

She pulled her hand from mine to slap my biceps as she laughed. Damn, I'd do anything to make her look that carefree on the regular. Her hand slid back into mine and she continued. "Anyway, life as an adult is weird, you know? I often felt lonely in Chicago, which is crazy considering how big the city is. Kylie is a good friend, but the other folks I know... It's like I felt that I was often just forgettable. And I'd see all these social media posts from 'friends' and they were always out for coffee, shopping, et cetera, but no one asked me." She shook her head. "That makes me sound whiny, and I don't mean it like that. Clearly they were allowed to invite whomever they wanted."

She scuffed her foot as she kicked a rock, and we crossed another street. Moving onto a brick sidewalk and the older part of town, she continued.

"And I also should acknowledge that I'm an adult and don't expect others to always do the heavy lifting. I'd ask them to brunch or whatever and we'd go, but it was like I just didn't quite click with them the same way they did with each other. It didn't feel effortless, natural, but like I was trying to manufacture a group of friends." She glanced over at me. "At any rate, I just felt adrift a lot, stressed from my job, wondering if I was missing the girlfriend gene, and finally I started writing a world I wished I was a part of—with women who were empowering, kind, and inclusive." Her sigh was heavy. "So you can see it was nothing dire I was escaping, just somewhere I felt like I could just... be."

We'd reached her front sidewalk, and I tugged her to stop midway up before she could tell me she needed to go.

"Jules, there's nothing wrong with writing a world you wished you could be in."

Her warm brown eyes met mine and she nodded.

"Babe—" Where had that come from? Moving on. "We all want to be seen. I don't know a person who doesn't."

"Even you?" she whispered.

I nodded, noting that she took a step toward me. I searched inward for willpower I didn't possess. Instead, I met her with another step until we were toe-to-toe. Damn magnetic pull gets you every time.

"You're making me crazy," I whispered.

Confusion flitted across her face. "How?"

A long strand of hair had escaped the pile on her head, and I reached up to tuck it behind her ear, running my finger along her jaw after I did. "I'm trying so hard to keep my distance," I whispered, not even sure if that was audible.

She started to step back, but I tightened my grip on her hand, which I still had, then let go to hold her hip.

"Why?" she asked, clearly having heard me.

My gaze roamed her face as I debated how honest to be. I decided to lay it all out. "Because since I came back, I've said Addie will be my priority. I can date when she's grown."

"Okay?" she whispered, confusion evident as she failed to grasp my faulty logic.

"But I really need to kiss you," I said, adding to the mixed messages because I couldn't hold back anymore but still wanted to give her time to say no. Hell, also allowing myself time to get with the program.

Instead of realizing I was a fool and telling me so, she looked up at me with a small smile. "I think I'm good with that," she murmured as she took the decision away from me and rolled up on her toes.

Fuck it, decision was made. I moved at once, tipping her chin and leaning down to capture my mouth with hers.

At first we just brushed our lips together. The brief sensation was like finding something I'd lost and needed a whole lot more of. I tilted my own head a bit more, and Jules immediately parted her lips as we came together again.

She tasted of coffee and a familiarity that I shouldn't have but wanted to never lose. Her hands swept around me to hold me against her, though she needn't be worried I was going nowhere.

I'd never had a first kiss—hell, any kiss—that made me feel as alive as this one. Just as I slid a hand up to thread my fingers in her hair, I heard someone clearing their throat and pulled back, sliding myself in front of Jules instinctively to block her from the prying eyes of what was to be certain another nosy Highland Falls citizen. What I found was that but more.

Looking at us from a mere six feet away on the public sidewalk were Jake and Ivy with giant grins. Their baby, Lorelai, looked to be sacked out in a sling on Ivy's chest. And, of course, jumping up and down and waving her stuffed elephant was none other than Addie.

Fuck.

Chapter 11

Meet the Fam

Jules

Wowza. Where does one even begin to focus their thoughts when the world turns upside down? However, it should be noted that I needed to commit every moment of that kiss to memory. That was romance-book worthy for certain. So inspiring that I wanted to transport myself to my computer posthaste and write a scene for Julian and Collette where they have their first kiss. Inspiration was finally striking while my lips were still tingling, though Julian was looking a whole lot like Noah, which could be problematic. Seemed like my hero still needed to be fleshed out.

And, at the same time, I wanted to burrow myself into the ground. How could I have my first kiss—but please not my last—with this man *and* have an audience as it happened? My face was certainly flushed, my neck likely red as well. I pressed my hand to my lips, still feeling the electricity, and met Ivy's happy gaze right before she sent me a wink. Ahhhh!

"Daddy!" Addie caught my attention as she was

dancing with her elephant on the sidewalk. "Who is your friend, and do you like my new skirt?"

Noah cleared his throat, his face betraying his unease at the situation. My stomach dropped. My reaction to our kiss was when could it happen again. Sure, we had stuff to sort, and I had no room in my life for a relationship, but I could handle some more kisses. Sign me up.

That being said, the man had just talked about how he was making his daughter a priority, which I absolutely agreed with, and now she was front row and center to our first lip-lock? If I'd had a Magic 8 Ball and shaken it right then, the prediction for any future mouth-on-mouth action would be "outlook not so good." I fought the rising anxiety in my chest and worked to act like all this was normal.

"Hey, Ads, I love the skirt." Noah's voice was warm with clear affection even as he clearly struggled with the whole situation.

Same, man. Same.

Addie spun so that the layers of tulle floated up and you could see the multicolored polka dots that filled the skirt. Below it, she wore navy leggings with silver stars that ended at her bright pink Crocs. It was an ensemble, that was for certain.

"This is my friend, Jules." He gestured in my direction.

"Hey, Ms. Jules, are you and my daddy one kissing friends?" Addie said, peering up at me with an innocent look. "Like my mommy and daddy two? But now I just call them both Daddy, though sometimes that's confusing." With that little bomb, she again began spinning and swaying on the sidewalk, twirling with Ellie the Elephant.

My reaction was to splutter as I fought needing a paper bag to breathe into. Did I answer her? Kissing friends? Daddy One? "Umm..."

Ivy reached over, tentatively putting a hand on my forearm. "Hey, Jules." Her voice was warm and held a hint of amusement. "Sorry for the interruption—"

"Are you?" Noah asked.

I looked from Ivy to Noah and noted the look he was giving her. It was one of annoyance mixed with affection.

She had the decency to look a little bit, heavy on the *little bit*, sorry. "Not like we planned this, Noah."

"Um." I looked around at my neighbors' homes, not wanting any of this to reach the ears of Lou. Seeing that we had so far escaped any more of this nosy small town's citizens joining us on this very public sidewalk, I made the only logical decision I could. "This is my house." I gestured up the path. "Do you guys want to come in?"

"Do you have a Chief?" Addie asked, a serious expression on her face as she locked her beautiful eyes on me.

"No." Noah answered for me. "She has a cat named O'Malley."

Note to self, Chief was likely a dog. Maybe I should follow up on that later. Did Noah own said pup? Jake and Ivy? How was I crushing on this man when I clearly had a lot to learn beyond the odd, instant connection I felt to him? Other known facts included that the man loved his kid, he could keep a secret, and was an excellent kisser. And I knew the info on his taxes. I guess people had dated with less knowledge, right? Hell, I was certainly trying to write a book with a less fleshed-out background for Julian. Maybe I should do some more character work?

Refocus, I chastised myself. Important note, would Noah even want to date? I mean, if I referred back to his comment about waiting for Addie to hit eighteen, the answer would clearly be no. But then there was that kiss...

I looked up as Jake cleared his throat, his eyes on Noah.

"Interesting that you know that tidbit about her cat," Jake said under his breath with raised eyebrows and a shit-eating grin. Thankfully he didn't catch Addie's attention, but the adults heard him just fine.

Noah scratched his nose with his middle finger.

"Yeah!" Addie squealed. "O'Malley and I can be best friends." She ran to my front door.

"Well, I guess we're all going in," Ivy said, patting her sleeping baby's bottom as she swayed. "Goddess knows we won't get her home until she sees the cat."

I fought hyperventilating again as I walked to the front the door. "Go ahead," I called to Addie.

She turned the doorknob and walked in.

"Babe," Noah said as he walked by my side. "You didn't lock your front door."

I looked up at him in confusion as we walked in the house and I kicked off my shoes. "Isn't that the benefit of living in a small town? Lou told me she doesn't lock her door most of the time unless she's sleeping or out of town."

"It's not safe." Noah's voice was growly. It was doing something to me.

Jake laughed as he and Ivy followed me into the house and kicked off their shoes too. "Noah, you know damn well your door often isn't locked during the day."

"I'm not Jules," he replied in a clipped tone.

"Patriarchal nonsense," Ivy muttered.

"Kitty," Addie exclaimed.

I looked past the living room to the kitchen. Addie's legs were sticking out of the entrance to the nook in my kitchen. We all headed in that direction as she pulled herself up and in.

"Momma," Addie said, peeking back out to look at us. "This is like a clubhouse."

Ivy stuck her head in to check it out. "It is," she replied. Looking to the side where my pile of pillows was, she gave a soft smile. "You must be O'Malley."

I couldn't see my spoiled cat, but his *mrow* was loud enough for all of us to hear.

Ivy glanced over at me as she continued to rub Lorelai's back in the sling. "Will O'Malley want company, or should I tell Addie to hop down?"

"I think they'll be fine." I stepped forward to aid in the introductions and popped my head in.

O'Malley was lounging against the jewel-colored pillows, leg up, giving his belly a good bath.

"O'Malley," I called. When he paused and looked my way, I nodded toward Addie. "This is Addie. Addie, this is O'Malley."

"May I pet him, Ms. Jules?" Addie was positively vibrating with excitement from holding herself back.

I smiled at her energy. I wasn't around kids a whole lot, but I could honestly say that so far I liked this one. "You bet, Addie."

"Gentle," Ivy cautioned.

Addie dropped to her belly on the cushioned platform and slid over to O'Malley. "Hey, O'Malley," she said in a hushed voice as she stretched out her hand.

O'Malley stopped his grooming routine and looked her way. He didn't move, so her hand crept closer, and then she ran her small fingers over his side. I knew Addie had won him over when O'Malley leaned into her and his purr reverberated through the space.

Addie looked to me, her eyes alight with joy as she said in a loud whisper, "He likes me!"

I grinned back at her and stepped away, content to let them continue their new friendship on their own. I turned only to see three sets of eyes fixed on me. Noah's gaze was wary, Ivy's was curious, and Jake's was amused. I guess wanting a relaxing afternoon was not in the cards.

"Um, you guys want something to drink?" I asked, unsure where to even start.

"Jules," Noah said, stepping toward me, "please don't feel like you have to entertain us."

I looked down at the counter for a moment, debating how much of myself I wanted to share. However, if I wanted to be different than I was in Chicago, if I wanted my life to be different, being open and honest was part of that.

I met Noah's gaze. "It's okay," I said softly. "I'd like you guys to stay."

Noah's eyes stayed locked on mine for a moment before he brushed my arm, gave me a quick nod, and stepped back. I looked to Jake and Ivy, who were watching us with rapt attention.

"That was electric, right, babe?" Ivy stage-whispered to Jake.

"Electric," he murmured back, reaching around to squeeze her shoulder.

I quickly made the choice to ignore what I didn't want to try to decipher and walked over to my fridge. Opening the door, I took a quick mental stock of what I had available. "Guys, I've got Sport tea, cold-brew coffee, soda, and water." Then I looked to my counter and nodded at the container by my coffeemaker. "I can also make regular coffee, and I have some blueberry muffin bread." I finally turned back to the three adults standing in my kitchen, wondering how this was going to go.

Ivy looked over at the spot where we could hear Addie chattering on to O'Malley, seemingly telling a story about a bird outside the window and his friends. "One, I hope you know that Addie will never want to leave here now. You might just have to let her move in."

I relaxed, which I realized was Ivy's intent.

"And I'd love some tea and some of that bread." She yawned, attempting to cover her mouth. "Sorry, little miss here was up most of the night." She patted Lorelai's butt.

"Is she okay?" I asked, pouring her some tea and putting together the shadows under both her eyes and Jake's.

"Think so. Likely teething." She gave me a small smile and a quiet thanks as she took the tea and the plate holding a piece of bread.

I gave her a small smile, then returned to grab some tea for myself. Within a second, I felt a hand on my hip as Noah came up behind me. "Sorry, babe, I'm grabbing stuff for Jake and me."

"Babe?" I whispered.

He was silent for a moment, which almost made me regret my comment. But then he squeezed my hip before grabbing two glasses as he replied, still in a low voice just for me. "Sorry, I think that's the second time I've called you that."

"Third, not that I'm complaining, just..."

"Confused?" He came around and leaned against the counter, looking my way.

I glanced over his shoulder, seeing Jake and Ivy had retreated to the nook and were talking to Addie and O'Malley, likely giving us a bit of privacy.

"A bit," I replied, slicing pieces of bread for the rest of us.

"I don't blame you." He hesitated. Was he regretting our kiss?

"I'm sorry," I blurted out.

His eyes drew together with concern. "Why?"

"You said you weren't ready..."

Noah shook his head. "Jules, I kissed you. And I don't regret it."

Whoosh, relief flooded my body. "You don't?"

He smiled at me. "I'm not sure what this is, and we need to talk a whole lot more, but please don't think that regret is anything I'm feeling whatsoever."

"Hey, kids, not sure what all you're whispering about, but I could use some caffeine sometime this century," Jake called over as Ivy smacked him, all while still patting the baby and swaying back and forth. Impressive multitasking.

Suddenly a wail worthy of an NFL linebacker came from the sling on Ivy's chest. Wowza, I had no idea babies could be so loud when they were so small.

"Uh-oh," Ivy muttered, which had Jake coming quickly to attention.

"What," Jake noted, his body tense.

Ivy glanced his way and gave him a look that could only be described as full of love. "Sorry, sweetheart, you've got to relax. There will be lots of uh-ohs as this little one grows."

"Ivy," he growled over the continued wails as Ivy swayed around the room, "you can give me sh—" He looked in Addie's direction. "...sheet for being overprotective later. What's the uh-oh about?"

"I think Lorelai has an ear infection, that's all." Ivy looked my way and shook her head, rolling her eyes in a clear commentary on Jake's caveman reactions. While I got where she was coming from, I also thought it was sweet.

"How do you know?" Jake had now stopped her, surrounding her with his arms as he peered into the sling.

"She's tugging on her ears," Ivy pointed out. "She had a slight temp earlier, but I thought it was no biggie and she was teething." She shrugged as she gave him a tolerant smile and kissed the underside of his jaw. "Babies get sick, Jake. It will be okay."

She looked back to me. "So sorry to cut our visit short, Jules. I absolutely want to get to know you better *and* have a moment to question that guy over there." She nodded toward Noah, who was standing against my island, somewhat frozen. Another mental note to add to my list—what was up with him right now? Did he not like seeing Jake and Ivy all lovey like they had been? I doubted that with what I'd witnessed that first night I saw them in the brewery. Hmm.

"Ads, we've got to roll," Ivy called. She looked at Jake. "You can take her home, and I'll head to convenient care and get this checked out."

"I don't want you to go by yourself," Jake growled.

Bless overprotective men. It could be hot as long as they weren't assholes. Another mental note to add to my ongoing list of things to ponder and/or add to my book.

Ivy attempted to reassure Jake. "Sweetheart, do you know how often I went by myself with Ads? It's no big deal, and I don't want Addie in the waiting room. Goddess knows what germs she'd pick up."

Noah still seemed frozen in place with an almost pained look on his face.

"Momma, I don't want to leave O'Malley. We're best friends. He'll be so lonely without me," Addie called from the nook, her voice trending toward a whine she was clearly trying to hold back.

Before I knew it, words spilled out of my mouth without a conscious decision to say anything. "How about Noah and I keep Addie, then you can both go."

Ivy stopped swaying and patting the fussy babe on her

chest and turned toward me with a glance at the still-silent Noah. She seemed to study him even as he didn't pipe up with any thoughts on my suggestion. Finally, she moved to a spot in front of him, her sway continuing as she walked and patted, Lorelai still fussing, but it was much quieter now.

"Noah," she said in a low voice, her comment making him focus on her.

Noah shook his head, then looked around to the nook, then at Jake, then Ivy again, before focusing on me. Clearing his throat, he said, "Addie and I can go to my place —you don't have to give up your afternoon."

"Da-ddyyyyyyyy." Addie poked her head out of the opening to the platform as she shot her parents a look.

I laughed at her incensed voice before looking at Noah. "I'd love you guys to stay."

He watched me for a moment, probably to determine if I really meant what I said, then gave me a nod before looking at Ivy. "We've got Ads; you guys go ahead."

Addie cheered and went back in her space without further comment to us, but some words were being mumbled to O'Malley. I heard "Silly parents" and "I've got you, sweet kitty." My poor cat didn't know what he was in for with that pint-sized dynamo.

"Excellent, guys. Let's go, babe." Jake grabbed their diaper bag and was ready to roll, looking all sorts of impatient.

Ivy hugged Noah, saying something in his ear before coming over to give me a squeeze. She whispered to me, "We'll chat later, Jules. Take care of him."

"I've got him," I replied, hoping I was telling the truth.

Chapter 12

Unpacking Some Baggage

N*oah*

We'd had a text from Ivy an hour ago with an update on Lorelai. They'd been sitting in the waiting room at convenient care for almost an hour, but after seeing a doc, the double ear infection had been confirmed. They'd headed to pick up some meds and get them in Lorelai as soon as possible so she could start feeling better. Jake had offered to drop them at their place and swing by to get Addie, but I'd let Jules convince me to tell them we'd keep Addie until dinner. Jules had made no moves to tell us to leave either, not that I'd wanted her to, thereby prolonging the longest breakfast date ever into one that was now stretching into early afternoon.

I looked over at Jules's living room. She and Addie had made a fort with sheets and blankets over the tops of chairs and the couch. *Bluey* was on the television, and Addie and O'Malley were set up to watch it from their cave-like location. Jules had just popped back over to check on them and was headed back my way.

And how was I doing? Pretty shitty if I was being

honest. I'd escaped any conversation about it so far. In the past three hours, we'd made homemade chocolate chip cookies, checked out Jules's new bird feeder, identified birds that were about, Jules had helped Addie make an illustrated "book"—printing paper stapled together—about Addie and O'Malley, and had some sandwiches for lunch. Then fort building had commenced and here we were.

I had a funny feeling my time of avoidance was at an end. It wasn't that I didn't want to talk to Jules, but I wasn't even sure where to start. The expressions she'd been giving me for the past few hours were wary, which was the last thing I wanted. Yeah, it was high time to make sure we were on the same page and get out whatever other crap we had hanging there, ready to weigh us down.

Then again, what did I say? I thought we had potential together and absolutely wanted to kiss her again but didn't think I should date until Addie was an adult. Oh, and I was carrying around several suitcases full of baggage of my own? That seemed like a great conversation starter. And to think this morning I just wanted to talk to this woman and let her share her own stresses. Now I was asking her to take on some of mine. Fuck.

Oblivious of my inner torment, Jules plopped down on the stool next to me at the island, still in hostess mode. "You have enough tea?"

"You don't need to wait on me, Jules."

"And you, Noah, have been avoiding a real conversation," she said bluntly, her foot knocking against mine.

I looked over at her and she, like she had ever since I met the woman just under a week ago, took my breath away. Her hair was still in a bun on her head, but far more than a few strands had escaped at this point. She'd kicked off her shoes when we got here and had been barefoot since. Her vibe was relaxed and unpretentious, and I was a huge fan.

I took a deep breath and sat back in my seat. "What would you like to talk about?"

She looked like she was going to give me shit, but I held a hand up when I realized how that sounded.

"Swear I'm not trying to avoid this, but there're so many directions we could take a conversation... The kiss, your writing, et cetera. What baggage do you want me to start with?" I worked to lighten the conversation, though it felt anything but.

She ignored my quip and leaned forward, clearly trying to keep this between the two of us. She didn't need to worry—*Bluey* was on and Addie had a cat with her in a home-made fort. She was in her happiest of places, and whatever we were discussing wouldn't even factor into her world over there.

"All those are important conversations, Noah, and I'd like to talk about each one. For what it's worth, it's not baggage to me but parts of you. For now, however, I'm more concerned about why you became clearly upset when Ivy and Jake had a sick baby and had to head to the doc." She watched me with a warm gaze, clearly trying to send reas-surance to me with telepathy. My original impression of the woman remained true—she was just *good*, down to her core, and I had a strong desire to know more.

I let out a sigh as I debated how to do this.

Jules's look changed, became a bit more closed off. "This really is none of my business, we just met..."

I shook my head. "That's not it, and I think I can speak for both of us in that we're building a solid friendship with..." I glanced over at her. "...the possibility of more?"

Jules nodded.

"Then you are absolutely entitled to ask questions when you are concerned." I thought for a minute. "But about my reaction to Lorelai's ear infection, I know I was being weird earlier. There's one answer for that, but it might lead to a bigger conversation."

"That's fine." She relaxed again.

My laugh was rough. "There's only so much childhood bullshit I want to dump on you in a weekend, Jules. I don't want to scare you off." It struck me when I said that how true the words were. Was that a normal thought about a friend? More to think on later.

"You won't," she promised.

I looked at the ceiling, searching for a way to put my fears into words. "Umm, well, you know the backstory of me moving here, right?" I remembered her telling me the other day she knew some of it, but I wasn't sure what details she'd heard.

I felt her hand on my thigh and looked over. "I know a little. You were in Africa and worked with a company to install wells but then moved to the States a year and a half ago."

"Yep, that sums it up." I thought back to my time after a college with a smile. "Addie was a surprise Ivy and I hadn't planned on, but the best surprise possible. When we found out she was coming, we'd already decided we were more friends than anything else." I took a deep breath. Jules already knew I'd been overseas for most of Addie's early years, but I still felt like a deadbeat dad whenever I talked about it. "I offered to stay, but Ivy knew how much I had looked forward to working in Africa, to making some type of difference." My voice trailed off as I thought of my parents.

Jules squeezed my leg, and I looked into her eyes, which held no judgment. "Why did you want to make a difference? Was that something your mom and dad instilled in you?"

I choked on the laughter that burst out at the image of my parents wanting to give to anyone but themselves. "Hardly."

She raised an eyebrow and furrowed her brow.

"Ivy and I come from a wealthy circle. And I'm sure not everyone with money is a self-entitled asshole, but my parents certainly are. They were infuriated that I didn't follow in my dad's footsteps and cut me off when I went to Africa, also cutting Addie off." My gut churned with the memory of the words they'd shouted at me, the absolute disbelief that I'd want a different life than them.

"My god, Noah. I'm so sorry." Jules's eyes were watery. She exuded kindness and compassion. My parents would eat her alive. Mental note to never let them meet her.

I slid my hand on top of hers to reassure her but also because it felt right. "Thanks. I wish I could say that was out of character for them, but that would be a lie. But in a weird way, they did inspire the need to give back. My entire life, I was surrounded by excess by the privilege of where I'd been born, not by anything I'd done to deserve it. So the idea of traveling to Africa, helping people have access to water, was born after I heard a presenter to my middle school class talk about his work over there. My parents thought I'd 'get over it,' but that was not the case."

Jules gave me a soft smile as Addie let out a peal of laughter.

"You good, Addie?" I called.

Her voice echoed out of her fort. "Yes, Daddy. *Bluey* is so funny. O'Malley loves this show, Ms. Jules."

"Glad to hear it, Ms. Addie," Jules called over, her eyes sparkling.

Damn, that was a good look on her.

"So you went to Africa." She got us back on track.

I smiled, acknowledging what she was doing. "Yes, and I did love it, but the guilt of not being here, of what I was missing, ate at me every single day." I tipped my head toward the fort, and she nodded in understanding. "Finally I came back—"

"And the rest is history?"

I tipped my hand from side to side. "I mean, kind of? I'm more grateful every day that I made the choice to come to Highland Falls, but sometimes things pop up that remind me of all I missed with Addie's first four years and that there's no way to undo that."

Jules looked off in thought but then turned my way with an expression that told me she got it. "Like a baby having an ear infection..."

"And Ivy having to take care of that on her own, over and over, for years."

Jules's eyes were watery again as she squeezed my thigh. "I don't know Ivy well, but she doesn't seem like the type of person to hold that against you."

I laughed. "Oh, she absolutely is not that type of person, but it doesn't keep the feelings of guilt at bay."

"I get that." Jules's voice was soft. "And the childhood trauma? How does that tie in?"

I ran my free hand through my hair. "I mean, beyond what I already told you about my parents..."

"Yeah, they sound like real peaches." Her voice was scornful. "I'd like to have a word with them."

The image of Jules going toe-to-toe with my mother and father was interesting. I immediately had the protective instinct that had popped up earlier to keep her away from them. I also had a warm feeling that she even wanted to *try* to defend me. The only person who had done that for me before was Ivy.

I smiled at Jules. "You're like a ferocious little kitten."

She blushed while attempting to deny it.

"No, that's a compliment." I tried to think of how to put my feelings into words. "I think it fucks with a person to grow up without a support system. I'm not sure if people know how lucky they are to have supportive parents at their back. Ivy, once we became friends, was all I really had. Well, along with an employee of my parents. I think that's why I was so upset when I found out last year that Ivy had really struggled to make ends meet after having Addie." I looked down at my hand on Jules's. I hadn't let go because it gave me the feeling of support. "I felt like I was no better than my parents—at least they had offered financial support when I was a kid."

"Noah." Jules's voice was firm. "Did you offer support to Ivy?"

I met her determined gaze and shrugged. "Well, yes, but she turned me down, so I started a college fund for Addie instead, but if I had known they were struggling that first year..."

"So how is that not supporting your child?" She didn't let up.

I slid my hand away so I could sit back on the stool and ran my hands over my face. I knew what she was saying, but it didn't change what I felt. I was overwhelmed, thinking of my parents, their dismissive nature, the memories of wanting to be righting the wrongs in the world while also feeling the tug to be here. It was a lot.

"Sorry, I'm not trying to tell you how to feel." Jules's voice was smaller.

Jesus, I was fucking this up. "No, babe, I don't think

that." I sighed in frustration. "I'm just trying to figure out how to put feelings into words, and it's all mucked up."

We sat there in silence, and typically that was hard for me. I wanted to fill it, to make everyone around me comfortable. That afternoon, however, it felt peaceful as I sorted out my thoughts. I was struggling to understand how to tell Jules where my mind had been, but if I needed some time, I somehow knew she was fine with that. The sound of *Bluey* floated in from the television, and the mouthwatering scent of chocolate chip cookies was still in the air. Interestingly, I noted that for it being only my second time in Jules's home, I was comfortable there.

"Before Addie, I didn't know if I'd ever have kids." My eyes welled up with all that I might have missed. Without hesitation, Jules slid her hand into mine and squeezed. "My parents were such shit role models; I had no desire to inflict that upon a kid."

Jules gave me space to think before continuing and waited patiently.

"Ivy and I had known each other for what feels like forever, but I think the main reason we got together was that neither of us has much, if anything, in the way of family beside our parents—and neither set is winning any awards. However, she'd be the first to tell you that mine make hers look tame. Once we realized we were better off as friends, she helped me plan for my jump to Africa and then"—I looked to where Addie was chilling out and got choked up— "the best thing ever happened."

Jules squeezed my hand but stayed quiet.

"My mother and father's reactions were predictable. They were taking any money I had coming and cutting me off if I continued to be 'foolish' in going overseas. They also said they wouldn't recognize Addie as their grandchild." I shrugged, downplaying how their coldness cut like a knife. "I didn't want or need their money and hadn't expected them to continue to support me financially anyway. But Addie..."

Jules gave up on the silent listening and let out what sounded like a small growl before speaking. "How could they be so cruel?"

I snorted without humor. "It's so par for the course with them; I wasn't even surprised. For my whole life, they've worked to control my actions. Most of the time it was easier to comply, at least by appearances, and do what I wanted out of sight. And honestly, when they said they were cutting us both off, I didn't fight it. I want them to stay as far away from Addie as possible, so that didn't have the effect they'd intended." I bit my lower lip, thinking back on what I learned upon moving to Highland—the truth Ivy had kept from me because she'd known what my reaction would be. "I just wished I'd known Ivy needed money."

"That's exactly why I made sure you didn't know."

I looked up to see Ivy walking into the kitchen from Jules's front door, which I hadn't even heard open.

"Iv—" I started.

"Nope." She made a slicing motion with her hand. "Sorry you're going to be here for this, Jules, but this stubborn man needs to hear me, and you get to be my witness."

Jules's smile stretched wide as she sat up. "Glad to."

"I feel ganged up on," I grumbled.

"Tough," Ivy said. "Noah, I know *exactly* what your parents are like, and I was so damn proud of you for growing up in that toxic bullshit but still being a kindhearted person who didn't care about the privilege he'd been given but still wanted to go out there and right some wrongs. *That's* the legacy you gave our daughter—a father she can look up to for his ideals. So what if we struggled at the beginning? Yes, I was stressed, and no, I never want to experience it again. That's why I'm cautious with money. But not one time did I resent you or feel like you weren't a supportive dad, Noah. You need to get past that. If I had really needed it, you have to know I would have gotten ahold of you." She looked pissed, which was not an expression Ivy wore often.

I put my hands up to get her to stop her soapbox moment. Otherwise, she'd keep going for certain. "You win, Ivy. I'll work on it."

She raised her eyebrow in my direction. "You better." Then she looked to Jules. "Sorry to crash your house, but Lorelai got some antibiotics in her and is sacked out for a late-afternoon nap. Jake is hanging with her, and I figured I'd come get Addie so you could go back to your day as planned." She waggled her eyebrows at the two of us, breaking the tension.

"You sure?" I asked, considering how tired Ivy seemed of late, though maybe the brewing ear infection was responsible for Lorelai's lack of sleep. "I wasn't here last weekend, so I'm happy to have Ads today and tonight if needed."

Ivy smiled warmly and leaned over to kiss my cheek. "You are the best, Noah, but we're good. Ms. Addie will be fine. And mister"—she gave me her best stern expression—"think on what I said. You need to let that stuff go. Goddess knows you are the father our little girl needs exactly as you are."

"Thanks, Ivy," I whispered, wishing it was that easy, that I could hear her words and believe them in the depths of my soul.

Jules sat quietly by my side as Ivy gave me a look that said she knew I wasn't there yet but would get there eventually. Then, as if she'd made some silent decision, she called out, "Ads…"

Addie's blond curls stuck out of her fort, and she looked our way. "Yeah, Momma."

"Time to hit the road. Little sis is at home snoozing, and Chief needs you on duty."

Ivy was a master. Giving Addie a job was the way to get things done without a fight. Tagging in Jake's pup was expert-level stuff. Even so, Addie sent a side-eye back in her tented area. "But Momma, O'Malley…"

Jules jumped in like the hero she was. "Oh, Addie, thanks so much for hanging with O'Malley, but it's time for his nap." She was on the move to the living room as she talked.

"O'Malley takes naps?" Addie's voice betrayed her disbelief at that statement.

"Of course he does," Jules said as she leaned past Ads and scooped O'Malley up. The cat looked up at her adoringly, which I completely understood. "He dozes most of the day, but in the late afternoon, he likes to get a solid nap in the spot that looks over the backyard so he can be well rested before dinner."

As Jules rubbed his belly, Addie looked at Ivy and me with delight. "I can hear his purr!" Her head swiveled back to Jules with a grin. "It sounds like an engine."

Jules smiled right back at Addie in a way that threatened to steal my breath. "He likes his belly rubbed, and he also likes his quiet time in the backyard nook."

Addie pondered that statement before nodding and turning back to us. "Okay, Momma. We better go so O'Malley can get his rest." Before she could skip off, she looked up at Jules. "Thanks, Ms. Jules. I like your house and your cat."

Jules beamed down at Addie. "Thanks, Ms. Addie. You are welcome here anytime."

"Can I give you a hug?" Addie asked.

Jules shot me a warm look before turning back to Addie. "Well, of course."

"It's important to ask and not just do it," Addie told her. "That's consent."

"I love that," Jules said. "Let me put O'Malley down. Do you want to give him a kiss goodbye first? I know he would be fine with that."

Addie nodded and they took care of that, then walked the lucky guy to the nook and let him hop to a spot by the windows where he circled many times before settling with his kingdom in full view.

Jules knelt to Addie's level and gave her a big squeeze that was returned. And with that, Addie was good to go.

She skipped up to give me a smacking, theatrical kiss. "Bye, Daddy. See you soon!" She grabbed Ivy's hand and skipped to the door with Ivy, who put a hand to her ear like a phone and mouthed, "Call me" to Jules.

And then there was silence.

Chapter 13

Book Club Gone Wild

Jules

I was at a loss. What did we do now? This day had been derailed in all the best ways, but I'd lost the courage I'd found before being interrupted by Noah's family. Before then I had a strong desire to get the man horizontal, not that I would have ever said that, just hinted strongly.

Now? Well, there was the pesky voice in my head brimming with writing ideas for the first time in eons. How did I share that with Noah? I mean, *your family was great, thanks for listening to my identity crisis, let's kiss some more later but you need to go right now* didn't have the best ring to it.

Damn.

"Jules?" Noah's kind—if possibly amused—voice pulled me back to present. I found his beautiful eyes watching me with crinkles at the corners.

"I'm so sorry, did you say something?" I felt heat rushing up my chest and to my face in the usual reaction that I couldn't control.

"No, no." Noah seemed distracted, and I couldn't figure

it out until he lightly ran a ringer up my neck before pulling back like he'd had an electric shock. "Shit, I'm sorry."

I worked to ignore the goose bumps that rose in wake of his touch. "For what?"

He shook his head like he was coming out of a trance. "It's not okay to touch you without permission—I just love the way your skin flushes."

I assumed telling him that I was down for touches up to and including that one, if not more, might make me sound too eager. "It's fine," I got out, my voice sounding like I smoked a pack a day. I cleared my throat and tried to get us back on track. "So what were you going to say?"

Noah stuffed his hands in his pockets. I toyed with the idea that he'd done that to keep from touching me, making a mental note to add that to my list of ideas for my book.

He cleared his throat. "Before I become a caveman who oversteps, I was going to tell you that you should clearly never play poker because you wear your feelings on your face."

I tilted my head and watched him for a moment. I mean, not the first time I'd heard that from Lou or Kylie, but from a guy? Apologies to the men of the world, but they didn't tend to be that observant in my experience.

"And what did I appear to be thinking or feeling?" Couldn't help it—I needed to test him a bit.

Noah's shoulders rose up in a shrug, hands still firmly in his jean pockets. "You looked conflicted. Like you might want me to stay but at the same time you'd like to be alone."

Dang, nailed it in one. Well, we were in the early days for this friendship slash whatever we called it, so maybe holding the real me back wasn't the right path forward. However, when had I ever been my authentic self with a guy I was interested in? Another note to ponder for my book. May all of my heroines live more evolved lives than me.

"Cards on the table?" I asked.

Noah nodded, distance still there, hands still in pockets. Adorable.

Well, I guess this would tell if he really wanted the honesty he proclaimed to. Watching for his reaction, I laid it out there. "I was thinking that I'd love you to stay and possibly figure out how we could move forward with being friends that kiss. At the same time, my brain is churning with some writing ideas for the first time in forever, and I really want to shove you out the door so that I can write."

Noah's face transformed, and it was beautiful. It smoothed out somehow, like he was at peace even while he threw his head back and let out a joyous laugh. His entire being transformed—shoulders dropped, hands out of pockets, body relaxed.

When his eyes finally met mine, I felt his stare down deep in my core where arousal stirred. Well, that was a long-dormant feeling of late. Tad inconvenient right now, however.

"Jules." He walked right up to me until we were toe-to-toe. "This okay?"

"More than," I whispered.

He threaded his hands into my hair, some more escaping from the mess on the top of my head while I lightly grasped his hips and worked not to just yank our bodies together. With his gentle directing, I tipped my chin up and our lips met again. Holy moly, I wanted to drown in that kiss. As my mouth slid open and his tongue found mine, a moan escaped. Him? Me? Who knew and who cared. A tingly sensation filled my entire body like I'd chugged several full-strength espresso shots. I felt *alive*.

Far too quickly, Noah slowed our kiss down until he pulled away, his gaze seeming to scan my entire face for something. Then he pressed a kiss to my nose and stepped back.

"Umm, not to be rude, but why are we stopping?" I whispered. My body wanted to stage a revolt, and my mind was in complete agreement.

Noah's smile was sweet laced with a hint of want—like he wasn't thrilled on the pause either even though he was the one who had done it.

You've only known the man for a week. My subconscious spoke up.

How long do you need to know someone before you can follow your gut? I asked back. I had known several guys in Chicago for a significant of amount of time longer than Noah and never felt as at ease as I did with him. Otherwise, no way would I be okay with kissing the man, much less attempting to convince him to give any of the fantasies currently swirling in my brain a go.

"I'm listening to you and what you said you needed." His voice was patient.

"You sure about that?" I thought of said fantasies again.

He smirked and laid a kiss on my forehead that I mentally cataloged for my book. Was there anything more swoony than a forehead kiss by a gorgeous man?

"Babe, you said you need to write. And while we still have lots to talk about, I believe when the ideas are there, you need to get them down, right?"

I suddenly had a vision of Noah in this kitchen in lounge pants and a tee, making breakfast for me while I typed away furiously at the counter. Could that be my reality one day? The longing I felt to make it so was strong.

"Jules?"

I shook my head, thinking I could write the vision instead, and looked to Noah as I drew willpower I wasn't aware I had. "As much as I'd like to say writing can wait, that isn't the best idea. Thanks for looking out for me."

Noah looked around at my place, Addie's fort still up and reminders of our afternoon visible on the counters. "Where do you write?"

"Umm, a variety of places. Today I was thinking of lounging in my bed."

He gave a small groan that I'd love to hear again, but then he stepped back and pointed to the stairs. "Go get some words down before I lose my ability to stay strong. I'll clean up down here and lock the door behind me when I leave."

Damn, also sexy to have this gorgeous man straightening up while I went to write. At this point it would be easier to catalog what wasn't hot. Hadn't found anything yet, time would tell, but I sure as hell wasn't looking a gift horse in the mouth.

I stepped up to him once again, rose up on my toes, and brushed my mouth against his. "Thanks, Noah," I whispered. "Text later?"

"You better believe it," he said. "Now go get that story out of your head and down on paper."

"Hope you don't mind if my new hero is heavily inspired by a single dad I've recently met," I said, shooting a wink at him. Who had I become? A person who winks?

Luckily he flicked me with a towel and replied with a smile. "I'd be disappointed if I hadn't inspired something in your writing. Now head up there." He pointed to the stairs again.

. . .

Hours passed, and I awoke to the sun shining in my window. It had a direct line to my face and pulled me out of my deep slumber. A glance around found O'Malley snoozing on the pillow next to me, my laptop buried in the comforter near my waist, and my clothes from yesterday still on.

I rewound my brain and remembered coming up here while Noah cleaned. I vaguely recalled his shout that he was leaving. The words were flowing and my fingers were flying. Sometimes that happened and time evaporated as the story poured out. I had no idea when I went to bed or if I'd just rested my eyes for a moment.

Untangling my laptop, I woke it up to see how many words I'd written before I'd gone to sleep. After my document loaded, I narrowed my eyes to focus on the word count on the bottom. Seemed I'd crossed the twenty thousand mark, which meant I'd cranked out over three thousand. Dang. I did a mental high five. That was far more than I'd gotten in one writing stretch of late.

I grabbed my phone off the dresser I used as a bedside table. At least I'd plugged that in last night. My first item I noted was that it was already ten in the morning. Damn. Good thing it was a Sunday. Second, I had a plethora of missed texts. Starting with Noah's first, I noted that it was from eleven p.m.

Noah: *Sweet dreams and thanks for being a sounding board today. We need to talk more about your top secret gig at some point, but I swear I won't share with a soul.*

I hoped he didn't mind that it had been almost twelve hours since he texted. I thumbed out a reply immediately.

Me: *Sorry for the delay, I was in the writing zone and crashed sometime last night in the wee hours before dawn. Glad to chat anytime even though it makes me nervous.*

Honestly, I liked sharing about my writing with you. Kind of nice for someone else to know.

Before I could even check the other texts that had come in, I saw that he was typing so took a swig of water from my bottle on the table while I waited. It didn't take long.

Noah: *Love that the words were coming to you so much that you were in a zone. Sounds like a good thing. Have fun at book club tonight. I think Ivy said it's going to be memorable.*

Holy hell, I'd forgotten about book club. I'd read the Pippa Grant book that they had mentioned the day after I learned about it but then fell down the rabbit hole of freaking out about my book being the May pick and completely flaked on meeting this week. Maybe that's what the other texts were about?

I stuck a heart on Noah's text and quickly clicked back to see the rest of my messages. Sure enough, there were a bunch in the group chat that was labeled The Coven. I opened it, wondering what could possibly make a book club memorable.

There were a handful of unread texts waiting for me.

Maggie: *Good news, ladies. Book club is on the move tonight! We're going to have our conversation of Pippa's newest at the mansion in Highland Woods, though the book conversation might be on the light side tonight. Maybe we'll meet again this week over coffee? The mansion is opening for a show, and I've got tickets for us all. Be there at 7, you won't want to miss this.*

A show? What kind of show would you attend for book club?

Emma: *Maggie, what are you up to? The park's website doesn't mention any events tonight, and Max just laughed at me when I asked.*

Hmm. That seemed suspicious.

Maggie: *Trust me, chickie. A women's group that some of my colleagues belong to have the mansion reserved for a show and they had extra tickets. They opened it up to a few groups of women in town, and our group is one. The mansion's bar in the solarium will also be open for those of you not pregnant or nursing. Let's go!*

Ivy: *I'm cackling over here because I know exactly what tonight's show is. Who needs a ride?*

Maggie: *Don't ruin the surprise, Ivy!*

Ivy: *I would never. I also talked to Maeve. She had some tees made by one of the café's customers who has some vinyl shirt setup. She and Allyson will have them available for everyone in our club at the café if you can get up there to pick them up before four. Otherwise, they'll text to arrange pickup. Wear them tonight and spread the word.*

Shirts? Shows? My normal anxiety about attending something for the first time was now being compounded by the unknown. However, there was also a quiet voice that was celebrating that I was included in this crazy group of women and whatever the evening was going to hold for us. I tentatively waded in.

Me: *Ivy, I could use a ride.*

There. The idea of not turning up on my own was extremely appealing. Some of my nerves abated.

Ivy: *Perfect. I'll grab a shirt for you too and bring it when I come. 6:40 good for you? That will get us there by seven.*

I sent her a thumbs-up and rolled out of bed. Time to get my day started.

. . .

That evening I was cocooned in the passenger seat of Ivy's Jeep as we crawled over the speed bumps on the park road leading to the mansion. Maeve and Allyson were in the back, and the car had been filled with chatter the entire fifteen-minute ride. They had been a last-minute addition, and as a result, we were running about ten minutes behind. Ivy assured me that we were fine to walk in late, that whatever this was, it wasn't a problem to enter after it began. I had a funny feeling I was the only one in the dark here—Maeve and Allyson both worked at the mansion, seeing as how the second location for their café was there, so they likely knew what we were headed to. And Ivy had told Noah it would be "memorable." Why they couldn't share, I had no idea, but they told me it was going to be a lot of fun. I had to trust them and pray this wasn't some strange book club initiation.

I smoothed down the white shirt I'd been handed to wear that matched the other girls. In red vinyl it read: Highland Falls Smutty Book Club: The spicier the better. And there were three chili peppers below the text. Sweet Jesus. It did look cute with my boyfriend jeans and red sneakers, and I had to admit the clear message that I belonged with this group of women was nice, if unfamiliar.

A thought popped into my mind just then. "Um, is my aunt Lou going to be here tonight?"

Ivy cackled. No exaggeration, the woman positively *cackled.* "Heck yes, she wouldn't miss it. She might have been early even."

Oh boy, that was telling. Something Lou would be excited about...

Minutes later we were parked and at the side door to the mansion while my mind conjured so many different scenarios. Even from out here, I could hear bass pumping.

Was it a dance party? I wasn't a great dancer but loved to do it. That could be fun.

Upon entering the space, Maeve immediately led us up to an unfamiliar gentleman who was standing just inside the door with a clipboard. The man had muscles upon muscles, and the fitted clothes he wore left nothing to the imagination. I mentally cataloged his look for any future inspiration I might need.

Mr. Muscles looked at our crew, noting our shirts. "You the last four for the book club?"

"Yep." Maeve spoke up. "We're in the party with Maggie Sullivan."

He nodded, crossing something off on his list, his forearms bulging as he did. Whoa. "Your seats are in the front on the left as you walk in, and the rest of your crew is there waiting. Think you can find it? We still have a few remaining guests that I need to greet or I'd walk you in."

"We've got it," Ivy assured him.

"Behave yourselves," he said with a wink as he gave us a wide grin.

"No promises," Maeve said as she ushered us all up the hall toward the music.

"Is he from Highland Falls," I murmured to Allyson. She shot me a small smile and shook her head, saying nothing more.

We reached the end of the hall and then turned to what was a large room that ran the length of the mansion. I'd visited this space as a kid with my parents as well as with Lou and Verdell. At a quick glance I could see windows to the lake on my right along with a bar in what I knew was the solarium, and in front of us were rows and rows of chairs filled with women all facing a stage at the far end of the room opposite where we were now standing. The lights were low and pulsing different colors. On stage were several men in different states of undress and...

Oh. My. God.

"Is that Aunt Lou?" I gasped.

Maeve let out a whoop. "It sure as hell is. Let's go."

How do I even put words to the scene in front of me? We were clearly walking into something that would have been perfect to film for the movie *Magic Mike*. The guys on stage were dancing in some choreographed routine. And center stage was my aunt Lou.

I looked over to my crew, which I was still standing with since I was frozen in shock. Legs? Who knew how they worked really? Maeve and Ivy had their arms raised above their heads as they cheered loudly, encouraging Lou. There were probably just under a hundred women in this room and, over on the right, was that Verdell?

My legs found the will to move to someone who represented safety as I hotfooted it over to the bar in the solarium. Verdell was sitting at the polished wood counter, calmly drinking a cup of coffee and reading the paper on his iPad in the midst of this mayhem. He seemed as at ease as if he were at home in his kitchen.

"Um, Verdell?" I asked, my eyes shooting from my uncle to my aunt. She was in the same T-shirt as the rest of the book club and some capri-length linen pants. A dancer was gyrating on her lap as she raised her hands to place them on his glistening chest to the roar of approval from the crowd. I noted that Ivy and crew had made it to the front and Maeve appeared to be recording the scene for posterity on her phone.

"Hey there, Jules. I wondered if you were coming," Verdell's smooth voice pulled my attention back from the stage.

I gave him a horrified look. "Does Lou know you're here?"

Verdell let out a deep chuckle. "Oh, sweetheart. Of course she does. I'm her driver. Well, the driver for Lou and her crew." He nodded to the front, and I saw the gray heads of Lou's best friends, Jeanie and Hattie, in the front where they were waving dollar bills at the dancers and, I narrowed my gaze, yep, they were stuffing the bills in the front of the dancers' pants.

Yeah, these women would absolutely need a driver. "So you don't mind?" I asked, still horrified by what was playing out before my eyes.

Now the dancer had pulled Lou up and somehow gotten her legs wrapped around his waist as he danced with her, his pelvis doing some type of thrusts as he held on to her ass to keep her secure and her arm was waving in the air like she was on a bucking bronco. I wondered what my mom would think of her big sister and then immediately dashed that thought. What if she wanted to join her? There would not be enough alcohol in the world to erase those memories.

Verdell made a rumbling noise of amusement. "Mind? Not in the least." His gaze was warm and followed his wife on the stage.

I looked at him in confusion, and he turned, took in my expression, and then covered my pale hand with his large brown one, immediately helping to relax me as I noted the size differential between the two of us. Verdell played basketball when he was younger and had coached for years. He would have been able to palm a ball easily. My distraction from the mayhem around me was only fleeting.

"Jules, I've been married to Lou for fifty years. We've been through times where a marriage between race was not accepted as easily as we are now. We've overcome arguments that occur when you put two very independent souls together. Our early years were volatile, but I knew one thing for certain then and still do today."

"What's that?"

"That woman is it for me. She makes my life interesting and keeps me guessing. And while she's having a hell of a good time right now up there, mostly she just loves being the center of attention. Whatever else happens, know this. She's coming home to me." He gave me a wink. "And I really like her spicy romance book club nights if you catch my drift. I have a feeling tonight's club will be no different."

I wrinkled my nose. "Eww."

He let out a deep laugh. "Not eww but worthy of celebration when you hit the age we are."

I mean, if I could remove the idea that we were talking about my relatives who were in their early seventies, I could get behind his words. Heck, I sure hoped I was sexually active when I was their age, but I could do without the dance party on the stage.

Looking that way, I saw that Kristine from the yoga studio was now planking with her arms braced on a chair on the stage while another dancer had her legs wrapped around his waist as he slapped her ass to the encouragement of the audience.

Maggie and Maeve were joining Jeanie and Hattie in the front row, passing off more tips. Sweet Jesus. I had zero desire for audience participation.

I was wondering if I could tell Verdell that I was going to sit here with him over here, hiding, until it was time to leave when I saw Ivy heading my way with concern clearly etched on her face.

"Hey, Ivy, sorry I haven't come over yet," I said, trying to make sure I was heard over the crowd, but this side room really allowed a view at a much lower volume than the main area. As Ivy glanced back at her phone, I wondered if Lorelai was struggling with her ear infection and Ivy needed to leave. As much as I wanted to hang out with these women, I wouldn't be opposed to going home and joining them another day.

"Jules, did Noah text you by any chance?" Ivy asked, her voice sounding strained.

"Why?" I asked, pulling my phone out of the depths of my purse. As the screen lit up, I immediately saw text messages stacked there. "He did," I murmured, tapping to open them as I felt Ivy press herself into my side. My heart raced, certain with everything in me that whatever was happening, it wasn't good.

Noah: *Jules, I'm so sorry, but I'm going to need to be out of town for a few days and wanted you to know I wasn't ghosting you.*

Noah: *Not sure how much you want to know or where our friendship plus more puts us right now, but my parents have been in an accident, and it isn't looking like they'll live through the night.*

Noah: *You know from our conversation that this is going to be strained. I'll call when I know more. But thanks for the past week and especially the past two days. You've been a bright spot, and I couldn't leave town without you knowing that.*

That message was sent a minute ago. I looked up to Ivy in horror. "Did you know about his parents?"

Ivy nodded miserably. "My parents know them and texted me, then Noah did so I'd know why he was going out of town." She wiped a tear away as it spilled over her cheek. "They don't deserve my sympathy, but he does."

My heart hurt for the poor man, then I thought of something and looked back to Ivy in horror. "He can't go up there on his own. He doesn't have any siblings or other family who will be there."

She nodded in agreement. "And that's why I came over here. You should go with him."

"But," I protested. "He's known you longer, or Jake…"

Ivy leaned in and met my gaze. "And you would provide the most comfort. I only had to be around you two for an hour to know that."

I bit my lip and looked from her to Verdell, who had been reading my messages over my shoulder and listening in unabashedly. He had clearly absorbed some of his wife's eavesdropping tendencies.

"This is the guy who bought your breakfast the other day?" he asked.

I nodded.

He gave a decisive nod and then said, "Go."

I looked to Ivy, and she gave me a sad grin as she lifted her phone. "Let's go. I'll tell Allyson and Maeve to catch another ride home on the way out and then we'll get Jake to stall Noah until I get you there." She hustled back to our crowd, who were celebrating the dancers just steps away from my bubble with Verdell but seemingly in a whole other world.

I hesitated, then looked at Verdell with teary eyes. "How can I comfort him? I haven't lost my parents, and Noah's relationship with his isn't positive."

"All the more reason for him to be around someone who actually cares about him." Verdell gave me a small push toward Ivy, who was coming back from our group. "Go."

I took Ivy's hand and ran from the room, energy and excitement at our back, sadness and uncertainty ahead.

Chapter 14

Facing Old Demons

oah

I glanced at my phone, biting back the unpleasant feelings swirling in my stomach. I'd texted Jake and Ivy to tell them about the accident since I wanted Addie to know why I'd be out of town. Jake had said he or Ivy would be by shortly to grab some of Addie's stuff before I left, but Ads was in bed doing the nighttime routine, headed for dreamland shortly. That was fine—I'd FaceTime her tomorrow. The problem I was dealing with was though they lived mere blocks away, we were closing on half an hour, and I needed to hit the road. They had a key to my place, so in reality I didn't need to wait, but I was.

You should be honest with yourself even if you couldn't be with anyone else, right? And the deepest truth that I didn't want to own was that I didn't want to go to Madison. Was I upset that my parents were in an accident that looked like it was going to take both of their lives? Of course I was. I wouldn't wish ill upon them no matter how fractured our relationship was. But did I think their current reality was going to make them want to have some healing last words with me before they passed to acknowledge their narcissistic behavior and leave this world with an apology on their lips and closure in their hearts? Nope. Wouldn't happen. If anything, I had a feeling that their finite time left would just serve to piss them off and they'd take it out on anyone around them. Well, if they could. I hadn't had any update since the first call, so I wasn't sure what I was walking into, but I knew the odds were that it wouldn't be good, and that made me want to run like hell.

Sometimes being an adult sucked.

The sound of a car door slamming brought me back to the present. I turned and grabbed my backpack and my hastily packed duffel. I had no idea how long I'd be gone, so I went with enough essentials for a week. I was just straightening up when I heard the front door open.

"Hope it's okay that I'm just going to leave you here to ransack the place for anything you need," I called out to Jake or Ivy, whichever one had finally arrived. "I'm going to get on the road so I'm there before midnight—" Anything else I was going to say evaporated from my mind as I turned to see Jules standing inside my front door, looking uncertain.

"Hey, Jules," I started, not sure what was happening, but then I looked behind her through the open front door and onto the stoop. I saw a small carry-on bag standing there. I looked from it to Jules, and a whole lot began to click into place, namely why on earth the meddlesome Jake and Ivy had taken so long to get to my place. Though now that I thought of it, Ivy would have been with Jules at book club. In all that happened, my brain had gone offline.

"Noah." Jules looked like she was beyond jittery. "I'm so sorry—I'm being beyond presumptuous." A flush was working its way up her neck, which I still loved. Her hands were flying around of their own accord until she'd grab them, wring them together, then let them loose once again.

I realized she'd been talking, and I'd tuned her out as I cataloged her movements instead. She seemed like she could be working herself into a state to hyperventilate or faint once again, so I moved forward to put what I hoped was a calming hand on her flailing ones. Piecing the suitcase and her behavior together, I had a guess as to what was going on.

"Jules, are you planning to travel to Madison with me?" I asked as gently as I knew how.

She nodded, clearly holding something back, and then lost that battle as it all bubbled over. "It's too much, isn't it? I mean, we've known each other for just over a week, what do I know about what you need, right?" She continued before I had the opportunity to answer. "That's what I told Ivy and Verdell. All I said is you shouldn't be alone, and you shouldn't!" She looked fierce at that comment. "But then Ivy was like, 'Oh, you should go.' And Verdell concurred. And I could barely focus because there were strippers—or maybe they were just dancers? I'm not sure—I didn't stay long enough to find out. But sidenote, Lou was on stage with them, and I don't think I have enough brain bleach in the world to rid me of that memory." She shook her head violently. "At any rate, now I'm here and Ivy took off and I feel like an idiot." She was close to tears, but I wasn't sure I could get past a few statements that just tumbled out of her. My brain pinged in so many directions it was hard to focus.

"Breathe, Jules." I took her hands, noting that hers were dwarfed by mine.

"I should be comforting you," she whispered and squeezed me back.

I gave her a smile. "You are, kitten. You cared enough to

be upset on my behalf and decided you needed to go on this hellish journey with me."

She took a deep breath. Then another.

"Now, I absolutely need to know more about the dancers/strippers, but I'd like to get on the road. And in case it's not evident, I'm more than okay with you traveling with me." The warmth in my body that started with realizing Jules cared enough that she wanted to ensure I wasn't alone hadn't dissipated. "It'll likely take just shy of four hours to get to Madison. But I have to double-check, are you certain you want to go with me?"

"Yes." She squeezed my hands again. "I'm the representative for Ivy and Jake, not to mention Addie— Oh!" She turned around to pull something out of her purse and handed me a drawing. I knew immediately it was my daughter's. She did have a signature style.

Jules unfurled it, revealing a drawing of a little blond girl with her arms out, a delightfully clashing outfit clearly indicating that this was my Addie—striped leggings and signature tutu the clearest signs. In her hands, she held a rainbow heart, and in her five-year-old handwriting, she'd written, "I love you, Daddy." Not all the letters faced the right way, but I treasured her writing as it was.

I looked to Jules, and she seemed to know my unasked questions. "Ivy and I left the show and swung by my house for my bag. I gave her and Jake a key so they could check on O'Malley for me, and then we went by their place so that Jake could run this out to us and also"—she turned, leaned behind her suitcase, and pulled out Ellie, Addie's Elephant —"Addie wanted you to have this."

A metaphorical hit to the chest, it was as if I'd had my breath knocked out of me. I knew I'd gasped. "But..."

Jules held up a hand. "Ivy said you'd try to leave this

here because you'd be worried about Addie being sad when she didn't have Ellie to sleep with. Ivy asked me to tell you that yes, that might happen, but the bigger lesson of Addie caring so much about you that she wanted you to have it because she thought you'd need it was not one you could say no to. She wanted me to tell you it would be good for Ads to know she was giving her dad comfort when she couldn't."

Jesus. The blessings in my life knew no bounds, which was an odd-as-fuck thought when your parents were in the hospital, not likely to make it. But with that reminder, I looked at Jules. "Thanks for doing this—bringing Addie's gifts but also wanting to come."

"So you're good with me traveling with you? You're sure?"

"I'm sure if you are; however, what about your work?"

"Already cleared with Sue. I can do some remote work to review returns for them as well as some other paperwork. She, uh..." Jules's face began heating up again.

I squeezed her hand to follow me out the door as I locked up. "She what?" I asked as we reached my car.

Jules remained silent until we were both seated and buckled in. After I programmed the address of University Hospital into the navigation app, I began backing down the driveway and she resumed her conversation, although haltingly.

"I saw Sue, um, coming out of the bathroom while, uh, Ivy and I were leaving the mansion."

I hooted, understanding her discomfort. "Sue was at the stripper show?"

"Well, remember, I don't know if they were strippers," Jules replied, sounding like she wanted to be swallowed by the passenger seat. "Maybe just dancers with very little in the way of clothes?"

I signaled to turn on the state route that would take us, eventually, to Bloomington. Then we'd head north to Madison. It would be a quiet drive for the most part, but the lack of traffic would hopefully translate to an arrival without delay.

I returned my focus to Jules. "We'll come back to that in a minute. So Sue was there?"

She almost whispered her response, like even she couldn't believe the way the night had unfolded. "Yep. Luckily, I didn't see her in the show, so I don't have those memories. But she asked where we were going, and Ivy filled her in. Before I could even ask, she told me to take the time I needed." Even while looking forward, I could see her shake her head in my peripheral. "I don't know what to do with a boss like her."

I reached over to grab her hand for just a moment. I needed to be connected. She sounded lost, and that wasn't something I wanted her to be, being all too familiar with that feeling myself. "Maybe just enjoy it?" I asked, trying to inject some teasing tone to get us to a lighter place.

We passed the next ten minutes in silence. Outside my SUV, dusk was upon us, the sun having set about half an hour ago. Both sides of the road had barren fields rolling to the horizon, too early in April for any hint of the crops that were to come. Our silence wasn't awkward but comfortable. I had the same feeling of "rightness" that had filled me up whenever I was around Jules from the moment we met. It was as if part of my soul recognized hers, which absolutely sounded like something woo-woo that Ivy would say. I made a mental note to never say that in her presence because I knew I'd never hear the end of it. I drove through the curves of the road, the only vehicle visible for miles. That peaceful bubble of denial of our present circumstances that I was enjoying, however, was not to last.

"What do you know about your parents' accident?" Jules asked as she slid her hand onto my thigh. Just her touch grounded me, and I had a feeling she knew that.

I sighed and ran through the events of the evening. Glancing at the clock, I saw that it was just a bit past eight. All this had unfolded in the past ninety minutes. Unreal at how quickly everything could change.

"One of the partners at my father's office called. My parents were headed home from a fundraiser when my dad lost control of the car and ran into a tree." Even as I said it, I could hear the lack of emotion in my voice. That likely wasn't healthy, but it was something to deal with later. "Ivy's parents called me shortly after. They were at the same gathering and saw the accident, then stayed at the scene until the ambulance got there and followed it to the hospital. They're the ones who told me the outlook was not good." I slid my hand onto Jules's on my thigh, squeezing it briefly before returning it to the steering wheel.

"Are they still at the hospital?" Jules asked.

"Yeah, they're staying until I get there or..." I trailed off, thinking Jules would get it. If my parents passed, there would be no reason for the Jameses to wait around.

"Oh, Noah. How are you doing with this?" Jules sounded near tears herself.

I quickly looked over to give her what I hoped was a reassuring smile. "Better than I should be," I said quietly. She looked at me quizzically, and I got my eyes back to the road. "I lost them a long time ago, Jules."

"It's not the same," she said quietly.

"No, it isn't, but in some ways this loss is less painful."

"How?" Her tone betrayed her confusion and doubt. I knew she thought I was lying to myself, downplaying the hurt. Maybe I was, but I had my doubts.

"This separation from them if they do pass and it sounds like, unfortunately for them, that is the likely conclusion, isn't their choice. They aren't choosing to leave me and their grandchild behind. But they *did* make that choice six years ago and they haven't changed their mind even though they had many opportunities to do so. That hurt more, you know? That they would rather go through life without us than with us just because I wasn't conforming to what they considered acceptable." My heart ached just thinking about it. There was nothing that Addie could ever do that would make me want to turn my back on her. Not for the first time, hell, not for the hundredth, I wondered why my parents were the way they were.

"I'm so sorry, Noah." Jules's voice had so much compassion laced through it; I felt it like warmth around me.

"For what, kitten? You aren't responsible for the actions of adults you've never met." I gave her a small smile in the dim light of the car, trying to reassure her.

She squeezed my thigh. "Silly, I'm not sorry for them, I'm sorry you've lived your life with parents who didn't reinforce to you on a daily basis the amazing person you have grown into."

The highway lay ahead of us like the yellow brick road taking us to the wizard, but there would be no wonderful land at the end of this one. I tried to take my brain to the end of our trip, of what I would find there, and just couldn't. Instead, I focused on Jules's words.

"Is that what your parents do for you? Remind you of who you are?" I tried to conjure up what Jules's mom and dad would be like, but I was coming up blank.

Jules let out a small chuckle. "I don't know, you could say that. My parents are flighty and forgetful. My mom loves to be dramatic, but I've never questioned their love for me. They might forget to pay a bill or to wear shoes out of the house when they're going to the store, but I know they have my best interests at heart even when I don't want to admit it."

"Sounds like a story there," I noted. I felt rather than saw her shrug.

"Yeah, I guess. My mom freaked when she came to visit me almost two months back. She decided I was overworked and not supported and begged me to move to Highland Falls so that Lou could watch over me after what Lou termed my 'Chicago meltdown,' though I think that is a high exaggeration." Jules's tone was tolerant and full of obvious affection even if she didn't agree.

"Why not move to wherever your parents live, not that I want you anywhere but Highland Falls," I said with a bit of a possessive growl.

"My parents are nomads," Jules said, sounding indulgent. "They retired to live in a motor home and are always on the move."

"Ahh." From what I'd gleaned from Jules in the short time I'd known her, I couldn't imagine her in a RV. She'd want far more stability than that. Sounded like both of us had parents completely different than we were, though not in the same way.

"Yeah, it's a good life for them, and I think retirement is the happiest I've seen them, which is saying something. I wish I got to see them more or that when I did see them wasn't time there and gone in a flash, but it is what it is," she said, her voice trailing off a bit at the end as she stared out the window into the dark.

I didn't want to interrupt her thoughts, so I concentrated on the road and the quiet music filling the car.

Within a few minutes, Jules's head dropped and I looked over to see that she had drifted off. I wished we were stopped so I could watch her sleep, though that sounded positively creepy. When she was awake, she often had a little wrinkle of concern between her brows, but in sleep it was gone. My hands itched to smooth that spot often, and I wished for a day where she wouldn't have whatever her stressors were on a daily basis.

For the next three hours I felt comfort from Jules's mere presence next to me with her adorable light snore, which I would never mention. Not being alone allowed the memories to come and not feel quite so painful. As scenes from childhood flitted through my mind, I wished I could say I saw at least a time or two where my parents had clearly cared for me, allowing me to find a small comfort in what was bound to be a hard night, but I didn't. Instead, I saw my upbringing for what it was—an inconvenience to them as I tried my hardest to make them happy but failed miserably every time. The one lesson they'd left me with was to ensure I didn't parent in any way like them.

Finally I exited Interstate 90 for our final ten miles to the hospital and began to wonder when I should wake Jules. I knew she'd be pissed that she'd slept through the drive, but it had been a gift. Unwittingly, she'd allowed me to begin the grieving process, such as it would be, before I even knew if it would be needed. However, in one way or another I'd been mourning our relationship for years.

As I did my final turn in to the parking lot for the emergency department, Jules started when the sound of a siren permeated even our peaceful bubble. She sat up, looked around, glanced at the time, and gasped. "Oh, Noah, I'm so sorry."

I pulled into a spot and put the car in park, undoing my seat belt as I turned to face Jules. I grabbed her hands, which were, of course, flailing as she murmured to herself, negative words about how could she have possibly fallen asleep on the job. It was adorable.

"Kitten," I began before she interrupted me.

"Three times," she murmured, though I'm not certain if she was speaking to me or herself.

"Three times what?" I asked because I had to know.

She looked at me in alarm. That told me she wasn't aware she had said that aloud. That was even better.

"Umm, three times you've called me kitten." She worried her lower lip between her teeth like she was uncertain what I'd think about that.

I leaned forward to kiss her nose. "That's because you are my ferocious little kitten. And I love that you thought you needed to be awake the whole way up to 'be here' for me, but honestly, just having you by my side was the comfort I hadn't realized I needed. So thank you for that."

She sat back, clearly more relaxed at my words, then turned toward the hospital. "Should we go?"

I nodded but didn't move. Finally I looked her way. "This is like Pandora's box, you know?"

Jules's gaze was warm and understanding in the parking lot lights. She reached for my hand once again. "I'm here for whatever you want to do."

I took a deep breath and said, "Let's go."

Chapter 15

Going Home

J*ules*

I absolutely was livid with myself for falling asleep on the ride up to Madison regardless of Noah's words that just the fact that I was next to him provided comfort. That seemed like a bunch of baloney, but now was not the time to press him on that. Instead, I held his hand while we walked through the automatic doors into the emergency room.

The bright lights were a harsh transition from the dark night outside. For an emergency room, it wasn't too chaotic. There was an information desk in front of us, a waiting room to the side with people in various states of alertness lining the chairs. As I scanned the room, I noted a couple who were my parents age, wearing a gorgeous dress and a tux. Call it a wild guess, but I'd put some money on them being Ivy's parents.

Sure enough, Noah headed straight for them. The woman had her head on the man's shoulder and had been dozing, but he noted Noah and jostled her awake. They both stood before we reached them.

"Mr. and Mrs. James," Noah began.

"Noah," Mr. James said, holding his hand out, and Noah shook it.

It was all so formal. I didn't even know where to begin with this. Lord knows that if the situation were reversed, any friend of my parents—much less Lou or Verdell—would have immediately pulled me in for a hug. Maybe these people weren't the hugging type? I decided to just blend into the background because they didn't seem to be concerned with who I was. However, that wasn't Noah's style.

"As I was saying, Mr. and Mrs. James, this is my friend, Jules. Jules, this is Ivy's parents, Mr. and Mrs. James."

I started to put my hand out but was cut off.

"I'd say it was nice to meet you, but the circumstances are horrid," Mr. James said, his voice laced with impatience. "Now Noah, I hate to be the bearer of bad news, but I didn't want you to hear it from some random ER employee. As we all expected, your parents didn't make it. They passed from complications of the accident about an hour ago. I told the person at the desk that you'd be here soon, but I had Barry at the law firm your dad and I use send over their wills and advance directives in case any of that was needed. You'll need to talk with the doctor to see what your next steps are and can consult with Barry tomorrow, considering the lateness of the hour."

I fought back a gasp at his delivery. It was like we, along with Noah's parents, had really put him out by having the accident occur at this time of night. What on earth?

Mr. James nodded to his wife to grab her purse, then turned back to us with the same borderline irritated tone he'd been using the whole time. "Bad business, this is. I told Steve he should have Diane drive or get a ride share, but there was never any reasoning with that man when he set his mind to something, as you well know. Hope you take after your mother in that regard."

Noah jerked at that last statement. "Are you saying this accident was caused because my father was drunk?" he asked with more than a bit of incredulity.

Mr. James brushed that off. "Of course not. He'd had several scotches but wasn't drunk. His reflexes might just have been better earlier in the night."

Noah gave a bitter laugh. "Because then he could have avoided the tree that just jumped into his path? Jesus, they could have killed someone else."

"Don't be ridiculous, Noah." Mrs. James was now involved and giving us a very disapproving look. "It was just bad luck. And with that, we really need to go. This was not how we thought we'd spend our evening. If you need anything, you know where we are. Let us know when the services are." She tugged on her husband's arm, but he still had something to say.

"Your parents were good people, and we are all worse off for this loss," Mr. James said, sounding as emotional as an airport employee announcing what flights were arriving. I was sure he felt that social niceties called for a comment such as that. "Call if you need anything." The words sounded hollow, and I knew they were not to be followed up on.

With that, they swanned out of the waiting room, and we stood frozen to the spot. All I could think was how Noah said Ivy would be the first to acknowledge that her parents were kinder than his. If that was true, what in the hell would his parents have been like? Jesus. I didn't even know how to process it. His parents were gone, and he had just been told like it was a random fact in the evening along with the small matter that it sounded like the accident had been because they were careless enough to drive when they had been inebriated. Where did we even start?

I turned to Noah, who was staring at the wall. Slipping my arm around his waist, I moved until we were pressed together and pulled him to me in the tightest hug I could. "I'm so sorry," I whispered to his chest.

I felt his head dip until his mouth was on the crown of my head. He bent to get his mouth closer to my ear. "Thanks for being here, Jules."

I tipped my head back to meet his gaze, noting the wetness of his eyes and wanting to squeeze comfort into this man and, at the same time, wondering how he and Ivy could come from cold and uncaring people like the two we had just met.

"Nowhere else I'd rather be," I said, knowing that was the absolute truth.

The next hour passed in a flurry of activity. We talked to the ER staff, the coroner, and the funeral home director where his parents had already paid for their final expenses. Apparently their wishes were to be cremated, and they had the urns and the niches where their ashes would remain already reserved and paid for. All that was set in motion, and Noah declined any type of visitation. There would be a graveside service on Friday, and he declared that would just have to work for all involved.

I watched him the whole time and could tell he was holding on by a thread. We'd left the hospital and were headed down darkened streets in an older area of Madison. The houses in this neighborhood, from what I could tell, dwarfed any that we'd see in Highland Falls.

"Where are we?" I asked quietly, not wanting to disturb

the fragile peace surrounding us but needing an understanding of what was next.

"My parents live—lived—in this village... Shorewood Hills."

We were only ten or so minutes from the hospital, and I'd assumed we'd go to a hotel, but it looked like we weren't done facing down all the demons tonight as Noah surely wouldn't be able to escape the memories in his childhood home. That was fine, that was why I was here—so he wouldn't need to do this alone.

Noah turned in to the lane of one of the giant homes and pulled up to a circle drive where he parked in front of the house. Within moments the car was off, and yet he didn't get out. His hands remained at ten and two as he stared off into the night sky before lowering his forehead to rest on the steering wheel.

"Noah? What can I do?"

He took in a slow, measured breath, then turned to meet my eyes, resting his left temple on the wheel. "I know it sounds too simple, but truly, you're doing it. Thanks to you, I haven't been alone."

"That doesn't seem like enough," I whispered.

"It's huge." He reached over and squeezed my knee. "Let's go in."

I grabbed my bags after an argument with Noah about him taking them and followed him to the front door. The house was Tudor in style and far bigger than anything I'd want to live in. As we got to the lit vestibule by the door, I saw him flipping through keys on a ring, trying one after another. It was then I remembered the hospital giving him that ring in the items he was able to take from what his parents had. Which told me he hadn't already had a key to their home. How often had he visited? At all? Had they been to Highland Falls? Had they met Addie? Somehow I knew the answer was no.

Questions swirled in my mind, but this was not the time. One rose up unbidden and didn't stay locked down. "Is this where you grew up?" I couldn't visualize a young Noah here, but what did I know.

"Got it," he murmured, opening the front door and swiftly walking to the wall to type a code into an alarm system. "Hope they haven't changed this code." He finished and then turned to me with a small laugh. "The date my dad's company went public and he went from rich to filthy rich. Most important day of his life, as he told me often." He shook his head.

"Wow." What did I even say? The picture he was painting of these pivotal people in his life was not rosy, for certain, but every time I learned something new, my heart broke for Noah—child version *and* the adult before me—a little more.

"To answer your earlier question, yes, I did grow up here." He reached for my hand and tugged me down the hall.

We left our bags at the bottom of a sweeping staircase and moved through a large living room to a wall of windows and doors on the back wall of the house.

"There wasn't a lot I liked about living here. It wasn't a relaxed space for a kid, much less loving, but we had some nice staff over the years, and we had this."

He opened a door and stepped through to a large porch on the back of the house facing... some type of water. I was so turned around; I had no idea what it was... A river? Lake? Pond? Whatever it was, it was beautiful to look at now in the filtered light from the moon, and I was sure it would be gorgeous during the day.

Noah walked me to the thick railing that lined the edge of the porch, and we leaned on it as he stared off into the dark. I hooked my arm through his to link us together. We stood in companionable silence for a while, two minutes or twenty—who knew, time was floaty. Finally he looked down at me and pressed a kiss on my temple.

"It's after two—we should go to bed."

"Okay," I agreed, my heart beating faster which was completely inappropriate right now, but I didn't seem to be in control of anything, so I went with it and prayed I could be cool. However, he hadn't stepped back, so my desires were getting a hell of a lot of mixed-up messages.

"Can I ask one more favor of you, Jules?" His voice sounded on the verge of breaking, and I wanted to smother him in hugs for the rest of his days, but I stayed stock-still.

"Of course, you can ask as many as you need," I said, wishing I could do so much more. Being able to read his mind would be helpful right now, but I was glad he couldn't read mine. I was here as a friend, but my body was shouting that being attracted to the man wasn't keeping me from offering him comfort. Good Lord.

"Do you mind sleeping in the same bed with me tonight?" Noah whispered.

His chin rested on the top of my head, which prevented me from looking in his eyes to see if there were any signs as to what he meant. I had to just go on what he'd said.

He let out a small laugh. "Sorry, that sounds like I'm making some type of move on you when you've been amazing all night."

"I didn't think that." I quickly spoke up, which was partly a lie. Also, a lie of omission was that I might be okay with that.

"I just mean not being alone tonight sounds really good."

Damn. I wanted to slap the side of my brain. The man lost his parents, and while they didn't sound like pillars of humanity, they were his parents. I was a writer for Pete's sake. How did I not have a better grasp of the human condition than this?

"Of course," I said and finally wrapped my arms around him like I'd wanted to do all night. While we stood there, I mused over the fact that I'd known the man just over a week. We'd kissed for the first time a couple of days ago. We were friends, sure, with several things standing in the way of becoming more—though that hadn't been ruled out. And now I was standing in his childhood home, comforting him after the loss of his parents. How did we get here? And more importantly, where did we go from here?

Apparently to bed, that's where.

Chapter 16

By Your Side

N*oah*

I lay still, watching Jules sleep in my child-hood bedroom, not that any part of this room showed a hint to the memory of the child who grew up here. It looked like a room that a decorator had likely come in to erase any trace of my existence shortly after I left for college, not that there had been much in the way of my possessions anyway. What I could say for the space was that it was comfortable and allowed me to get my thoughts together, not that I slept much. Was that due to everything swirling in my brain or the sleeping beauty next to me? It was impossible to tell.

Last night I'd asked Jules to sleep in my room and immediately wanted to take it back. Not that I hadn't meant it. The reality had been that I knew I didn't want to be alone. But Jesus, the woman had known me for just over a week. Who did I think I was to ask for more than she was already giving me? I felt unbelievably selfish. I didn't know what Jules was typically like as a friend, but she seemed to be kind on a level I hadn't experienced. She'd uprooted her entire life for the next few days to make sure I wasn't alone. That wasn't something I'd forget. And while I hadn't gotten a lot of sleep, it had been comforting to have her next to me, her light snore reminding me that I wasn't here by myself.

I moved as slowly as possible to the edge of the bed, not wanting to disturb Jules's sleep but needing to see what was what in the light of day. My mind jumped from work items I needed to deal with to talking to the lawyer—did Mr. James say his name was Barry? And Jesus, the memory of Jules's face upon meeting the Jameses. I hadn't met her parents, but Ivy's and mine were typical for their crowd, though anything but typical for the folks I'd met in Highland Falls. In some way it was reassuring to see her reaction. It confirmed for me that they were just as bad as I'd imagined. In other ways I was almost ashamed, like it reflected on me how Ivy's parents and mine had always behaved. Of course that made no sense, but it was there.

Sighing, I continued down the hall to the kitchen. At least I could get coffee started and potentially some breakfast. I came up short when I saw an older woman bustling around the kitchen, then sighed with relief as I realized it was Mary. While my parents had a revolving door of staff over the years, Mary had been here since I was small. She was old enough to be my grandmother and had cooked and cared for me far more than either my mother or father ever had.

And then I realized she didn't know. Damn. I hadn't counted on having to tell her.

I cleared my throat so I wouldn't startle her, and Mary turned, surely expecting one of my parents, but her face absolutely lit up when she saw me.

"Oh, Noah." She rushed forward, folding me into her arms. I immediately relaxed into her embrace, remembering when she'd surrounded me as a kid. Now I towered over her. "Your mother didn't tell me you were coming."

I kept my eyes closed for just a moment, selfishly soaking in this feeling, which felt a whole lot like love. Mary's scent was always sweet, like she'd just baked cookies, combined with a light floral smell. It was the background of the majority of my happy memories in this house.

Taking a fortifying breath, I stepped back and looked down at her. "I have bad news, Mary."

She stiffened a bit and nodded. As I began to fill her in, one of her weathered hands reached out for mine. Was she getting strength from me or giving me some because she sensed I needed it? I had a feeling it was the latter. When I finished telling her all that I knew, she blotted her eyes, then seemed to take stock of what was needed.

"I don't what the will says yet, Mary," I shared. "And I have no idea how many folks my parents were employing now. While I'm sure I am not getting anything from them, I hope they've provided for you all, and if I have any say, I will ensure it."

"Oh, Noah," Mary said, "you don't think they've left you everything?"

I gave an incredulous laugh. "They didn't hesitate to cut me off when they were alive, I cannot imagine they'd want me to benefit from their deaths—which is just fine with me."

She shook her head but didn't say anything, which was nothing new. I knew Mary didn't approve of my parents' behavior when I was younger, but she never said a word against them. "Okay, let's think. What needs to be done? I can help you."

I put up a hand. "Oh no, I'd never ask you to do that."

She shook her head, dismissing my protests in one smooth move. "Shush, you. I know this household like the back of my hand. I also know where your mother keeps everything. It will be faster for you if I help. And the first thing you need is Barry Foley. He's your parents' lawyer, and his number is in your mother's book. Once he comes and looks over all their paperwork for you, you can get started with whatever needs to come next." She moved off to my mother's study, presumably to get her book.

I pulled out a mug and poured myself some coffee. It had been, what, almost two years since I last saw Mary? She had to be in her late sixties now, but she'd looked essentially the same since I was small. Her short stature and roundness had always given me comfort. We kept in touch through monthly letters when I left for college and hadn't ever stopped. Mary wasn't a fan of technology, so pen pals was the option I was left with.

I'd stopped in Madison when I came back from Africa, checking to see if my parents would want to be part of my life now that I was back. I thought I knew what their response would be but wanted to give them a chance. Why, I had no idea. I think most of my life had been spent hoping against hope that they'd become what they were not—loving parents who wanted the best for me.

I had still been let down—my original instinct was correct. They'd declared they weren't supporting me since I was "insane" enough to stay in this "charity work" instead of making real money at my dad's firm. Their words, not mine. Trying to explain to them that I didn't want their money, didn't need it, was fruitless. I just wanted them to care about what I was doing, to be part of my life. To them, money equaled their "love." I'd been crushed—it had felt like a final nail in the coffin. Not a great way to put it now, but there you go. But Mary had understood my broken heart and had sent me off to Highland Falls with my favorite brownies of hers and a hug to tide me over until her letters began again, closer to home now, to remind me that someone was proud of me even if my parents weren't.

What would she do now that my parents were gone? Did she have enough money set aside to retire? I hated the idea of her working some job she didn't enjoy.

Hearing someone enter the kitchen, I looked up, assuming it was Mary, only to see Jules with a tentative look on her face.

"Hey," she said with a sleep-softened voice. I could tell she wasn't sure of her surroundings. To be fair, even though this was my childhood "home," neither was I. It certainly wasn't the type of place that made you want to sit down and relax. Instead, it inspired you to sit up with your best posture and mind your manners.

Jules's dark hair was tumbling over her shoulders in waves. Her "pajamas" consisted of black leggings and a crazy-big graphic tee. Reading it, I bit back a smile. It said READ ROMANCE, FIGHT THE PATRIARCHY. Her feet were bare with dark polish on her toes. That seemed to be an intimate detail I shouldn't know, but then again, we'd slept in the same bed. Heavy emphasis on slept.

"Hey, did you get enough sleep?" I immediately moved to grab a coffee mug for her. I held it up, wordlessly asking if she wanted some.

"Sure," she said, reaching for it, but I stepped around her to fill it up. I felt an inherent desire to take care of this woman, foreign to anything I'd experienced before.

"Let me," I murmured as I grabbed the pot. "We don't have the makings of a vanilla latte here." I thought of her order at the Sanctuary. "But there's creamer and sugar."

I turned to pass her the filled mug to find her staring at me in wonder. "You remembered my order?"

"Sure," I replied, not certain why that would make her eyes well up, but I'd take it.

Instead, she shook her head like waking from a dream, took her coffee, and put it on the counter to my side. Then, with uncertainty positively pouring off her, she stepped to face me and slid her arms around my waist. I had to admit, just holding her made me breathe easier. I relaxed into her embrace, sliding my arms around her as well.

"What is this for?" I murmured to the crown of her head.

She squeezed her arms around me, then spoke into my chest. "You lost your parents."

I shook my head at her kindness, frankly more than they deserved to have directed their way. That sounded terrible, but it was the reality I'd long accepted. Likely I needed to look up a therapist and process some of this shit, but for the most part I felt okay with my mental state. Whether that would hold true as I processed, who knew.

"Jules, you are beyond kind, but I'm doing all right. I promise. Sad, sure, but as I said, at least this wasn't them *choosing* to separate themselves from me. In many ways, that was harder." I stepped back and looked down at her, tipping her chin up so she'd meet my gaze.

Her warm brown eyes met mine. "I feel like you have more to process here."

I gave her a small smile. "I have zero doubt that you're right about that. And when that happens, I'll work through it. But for now I'm fine."

She studied my face like she was searching for the truth. Whatever she was looking for, she must have found it because she gave me a decisive nod before putting her head back on my chest. We stood there in companionable silence, and I felt a peace that was unfamiliar to this space. I could only assume it was due to the presence of Jules, and maybe the fact that I wasn't bracing to be told I was a disappointment—which was its own mindfuck.

"Noah, I found— Oh—" Mary's reentry into the kitchen was accompanied with her dropping something on the floor, causing Jules to spring back from me like we were teenagers who had just been caught making out. In Jules's defense, I hadn't warned her to Mary's presence, so she hadn't known anyone was in the house.

"Oh, I'm..." Jules stuttered, clearly not sure what to say to this grandmotherly-looking figure in a work dress, staring at us with a pleased expression on her face. If I could see into Jules's brain, I was certain she was running through all the possibilities of who Mary could be.

"Jules, this is Mrs. Doyle—"

"Mary," she said. Stubborn woman.

"My apologies," I gave Mary an indulgent shake of my head and smiled at her. "Mary, Jules. My parents would have been lost years ago if Mary hadn't taken charge of their household. She runs this place."

Jules put her hand out, but Mary wasn't having any of that. She walked up to Jules and pulled her in for a hug. "Come here, sweet girl. You're going to need to tell me why I found you in our Noah's arms. Then we're going to conspire against the man and take care of him while we figure out what is to be done after his parents' passing."

Jules let out a laugh and looked from Mary to me, her eyes twinkling. "I think you and I are going to get along just fine."

"Oh boy," I said, grateful for the lightness of this moment. "I think you two together equals trouble."

"You know it," Mary said with a wink. "Now both of you, sit. Noah, here's your mother's book so you can contact Barry Foley. Jules, what do you want for breakfast?"

With that, I lost Jules to a flurry of a conversation about everything Mary could whip up at a moment's notice. I knew she'd make me an omelet, so I excused myself to call Barry and wrap my brain around what needed to happen next.

Coming back into the kitchen twenty or so minutes later, I found that I was incorrect in my assumption that I'd be having an omelet because Jules was behind the counter with Mary, and they were making pancakes. I leaned against the wall and took the time where they didn't know I was there simply to observe. There was a lot of laughter while Mary gave Jules gentle advice on how big to make the pancakes and how to know when to flip them.

"Yes, that one looks good." Jules cheered as she looked to Mary.

"Couldn't make a better-looking pancake myself," Mary said as she moved the completed pancake to a stack on a platter.

"Can we put some chocolate chips in a few?" Jules asked as she ladled some batter into the skillet.

"Sure, though maybe we should tell Noah to come from the back of the kitchen to join us and then we'll know what he wants on his," Mary said without turning around. The woman had always been all-knowing since I was a kid.

Jules looked in my direction and I raised my hands.

"Busted, and I'll take whatever you give me." I headed to join them at the counter. "And Jules, I hope you know Mary is already playing favorites—she sure never taught me how to make any of her secret recipes."

Jules looked to Mary, "Is that true?"

Mary laughed. "That you're my favorite? Of course.

Now flip." She pointed at the pancakes and revealed the truth of her feelings for me as she moved to my side and gave me a small hug. "Now Noah, don't you go telling lies. I taught you to cook when I could."

I nodded and looked at Jules's confused face while she poured the last pancakes into the pan. "The truth is, I haven't learned how to make her pancakes, but she used to teach me basics when my parents weren't here."

Jules drew her eyebrows together in a clear sign of confusion. "Why only then?"

I looked to Mary, who shrugged before she spoke. "Not to speak ill of the dead, but Noah's parents wouldn't have approved of him learning to cook."

"Why?"

I thought of how to phrase it without them sounding like entitled asses, but that was difficult at best. "They wanted me to work for my dad and make enough money that I could always have someone to work for me and do tasks like cooking and cleaning."

Jules didn't look any less confused than before. "I thought you mentioned you enjoy cooking?"

"Yep." Best to leave it at that.

Mary clucked her disapproval at the memory of my parents. Looked like their passing might make her blunter. That was going to be enlightening.

"Did you talk to the lawyer?" Mary asked as she helped Jules plate the final pancakes. A plate was slid to me at my stool at the island, then one for Jules. I cleared my throat, trying to tell Mary to make her own plate, but got a "mind your business" look back from her.

I rolled my eyes at her like my ten-year-old self had done so long ago before answering her question. "I did. He's swinging by here in half an hour to go over the will." I took a bite and groaned in pleasure. I hadn't had Mary's pancakes in years, and they were just as good as I remembered.

Jules took her first bite next to me and let out her own noise of pleasure that had me sitting up and praying that my current pair of joggers would not make my sudden arousal visible to all. My brain was all too happy to catalog that noise and pray I could get more from her in another setting. Jesus. Not. The. Time.

Luckily, she put down her fork to take a sip of coffee, then turned to me. "Should I make myself scarce when he comes? I mean, I need to get some writing done..." Her eyes flashed in panic as she glanced toward Mary, not that Mary was even paying attention. She'd already started cleanup and was happily humming to herself as she got her kitchen back in order.

"It's fine," I whispered, reaching over to squeeze her knee. "And if it's all the same with you, I'd love some company. I'm sure it's going to be another chance for them to insult me, but it would be nice to have someone by my side while that happens."

Jules laced my fingers with hers. "Then by your side sounds good to me."

Chapter 17

Surprising Parental Decisions

Jules

I was having an out-of-body moment as I sat next to Noah in his dad's home office. How had I gotten here? Last week at this time, I'd met Noah of course, but we hadn't even shared a meal yet. I thought the biggest thing that could happen to me was finding the path forward in my current book. Well, let's just say my life had taken a turn, though the story was finally less murky, so there was that.

The lawyer—Barry—was going over the details of the will. Apparently, much to Noah's surprise, he was the executor. I think he had been under the impression that he wouldn't even be named in it due to the way his parents had treated him during, well, pretty much forever, but especially over the past ten or so years.

"I'm not sure I understand, Mr. Foley," Noah was saying.

"Barry," he said. "And what are you confused by?"

Noah looked my way with confusion etched all over his face. Clearly I should have been listening more closely instead of contemplating the origin of our—well, whatever this was.

I squeezed his hand. He'd grabbed mine as soon as we walked into this space. Whether that was due to memories of his dad or the nature of this meeting, I wasn't sure and didn't really care. My gosh, I'd kissed this man only five days ago. I slept by his side, just slept mind you, last night. What was this world? This might be a faster relationship track than even the books I wrote.

Actually kidding, that was so not the case. Goddess knew, as Ivy was prone to say, in my books if my hero and heroine found themselves in the same bed, *sleep* would be the last thing on their minds. We had an only-one-bed type of situation, and I clearly didn't use it to its full benefit.

However, in actual reality, I loved sleeping next to Noah. I was honored that my being with him helped ease his grieving—recognized or not—in any way. The fact that he even asked for what he needed meant a lot to me.

Focus, Jules, I chastised myself. I tuned back into the present conversation and this gorgeous man. Whatever was happening between us, and my ruminations about it, would have to wait.

"Do you know what provisions are in place for the household staff?" Noah was saying.

"They'd cut back a lot from when you were younger, but the remaining staff all get a year's pay and benefits covered for that time," Barry said as he scanned the document in front of him. Looking from it to Noah, he went on. "And as I said before, the remaining estate—this home, their vehicles, all investments, et cetera—goes to you, their sole heir, along with a trust for your daughter"—he consulted his papers—"Adaline, when she turns twenty-five."

Record scratch. *What?* Noah's hand in mine was trembling. Now I understood a bit more why he was freaking out. *Daaamn.* His parents really knew how to shake his foundation even when they were gone.

"Barry." Noah's voice was scratchy as he spoke. He cleared his throat and went on, though that still didn't get rid of the tremble. "I'm not sure how well you know what my relationship was like with my parents since college, or really ever."

Barry looked up at Noah over the top of his glasses. "Noah, to be blunt, your father wasn't an easy man. And from what I observed, your mother was his match."

Noah nodded.

Barry continued, a look of compassion in his eyes. "And also, from what I knew of them, appearances were rather important."

Noah gave a wry laugh before stating, "Understatement of the century."

"So don't you think that, even in death, they wanted to make sure everything looked a certain way to the folks they associated with?"

"But—" Noah began before Barry spoke over him.

"Sorry to interrupt, but let me get through this, and then if you have any questions, you can ask whatever you need."

Barry looked at Noah, and they had some type of nonverbal understanding before Noah nodded and Barry continued.

"So from what Mrs. Doyle has shared with me, you have done quite a bit of good work in this world already. I know your parents had different plans for you, but you have forged your own way. I would be remiss in failing to tell you that I admire that."

Noah's hand in mine trembled, and I looked over to see that his eyes were watery. I wondered how often Noah heard something like that. He'd given up a lot to help others, and his parents had looked down at him in disdain rather than sharing any admiration. Mental note to tell him how amazing what he's done so far in life is as soon as possible.

Barry looked over his papers, then straightened them and gave Noah a serious look. "I'm not here to tell you what to do necessarily, that's all you. But if it were me, no matter what the relationship with your parents was like, I wouldn't look a gift horse, so to speak, in the mouth here. Whether or not you and your parents got along has no bearing on this will. You are the main benefactor once we settle their estate. After that, do with the money whatever you'd like. Keep it, give it all to charity, dance in it as you rain dollar bills down, it's yours." Barry gave Noah a look filled with such kindness, I wondered how on earth this man could be someone who worked for Noah's dad or Ivy's. Maybe that was just business, but in actuality he was truly kind? Who knew.

I glanced at Noah and saw he was visibly shaken. While it wasn't in my nature, to say the least, I spoke up. "Mr. Foley, would it be possible to give us a few minutes?"

Barry looked from Noah to me, then nodded. "Sure. I'll just step out and make a call. Be back in five minutes or so." He stood and walked out, putting a hand on Noah's shoulder and squeezing it as he went.

Once the door was shut, I immediately stood up. Noah looked up at me in confusion, but I didn't give him a chance to say anything. I grabbed his hand, pulled him up, and tugged him to me so I could hug the man. Hard. I squeezed my arms around his waist as I tried with all my might to pour in some comfort from me to him. I didn't know how, but I knew it needed to happen. I took all the memories of being comforted by my parents, by Lou and Verdell, by my grandparents when they'd been alive, and worked to make

Noah feel even a smidge of that solace I'd found in all of them.

At first he was tense, but as he relaxed into me, he dropped his chin to the top of my head. His breathing deepened, and then I felt the first shudder. I tightened my arms. Another came, then another. His arms wrapped around me, and I let the man cry for the parents he lost—years ago and also just yesterday—in my arms. My heart broke for the little boy he'd been, just wanting to please his parents, and the man he was who'd simply wanted the same.

After a few minutes, his heart rate slowed, his breathing evened out, and he stepped back.

"Thanks," he said, emotion still clear in his voice.

"Of course." I wiped the moisture from my own eyes.

He shook his head. "I stand by what I said yesterday—I lost them some time ago. But as Barry was reading the will, I realized that for so long I've had the *hope* of them making a different decision one day. Realizing I've wished for them to see what I'm doing and know that what I do does make a difference. And now that's gone. I guess it's nice that they didn't choose to cut me out of their will, but it isn't like money is equal to their love in my eyes." He paused, then sank back into his seat. "It's just so final."

"However you need to grieve, do it." I said, sitting back down and taking his hand. "If you need to cry, cry. Shout it out? Sounds good. Pound something to oblivion? We can find a rage room or"—I glanced around the room—"I'm sure there is something ugly but worth a small fortune in this house that we could destroy."

He let out a laugh, which thrilled me that I could make that happen.

There was a knock at the door before Barry stuck his head in. "Good to resume?"

Noah grabbed my hand and squeezed it. "You bet."

Several hours later, I sat in a ridiculously comfortable chaise on the deck overlooking what I'd been told was Lake Mendota. It was a warm day for April, though I had a blanket on my legs to ward off some of the chill still in the spring air. I was typing away at my laptop, my story flowing once again. My hero, Julian, came from money, Noah's parents' home—now Noah's?—was providing all sorts of inspiration for me.

I'd transported this home to the setting of my book. In the scene I was currently writing, Collette had helped Julian organize a fund raiser, and they were holding it at his home. As they stood on the deck, overlooking a river, Julian turned toward Collette, brushing back a hair the wind had blown into her eyes. Collette threw caution to the wind and rose up on her toes to press her lips to Julian's for their first kiss.

My fingers flew over the keys, the entire scene unfolding faster than I could type it. After being stuck on this story for so long, I was grateful my characters were finally cooperating. I felt like I was in the zone for the first time since my last book, and that gave me such relief. Readers were waiting on this story, and I didn't want to disappoint anyone.

I heard the door open behind me and looked over to see Noah headed my way with a plate and glass in hand. "Hey." I stopped typing and focused on him. "You doing okay?"

He'd wrapped up the meeting with Barry, which had left him with a list of next steps and people he needed to call. He didn't need me for that, so I'd excused myself to go write but also to give him some space to do whatever he needed to do. I'd also told him I'd check in with Ivy and Jake so they'd know what was going on up here and to get a time he could FaceTime with Addie later today or tomorrow.

"Yep." He slid the plate my way. Two giant pieces of avocado toast were there. "One's for you," he said, picking up the other piece.

I took a bite and closed my eyes in pleasure. How could something as simple as avocado smashed on bread, topped with what looked like everything-bagel seasoning, be this good?

"That's Mary's homemade sourdough," Noah said before taking another bite.

Answered that question. I wondered if Mary wanted to move to Highland Falls so I could continue to eat all her food daily. She could find a spot at the Sanctuary Café, though I'm certain she actually had a life here in Madison that she wouldn't want to leave just to keep me in bread and other baked goods.

I set the remainder of my toast down so I wouldn't inhale it all in the matter of a minute. Turning to Noah, who was sitting on a chair next to my chaise, I looked him over. He seemed more relaxed than he had even this morning.

"How are you?" I asked since he hadn't really answered me when he came out here other than to take care of me.

His toast gone, he wiped his hands on a cloth napkin and met my assessing look before turning to the water and putting his feet up on the rail. "Better." He paused, and I didn't interrupt because I sensed he was getting his thoughts in order. "Ivy has always told me I'm the type A to her type B. I thrive on order, on knowing what comes next.

It's why I can manage projects for the company I work for so well. I love spreadsheets and lists."

"You're speaking my language," I said, to which he laughed.

"I can see that. At any rate, it was hard to sleep because I didn't know what I didn't know, so to speak. Things like who would oversee the estate, what my role would be, how we needed to proceed, what would happen to Mary. Meeting with Barry gave me actionable steps. And, as shocking as my parents leaving me money might be, it also means I can hire people to help sell what I don't want or need, that my entire life won't have to be moved to Madison while I finalize their estate, and that Mary and any other staff they still have will be taken care of."

I paused, thinking of all that he was saying and what he wasn't. "It means you can get closure sooner versus later."

He looked my way, relief evident on his face. "Exactly." He looked from me to my laptop. "How is the writing going? Can I get you anything?"

It was odd to have someone want to take care of me. I hadn't really had that before. My parents were amazing, but I was far more likely to take care of them than the reverse. As Lou would say, *Bless their hearts*. They'd forget their heads if they weren't attached.

Add that to the fact that I had a strong feeling that I should be taking care of Noah, he was the one who'd experienced a loss here. So rather than beat around the bush, I said just that. "Noah, I feel like I'm falling down on the job here. What can I get you?"

He gave me a soft smile. "This has likely been the strangest start to dating ever."

"We're definitely dating then?"

Good grief. That was romantic, wasn't it? I swear, I could do this so much easier on the page. Real life was hard.

He nudged my foot with his. "If you'd like to be, we are. I'm just sorry we've jumped straight into the deep end of the heavy things going on in my life." He looked worried, like the chaos around him was going to make me want to say this was all too much. "And I have no answers for how I'll balance this with what I want to be for Addie, but I'll work on that."

Dang, the man tugged on my heart even when he wasn't trying to. His gorgeous blue eyes were dark, almost gray. I think I had once cataloged them as reminding me of a stormy sea. Note to self, use that in a book.

"Just so I'm on record here," I said, working to keep my eyes on his even though I was feeling way out of my depth, "I'd like to be dating you too." I looked at my open document, saved my work, and closed the laptop so I could slide it to the side. "Now, what can I help you with on your list?"

Noah looked at my laptop, then back to me. "I don't want you to stop writing on my account."

The way this man cared for me was something I'd have to work up to getting used to. "I'm good. I need a break."

"In that case..." Noah held out a hand for my laptop.

I passed it over, and he put it on a table along with our plate from the avocado toast and both our drinks. Then he slowly lowered himself onto the chaise with me, sliding under the blanket and facing me while on his slide.

"I was wondering if we could find a way to pass a bit of time together." The expression on his face could only be described as mischievous.

I immediately wondered if that was what Addie looked like when she was up to something.

"Whatever could we do?" I asked nonchalantly. "Look at the water?"

"Good idea, good idea." His voice was thoughtful as his gaze roamed over my face before he tucked a strand of my hair behind my ear. "But I have something else in mind."

"You do?" I asked, playing innocent. "Whatever could you be thinking of?"

He lowered his mouth to mine, hovering just above my lips. "This," he whispered, pausing so I could tell him if I wasn't interested. Like hell was that happening, so I pulled him flush with me, entwining our legs together under the blanket.

His lips met mine, and I wanted to fall into them. They parted, letting his tongue dance with mine before he backed off and nipped my lower lip. There was a moan—from him or me, who knows—before he began kissing down my neck. I arched my head to give him access as his hand slid up my shirt and I held his head to my neck, wishing for more room than this chaise provided.

Too quickly, his kisses slowed down, backing off in intensity far before I was ready for that to happen. I opened my eyes to meet his. "Why are you stopping?"

He tried to hold back a smirk and failed miserably. "Mary should be back from the store any minute, and I didn't figure you wanted to do this with her one room away from us."

"Do this? Make out?"

He gave me an indulgent look. "I mean, sure, that was part of it. However, that kiss just went from zero to ninety in a matter of seconds. I have a feeling that if we'd continued, clothing would have been shed in the cool April air. Am I wrong?"

I chuckled. "No, my fantasies were already heading there."

His eyes darkened as he leaned forward to place another kiss to my neck. "I think I need to hear more about these fantasies."

"Maybe tonight?" I said breathlessly.

"Noah, Jules, I'm back," Mary called from somewhere in the house.

I groaned.

"Tell me about it," Noah commented before swinging his body up to standing and offering me a hand. "Ready to head in?"

Chapter 18

Game On

Noah

I lay in an empty bed, staring at the ceiling in the light of the morning and wondering what today had in store. Two nights ago I'd thought—hoped, dreamed—that things with Jules would be heating up. I mean, they had on the porch and once we'd headed to bed, I'd assumed that would continue. Unfortunately, she'd gotten a call from Sue around seven, pleading for her to tag in on some last-minute tax prep. She'd sent me big eyes of apology and a promise that Tuesday night would be different.

Tuesday and Wednesday had been filled with the minutiae of learning everything I needed to do between my parents' passing, the service on Friday, and everything that would come after. Jules had alternated between helping Mary and me, working on taxes, finding time to get more words on the page for her book, and making sure to take care of herself or Sue would personally hold her accountable.

Mary and I were able to get many things crossed off my

to-do list while also making sure Jules didn't get so far in the zone on either of her jobs that she forgot to take care of herself. I'd watched the woman, which was no hardship. I had a strong feeling that if left to her own devices, she'd sit down at her laptop to work and only stop typing when she completely ran out of steam, even if that meant she'd go hungry, thirsty, or end up with a sore neck and back. More than that, I enjoyed doing things for her. She was so grateful for even the smallest of gestures, it made me want to do more.

I'd looked forward each day to the moment we could go to bed, and then one wrench and then another was thrown in the works. Tuesday Addie had a nightmare. Ivy and Jake had talked to her, but she was convinced I needed her. We'd texted back and forth, and our solution was an extra-long FaceTime past her bedtime and mine. It had done the job, and I got to see her little blond head sacked out next to Jake as he and I had teamed up to tell her a Little People story, a tradition he'd had growing up that he shared with Addie. Since she loved them so much, he had taught me his tricks, though this had been our first joint story.

By the time I'd finished and headed to bed, Jules had been sacked out. She'd been up late on Monday, doing the work for Sue, then ran herself ragged all day even though I'd tried to ensure she found time to rest.

Instead of the day ending the way I'd fantasized, I'd stood in the door, watching her sleep like some creeper, her hair spilling over the pillow. I noted that, similar to the nights before, she slept with the duvet pulled up to her chin and her feet kicked out of the covers at the bottom. It made me smile and wonder what else I could learn about this woman the longer I spent with her. Each day I uncovered more, and every quirk or fact learned just made me greedy for more.

I'd slid in next to her and was hit with the notion that lying in the same bed next to her didn't feel anything but right. Like, I'd slept next to the woman for three nights and didn't want to think of sleeping alone.

I needed to slow this train down. Was it the current circumstances that had accelerated whatever this was, or was it just the two of us? My conversation with Addie last night reminded me of my priorities, but didn't I have room in my life for Addie *and* Jules? And yet, if I did, how did I go about making sure I didn't fall down on the job of parenting ever again?

Wednesday had been a lather, rinse, repeat of Tuesday, but I crashed out when it was time to go to bed. There was only so much energy I had in me and then it was gone.

Thursday morning dawned, and a glance at my cell told me it was still early. I wondered why Jules was already up—we had nothing on the docket for the day. The plans were in place for the visitation the following day. I'm sure it wasn't as elaborate as they would have planned for themselves. It was understated and elegant, Mary made sure. But beyond that, I didn't need a drawn-out affair that made me have to spend any extra time with the toxic people my parents had surrounded themselves with. I was dreading the next morning, but knew it was a necessary step to moving on. And, as Jules had mentioned and Mary had agreed, moving on for me would likely need to be processed with the help of a good therapist. The baggage I was carrying was more than a carry-on.

Yesterday Barry and I had talked to my parents' staff and explained what the plan was for them moving forward. Barry was reaching out to a real estate agent he knew as well as an auction house up here that would help me sort out what I wanted to keep and sell.

Honestly, there wasn't much here that held great memories for me, so I just wanted to wash my hands of all of it. However, Mary and Jules had asked me not to be hasty, though a small part of me wanted to bury my head in the sand and ignore any it all. Irresponsible maybe, but it was a desire I was working to ignore. We'd brainstormed together, and the current plan was to go through the house, selecting the few items I knew I wanted to keep. Then Mary was going to work with the estate folks on my behalf and ensure we were in contact by video when they were getting the sale together. I'd likely come back up for that.

All of it seemed exhausting, but with the help of Jules and Mary along with the advice of Barry, it was coming together. But that brought me back to Jules. I pulled on some joggers and a tee and headed out to find my missing bed partner.

The house was silent. Mary wouldn't get here for about twenty more minutes, which would be seven. There were no signs of life as I made my way downstairs to the kitchen. Once I entered it, I looked beyond the counters and found her exactly where I'd suspected. She was bundled up on the chaise on the deck overlooking the lake. It looked like I was about half an hour too late for sunrise, but I wasn't entirely sure Jules had seen it either—her fingers were currently flying as she typed out what I was assuming her novel on her MacBook.

While she had a blanket around her shoulders and across her lap, it still looked chilly. I glanced at the coffeemaker and saw that it hadn't been started. I got that going and jogged back upstairs to grab one of my hoodies. Back in the kitchen, I toasted up an everything bagel, slathering chive-and-onion cream cheese on it as she'd done yesterday. Once the coffee was ready, I doctored it up and headed out the French door.

Jules was so far into the zone that she didn't seem to register my presence on the porch. I put the coffee and bagel on the empty table next to her. As much as I didn't want to disturb her flow, I could see one arm protruding from the blanket as she typed, and it was covered in goose bumps. That would just not do.

"Babe," I whispered. No reaction. God, her focus when she wrote was sexy as hell. And I never thought that would be something that turned me on, but here we were. "Jules." I spoke louder this time. Still nada. I leaned forward and lightly tapped her shoulder. She started and looked up at me, blinking several times.

"Noah?" she said in confusion.

This woman. I wanted to wrap her up and take her back to bed, but I also knew she'd struggled to get into this book, and that didn't seem to be the truth anymore.

"Hey, babe, I thought you might be cold." I held out my hoodie, and she pulled it on with a sigh of relief.

I pointed to the coffee and bagel. "I also brought you something to give you some fuel as you write."

She looked from the side table to me, her gaze becoming warm. "Thank you," she whispered.

I leaned down and pressed a kiss to her head as I racked my brain, trying to pinpoint if I'd ever felt like this about someone else. My feelings for Jules ranged from wanting to spend unending days in bed, having what I knew would be amazing sex, to pure affection as I watched her simply move through her day, to ease and comfort as we sat and talked.

This was new. I hadn't dated a ton of women in my life —growing up, I had zero desire to inflict my parents on anyone. In college there were some short relationships, but nothing long term. There was Ivy, but that was clearly stronger as a friendship than anything more, we were just in denial at first. And then for the past six years I'd had other work at the forefront of importance: my job in Africa and being a dad. But I'd never had the ease of friendship along with the heat of something more with the same person. And somehow I knew this was a rare treasure and needed to be treated as such.

"Keep at it. I'm going to get some things done inside." I started to head back to the door.

"Are you sure? Is there anything I can do to help?" Jules asked, her teeth coming to bite her lower lip once again. I noted she tended to do that when she was uncertain.

"Positive." I stepped back into the house before she could find a reason to stop writing. As I closed the door, I saw her head bend and her fingers begin flying across the keyboard once again. I leaned against the wall, watching her for a moment before I heard a throat clearing behind me.

"Hey, Mary," I said without turning.

"So tell me about Ms. Jules," Mary said, her voice heavy with amusement.

I looked to her. "What's so funny?"

She shrugged, then began to pull out ingredients from the fridge. Looked like I was getting my omelet today. "I just used to wonder what you'd be like when you fell head over heels in love. Now I know."

"Oh, that's a bit dramatic, Mary," I said. "I wouldn't say *love* yet."

"Is that so?" She cracked some eggs in a bowl and began whisking while heating a skillet on the stove. "What would you say then?"

I felt nerves flooding my body. What the literal hell? "Umm, a strong like?"

Mary's expression could only be described as tolerant. Truly, it said she thought I was an idiot. I wouldn't say she was wrong.

"Come on, Mare. You know what my model was for relationships growing up..."

"You hush. You had me and Mr. Doyle." She tried to give me a glare.

I snorted a laugh at her instead. "Yes, Fred has long shown me how to be ever-suffering in your love life."

She leaned over to my spot on the counter and whacked my arm. "You watch yourself, young man." Her eyes were alight with amusement.

In truth, the few times Fred did come to visit Mary over the years that I was around, they were great models of a healthy relationship, it just wasn't one that I saw often. Fred was a hilarious foil to Mary's quiet and often proper demeanor, at least that's the way she was here. I hadn't seen her in her own home to know what she was like there. However, if the past few days were any example, she was far more relaxed. Fred liked to poke her buttons to get her to tell him to get in line. Whenever she did, he'd swoop in and kiss her on the cheek.

I shrugged and pulled the bowl of grapes she had on the counter toward me, plucking a few off the stem and popping them in my mouth. Once I finished chewing, I shrugged and looked at Mary, uncertain on how much to share. "I'm working on it. It's just one, ensuring that Addie comes first, and two, making certain I'm what she needs."

"What who needs?" Jules's voice made me sit up and look at Mary in alarm.

"Oh, just the estate service that the young man, Barry,

found for us. They need some info from Noah here." Mary didn't look up as she whisked the eggs, impressing me with how she thought on her feet.

Young man, Jules mouthed at me with a smile. Barry was, at a minimum, sixty.

I simply shot her a wink, then bumped Mary's hip with mine. She was saving me now as she had through childhood. In turn, she gave me a look that told me we'd be talking more later.

"Jules, how does an omelet sound to you this morning?" Mary asked as she continued bustling around the kitchen.

"Like you need to run away from Madison and come live with me," Jules said with a happy noise that made me want to escape to somewhere far more private.

"She's a keeper, Noah," Mary said with a calculating smile.

I shook my head and got a cup of coffee to start my day.

Hours later, after a full day of work for Jules, organization and planning for Mary and me, and a delicious lunch and dinner that made me remember the good parts about being home, I stood in my en suite, brushing my teeth as Jules rattled off items on a list, reminding me of what we had ahead. We were going through last-minute prep for tomorrow's services: the time the minister would meet us and whether tips were needed for anyone from the church to the funeral home to the cemetery. I'd finally conceded to let Mary prepare some food to have at the house. I told her I had zero desire to mingle with my parents' friends, but she seemed to think it was important, so I let her have that. Maybe I could be rude and hide out in my dad's office until everyone was gone.

As I put my toothbrush down, I looked at myself in the mirror. Jules's voice filled the space as she listed off all the dishes Mary was whipping up for tomorrow—all my favorites, I should note.

Staring at myself, I noted how intimate this felt. Preparing for bed, going over plans for the next day, and Jules sitting in my bed in her oversized T-shirt and underwear but no pajama bottoms. I knew that because she'd borrowed the shirt she was wearing from me just a bit ago. She'd done laundry today, much to Mary's dismay. Jules told her that laundry brought her peace when her mind was stuck—whether she was struggling with accounting or writing, I wasn't sure, but Mary let her have it. She'd come to me an hour ago, sharing that her pajamas set was in the last load in the dryer and not quite done, so I'd given her my Homestead Brewery tee to wear. I had no idea that it would captivate my attention like it had. Now I wanted more than anything to see that shirt on the floor.

"And I think that does it," she called from the bedroom. "After we get through tomorrow, we can head back to Highland Falls if you feel like you're ready and Mary is on the job up here. You'll likely need to make one, possibly two, more trips up here to close everything out, but between Mary, Mr. Foley and his office, and the folks he helped you hire, I think they have it well in hand."

One more glance at my reflection and I couldn't help but note the resolve in my eyes. We were in my bedroom, alone and without distractions. For the first time in the past few nights, we were ready to go to bed, and neither one of us was asleep, working, or calming an almost-six-year-old to go back to dreamland. Maybe I should wait until we were back in Highland Falls, but there was no telling what would cockblock me there. For all I knew, Lou would move into Jules's house and have a slumber party. No, I was a firm believer in taking the opportunities that came, and if Jules was still interested in continuing what we started *days* ago, I was all in.

I walked back into the bedroom and took her in as she sat up against the headboard, consulting a list she had written in the tablet on her lap. She was gorgeous while also appearing like the girl next door. There was an innocence about her that was sexy as hell. Before I could say anything, she sensed my presence and looked up. I couldn't help but watch as she clocked my gray joggers and lack of shirt, her eyes roaming my torso before finally meeting mine. Her cheeks had an adorable flush on them that went down her neck, and I wanted to tug off my shirt that she was wearing to see if the color continued down her chest.

"Hey, Jules," I whispered, slowly moving toward my bed.

"Hey, Noah," she whispered back as she blindly reached out and put the list on the bedside table while keeping her gaze locked on mine. Then she bit down on her lower lip, clearly debating her next move, before reaching over to grab the covers and throw them back, welcoming me to the bed.

I slid in next to her, not turning off the lamp on the bedside table. If this was happening, and all indications seemed like green lights in that regard, I wanted to see Jules, not grope around blindly in the dark. The only glow in the room was a soft light from the bedside lamps, but it still worked for me.

I turned in her direction once I was settled to find that she was still watching me with a shy smile, but she seemed to have something she wanted to say. Her body language made it pretty evident when she was holding things back, but I was learning she'd speak up with a small amount of encouragement.

"What's on your mind, kitten?"

Her face transformed with a smile almost immediately. "I don't know why I find it sweet that you call me that."

"Doesn't have to make sense to work for us, right?"

She gave a slow nod, then looked up with a more tentative expression. "Um, it's just, I want to make sure you don't think that just because I write romance that I'm..."

I had a feeling I knew where she was going with this. "That you're some sex kitten in the bedroom?" Yep, the flush intensified even while she nodded her head. "You mean you don't like to straddle your partners while they sit against the headboard and you chase your climax like Clara and Josh in book two of your Sleepy Valley series?"

She shot up in bed and looked down at me in what could only be described as shock. "Um, what?"

I moved to a sitting position to mirror her and gave her an innocent shrug. "Or maybe like Anna and Clayton's sex *in public* at a deserted pond after skinny-dipping from your first book? Is that something you're interested in?"

"You've read my books?" Jules asked, mixed emotions everywhere. This wasn't how I'd intended to tell her, but here we were. It wasn't something I'd kept from her intentionally, but now that it was out...

"I started reading your books the night you told me about them," I confessed. "I've never met an author, and I thought it was beyond cool that you've written and published your books. If all this"—I gestured around us—"hadn't happened, I'd be much further along in the series. I tend to devour books I like."

She looked down at the duvet. "I'm not sure what to say."

I leaned over, putting my finger under her chin to tilt it up so she could meet my gaze. "What you should say is that you know you are a damn fine writer. I love your books; they make me want to keep reading because the town you've written is delightful, as are all the characters."

She tried to look away as if she couldn't take a compliment, but I kept her gaze locked on mine. It occurred to me if she only had one friend that knew she wrote as Jules Jenkins, she wasn't used to hearing to her face about how her writing impacted other people, so I was doing that for her right here and right now no matter how much I wanted to heat up the sheets with the woman.

"Jules, I've been a reader all my life. I think it's absolutely a gift that we get to disappear into books and be captivated by other people's stories even when they're fictional, or maybe especially because of that." I paused to let that sink in. "I've read all genres and don't discriminate. That being said, the romance genre was new for me, but now I don't know why I hadn't read any earlier. The knowledge that the book will work out in the end is comforting. And the sex scenes are, no exaggeration, fun as hell to read." I squeezed her hand. "I think you're an excellent writer, and I'm guessing your sales numbers confirm that, which is why I'm already on book three and have book four downloaded and ready to go."

Her body relaxed as I spoke. When I paused, I noted that her eyes were a touch watery.

She blinked a few times before she spoke, her voice soft and warm. "First, though I'm a bit mortified to realize you've read my writing, thank you."

"Mortified, why?" I asked, completely confused.

She bit that darn lip again, looking up toward the ceiling. I leaned over and tugged it out. Then, giving in to the urge I'd had every time I'd seen her do that little move, I leaned forward and pressed a light kiss on her lip.

Sitting back, I gave her a smile while picking up her hand closest to me and clasping it in my own. I was attempting, in my own way, to do what she had done for me all week—send her positive energy while she dealt with something difficult for her.

It seemed to work because then she spoke up. "Mortified because in so many ways, writing is like laying my soul bare even when it's fiction." She took a breath, then continued. "I feel like there is more *me* on the pages of my novels then anyone would ever guess. People who read my books always ask which character is based on me or real people in my life, but what they're missing is that the characters aren't formed from real people, but all the books are essentially *who I am*. They encompass my wishes for the world, what type of friends I'd like to have, what I think would be an ideal partner, the types of houses I'd like to live in, et cetera. Like"—she waved her hands around—"it's all there—my deeply held beliefs. I have no idea if everyone is like that when they write, but I am."

"So what you're saying about the scenes you write..." I teased her, knowing she would get where I was going.

She absolutely did as she used her free hand to playfully slap my chest. "Shush, some people online always write to me about the sex scenes—where is the inspiration for them coming from?" She rolled her eyes and shook her head. "Good Lord. I mean, does Stephen King write the murders in his books from real life?" She raised an eyebrow at me. I figured now wasn't the time to tell her how sexy she was doing that.

"I've had sex, of course."

I gasped in fake shock just to fuck with her.

She went on like she hadn't heard me. "And like anything else I have experienced in life, it informs my writing to an extent. But my scenes aren't written from life, and I would put money on most romance writers being the same way." She gave me an impervious look before finishing. "Because look at the number of heroines in hetero romance books having an orgasm *every single time* they have sex, much less from penetrative sex? I mean, do you know the average of that in real life? It's abysmally low, so clearly there is fiction at work here, and that doesn't even begin to touch the multiple orgasms or the speed of which any of that happens." The smug expression she wore combined with amusement dancing in her eyes made me want to kiss her repeatedly. "Or"—she lowered her voice—"the size of the heroes, and I don't mean height."

"Is that so, Ms. Jenkins?" I waggled my eyebrows at her.

She laughed at the use of her pen name. "It is."

"I think I might have to give you some new data points," I said, tugging her down to lie in the bed and then joining her on my side.

She placed a hand on my chest, and I froze. Maybe I'd read her wrong.

"Noah," she said, her tone serious. "I know we escalated things the other day on the patio, but you've had a lot going on this week. If you aren't ready for this step, that's totally fine. We can wait."

I relaxed, realizing she was indeed at the same place I was, she was just trying to protect me once again. While I appreciated it, I also wanted her to look out for her own desires. I had a feeling that Jules had spent a lot of time putting her own needs last.

Instead of addressing that with words, I decided to answer her with action. Leaning forward, I bypassed her lips and found her neck. Jules immediately arched into me, tilting her head to give me better access.

"Hey, Jules," I whispered between kisses.

"Yeah?" she replied breathlessly.

"If I'm ready for more, are you?" I asked because I had to check.

She huffed out a small laugh. "Hell, yeah." Her fingers entwined in my hair, holding my mouth to the crook of her neck.

I pulled back. "Then please lose the shirt, kitten."

She looked up with a challenge evident in her gaze. "How about you help with that?"

I tugged her shirt, scratch that—my shirt, up and over her head and tossed it on the floor just as I had fantasized. I was right—it was the perfect spot for it. Then I kicked my joggers off, noting the delight in her expression when she noted that I was commando. "Game on, babe."

Chapter 19

Finding Pleasure

Jules

Pinch me. I mean, not really. No kink shaming here, but I was not a fan of pain during sex or otherwise. But surely I was dreaming. As much as I wanted to climb this man like a tree, I still was struggling to believe he wanted this with me. It wasn't that I had a low opinion of myself, though goddess knows it could be improved upon, it was just that Noah was giving all the vibes of a romance hero. He seemed too good to be true, like my fictional world was dreaming up the guy for me.

That being said, who was I to look a gift horse in the mouth? Noah had kicked off his joggers and was lying in front of me without a stitch of clothing. Me? I wished for the confidence to run my tongue over his torso like I was lapping up an ice cream cone. However, that was not in my wheelhouse, though I absolutely wrote heroines who would. Instead, I dove at the man and kissed him like he was a soldier getting ready to head out to the field and I wouldn't see him for weeks on end. Still required some confidence, but I had enough for this.

Noah's arms wrapped around me and pulled my body flush with his. Mm-hmm, I could feel how aroused he was, which only served to make me even more so. I slid a leg between his and ground down. The infuriating man put a hand on each of my hips to hold them still. I'm sorry, what? I opened my eyes, prepared to lodge a formal protest when I saw him watching me with amusement.

"Not so fast, kitten. I promise we will get there, but we need to have some fun first," he said with a heated look that promised I wasn't alone in the want that was racing through my veins.

"I thought that was what I was doing? Having fun..." I gave him a pleading glance. He leaned forward to press a kiss to my nose and then began sliding down my body.

Hooray, my happy place cheered. Yes, I did say happy place. Double yes, I also wrote sex scenes on the regular. And I have no issue with correct terminology for anatomy, but since I'd hit the age where I became sexually active, I didn't think of my *vulva* or *vagina* if I was thinking in terms of sex. Not even my *clit* or *clitoris*. I had no idea why, but in my head, I called it my happy place because if the guy, or my vibrator, knew what they were doing, the end result for me was pure happiness.

Back to the matter at hand. Noah's tongue was doing goddess's work at the moment and tracing its own path down my body, over my mound, and... *yes...* right to my happy place. I sighed in absolute pleasure. The man's tongue pulsed over the perfect spot, the right amount of teasing and suction to get me just to the edge. However, right as I was almost at the point of tipping over that cliff into a world of pleasure, he moved back up.

I shot my head up and looked down at the gorgeous man

working his way back up my body. "What is happening?" I asked in a throaty voice.

Noah was kissing the softest places of my stomach, the ones I used to be more self-conscious about until I did the work to decide that my body was beautiful as is and screw the parts of society that tried to invade our minds to tell us otherwise.

So yeah, Noah was spending some time there when I needed him farther south. Instead of answering me, he moved to my breast and pulled my nipple in his mouth. A pulse shot down to my happy place. After a few moments, he laved the same attention on the other side. Amazing, yes. Was my happy place begging for more? Also yes. I arched into his mouth, feeling both filled with arousal and also left wanting.

Finally he started moving again, but still not in the direction I needed as his face appeared above mine. "Hey, kitten," he whispered before his head descended so that his mouth could meet mine.

While I wanted to lodge a formal protest that an orgasm might feel really good about now, I fell into the kiss before I could think too hard. To be honest, kissing during sex was typically the first act on my mind. The path taken to get to more. But this was, well, something else. Like I could envision leisurely days of lying on a couch with Noah, legs tangled together, just kissing. I loved how he varied from heated kisses to leisurely pecks that made me want to chase him for more. And yes, I wanted to get back to his mouth on my happy place, but I also loved this. It felt more intimate. How was that possible?

I pulled my head back to catch my breath after a particularly intense moment and met Noah's smile with my own. "Noah?"

"Yeah?" He pressed a kiss to my neck.

"I, um..." I squirmed for a moment, trying to just say what I wanted.

He tugged on my earlobe before whispering, "Say it."

Damn him, how does he know I'm holding back?

His tongue was making patterns on my neck that were causing goose bumps to spring up across my arms. Maybe I didn't have to say anything, but could just nudge his head where I needed it to go?

"Come on, kitten." He moved across my neck and up the other side. "Give yourself the same permission you give your heroines. What do you need?"

I closed my eyes, the pulse in my happy place telling me what it needed for certain. Finally I thought screw it and took a deep breath before opening my eyes to meet Noah's. "I need to orgasm."

He pressed a kiss to my lips. "That's it, babe. And how do you want that first one to happen?"

My gaze stayed locked on his unwavering one while I contemplated his *first one* comment. "I need your mouth on my happy place."

His mouth hitched at the side. "Happy place?"

I wrinkled my nose at him. "Well, it was on the way to being that, but *someone* moved back up."

He barked out a laugh and then brought his fingers up in a salute. "Aye, captain. Happy to follow your orders anytime." And he started to slide back down before I grabbed his arms to halt his descent.

"But I really did like kissing you," I said, not wanting him to think I was only here for sex.

He gave me a look filled with warmth. "I like kissing you too, Jules. But we've had some practice at that over the past week, yeah?"

I nodded.

"So maybe it's time to add some more ways to connect to our repertoire?" he asked, and what could I do but nod again?

With that he slid down and got back to business. I didn't know if it was because I had almost climaxed already that my body went from a low level of arousal to the edge of the cliff so quickly, but before I even knew what was happening, my entire body was tightening up and ricocheting over the orgasm mountain. Without even realizing it, I'd pressed my core tightly to his mouth, chasing that elusive feeling as pulses shot through my body. Noah stayed still, just giving me enough pressure to keep the sensation going until the sensitivity got too much and I tugged on his hair to pull him up.

His mouth moved to my inner thigh, kissing me there, then my hip bone, stomach, ribs, breasts, before meeting my mouth. "You good, kitten?"

"I need you," I said, feeling at once relaxed and empty, ready for more.

His eyes twinkled. "Look at you asking for what you need." He leaned over, getting a condom from the bedside table where apparently he'd placed one earlier. He got it on quickly and kissed my jaw. "Position preference?"

I started to say *any*, but had a feeling he'd call me on it, so I quickly gave a light push. He took the hint and rolled to his back, and I slid over his waist to straddle him, then sliding up to make room for his cock.

"Ready?" I asked, looking down at this sexy-as-hell man and thanking the goddess above that we were here.

He winked at me, sliding his hands to my hips. "Ready," he said as I centered myself over him and slid down, letting him fill me up.

I wasn't living in one of my books, but if I had to describe this feeling in one of them, I would have written something sappy like *I felt like I was coming home*. I know that made zero sense, but how do you describe the incredible feeling of *rightness* I was experiencing?

I'd had sex for the first time in college at nineteen. In the past eleven years, I'd had several partners. It had been varying degrees of good, but this was so far beyond that it brought tears to my eyes. Maybe it was Noah. Maybe it was the fact that we'd only known each other for a short time but had grown incredibly close because of some difficult shared experiences. Maybe it was because he'd made me speak up for what I needed, but this was a different level of connection than I'd ever had.

I continued to move up and down with Noah's hips, but his hands on mine led me to do more of a low thrust with a grinding action that... *Ohh*. Tingles started building in my body, emanating from my core and radiating outward as I felt a warm sensation building until it filled me up.

My eyes shot open to see Noah looking up at me, my hands braced on his chest as I rode out that roller coaster of feelings. He gave me a smug smile as I dropped down on his chest. His hands moved to my shoulders, and he continued to thrust a few more times, then froze and let out a quiet moan right by my ear before we both lay still but breathing hard.

After a few moments, Noah kissed the top of my head and rolled us to the side. He slid out and dealt with the condom before climbing back into the bed and lying on his back, helping to position me until I was on my slide, head to his chest, still peering up at him, and he pulled the duvet over both of us. He leaned his head back, eyes closed, and took a deep breath.

"What on earth was that?" I whispered. I mean, it was like an orgasm but different at the same time.

Noah pried one eye open as he looked over at me. "That was sex, kitten. And some pretty excellent sex at that if I do say so myself."

I slapped his arm and rolled my eyes. "No kidding, Noah. I mean..." My voice trailed off as I lost the courage to say what I meant. *Dammit, Jules. Why was it so hard?*

Noah squeezed his arm around me, and I looked at him and felt reassured enough to be an adult and get my words out. "Okay..." Deep breaths. "At the end there, it was like I had an orgasm but also not the same. It was warmth throughout my whole body, just like it felt *amazing*." Gathering some more courage, I continued. "Like, I'm thirty years old, Noah. This isn't the first time I've had sex. And, as you know, unlike the majority of the population, I even write about people doing that. But whatever that was at the end, I've never experienced it before."

Noah rolled us both to our sides and put his finger under my chin, tilting it up and placing the barest of kisses on my lips. "One, how is it you can write sex scenes in your books and, from what I can tell, not be the most comfortable talking about it in real life?"

I looked down and mumbled my answer. "I drink wine or beer."

Noah's laughter filled the room. "I'm sorry, did you say you have a drink before writing a scene like this in your books?"

I met his amused look with a stubborn one of my own. "Well, it works."

He pulled me to him and gave me a lingering hug that soothed my soul. "I'm not making fun of you, Jules. I love that you've found whatever you need to do to make it work."

His lips kissed my bare shoulder. "And I'm not an expert on the female body, but I think what you're describing is a vaginal orgasm, which I believe but could be wrong, feels different than a clitoral orgasm."

"Whoa," I said, contemplating all the miracles that our bodies had for us. And then, as my brain was wont to do, I immediately began to contemplate how I could work this into a book.

After a few moments, Noah squeezed my waist. "Did I lose you there?"

I shook my head. "Sorry, I began to think about writing."

A huff of laughter came from him. "Should I expect to see this scene in a book one day?"

"No, not this scene. Like I told you, I don't write my actual life, especially in sex scenes."

"But..."

I bit my lower lip and looked up before continuing. "Maybe the way you made me feel or the confidence you gave me?"

His smile was immediate and soft. "I'd love that." He rolled over and picked up his phone, looking at the lock screen, then rolled back to me. "It's ten. Do you want to go to bed, or do you want to write a little?"

My heart rate rose at his question as I looked up with what I knew was incredulity. "You don't care if I write?"

He wrinkled his brows as he looked at me in confusion. "Why would I care?"

I shrugged, trying to examine where that feeling was coming from in me. "I'm not sure." I paused, and then a memory came to mind. "I guess the last guy I dated seriously, Bryon, expressed his displeasure to me when, during tax season, I needed to work late into the night. He said I wasn't prioritizing our relationship and broke up with me shortly after that. So maybe that made a bigger impact than I thought?"

"When was that?"

I gave that a few seconds of thought. Wow, I hadn't thought of Bryon for a while. "Two years ago. I was crushed at the time, but upon reflection we absolutely weren't right for each other, and he did me a favor."

"Sorry that happened. And yeah, if you were neglecting your health—meaning sleep—for weeks on end while also choosing work, writing or accounting, over me every single time, then we might need to talk. But when you're inspired" —he waggled his brows at me—"feel free to pick up your laptop."

I laughed but then sobered, feeling the tendrils of inspiration for my story flowing through my veins. "Um, if you don't mind, I'd love to grab my laptop. Not that you should get too full of yourself, mister, but I do have some ideas I'd love to get down while they're actually in my brain."

He rolled toward me and brushed my mouth. "One request."

"Name it."

"Are you able to write in bed? Like sitting here while I sleep? Because I'm beat, but I'd love to go to bed to the music of you typing out a story." His expression was one I'd only seen a few times from him—all while we'd been up here dealing with everything to do with his parents—he was tentative, unsure. Like he was verbalizing what he wanted but was didn't know if it would matter. That was a learned behavior, and my heart hurt for the little boy who didn't get what he needed from the people he should have been able to expect it from. I was also grateful to Mary because without her, I think his childhood would have been devoid of any type of affection.

"I can absolutely type in here."

Noah's smile was bright and instantaneous. He hopped out of bed before I could say anything and moved across the room to grab my laptop from where it was charging on a dresser. He hesitated, then also grabbed my AirPods. Sliding back in next to me, he handed both over. "I think I've seen you with your earbuds in when you've been writing," he said by way of an explanation for bringing them as well.

"Yeah, I listen to a different playlist for each book," I explained, unbelievably touched that not only had he paid attention but cared enough to try to ensure I had everything I needed.

He leaned over to turn off the lamp on his side of the bed, then slid down and got comfortable next to me.

"Do you need my lamp off?" I asked.

"Nope. Benefit of my work in Africa and our sleeping quarters where people were working different shifts is that I can sleep through anything." He paused, then looked up. "Do we need to talk about tonight though? I just realized we got a bit offtrack. Because I loved what happened here."

I gave him a soft smile. "I did too. Thanks for checking in."

"Enough for a repeat?"

I raised my brows at him. "Right now?"

He snorted. "No. I need to sleep; you need to write. But soon?"

I nodded. "Soon." I leaned down and gave him a quick kiss.

I woke my computer and opened my current novel, then read over what I'd written earlier that day and thought of what needed to happen next. With a glance to my left, I noted that Noah was already out. I pulled up my playlist on my phone, made sure the volume was set low enough he wouldn't hear it through my earbuds, and focused on letting the story flow out.

Ahead of us we had a funeral, decisions about dating, and my secret profession that needed to be shared with those I cared about. But for now it was just me with these characters and a man I was growing all too fond of who supported me with his mere presence in a way I hadn't known existed out of the fictional worlds I created.

Chapter 20

The Family You Made

Noah

I woke up refreshed and with a clear mind. In other words, the absolute opposite of how I'd assumed I'd start the day of my parents' funeral. Part of that was due to the time with Jules before I went to bed. Damn, I knew from her books what her romanticized version of sex was, but that was something different for me. The connection I already felt with her was why it was another level, but I also knew that as we got to know each other, our connection would grow. I couldn't imagine how what we'd shared could be improved upon, but I was happy to find out.

As for the funeral, thanks to Jules, Mary, and Barry—loved that their names rhymed—this day was planned, and I wasn't stressed about the actual event. How I felt about it had varied as the week unfolded. Mainly, if I was being honest, I wanted it to be over.

There was some work to do with a therapist. After talking to both Mary and Jules the past week, I was realizing there was part of my younger self that felt I had somehow failed my parents. If I was really examining Past Me, I even felt that to an extent after college when I chose to go to Africa.

Jules and I had talked during the week when scheduling the minister, and I realized I had quite a bit of repressed resentment. It came up when we picked the pastor from the local church my parents had attended weekly without fail. I told Jules that the mindfuck I had struggled with all my life was that there were people like my mother and father who purported to be Christian but also behaved in a way that was so far from Christ it wasn't even funny.

I could look back now and realize that if we wanted to look at what all those kind Sunday school teachers had taught me about Jesus growing up, not the example my parents and their friends had set, I had actually been following what they'd said Christianity was supposed to stand for in giving back by working in Africa. It was my parents who had lost their way, and that gave me a measure of comfort, which was something I clearly needed to unpack a bit more and likely with a professional.

I think the final straw of my relationship with my mother and father was when they turned their back on their grandchild. Addie was all that was pure and good about the world—I'd known that before she was even born. All children are. For them to make that choice spoke volumes.

How I couldn't realize I'd been a kid too and deserved more than I'd been given was something I'd have to process in the future when I wasn't dealing with everything else currently swirling around. But I'd face that back in Highland Falls, where I felt at home. A tug at my heart made me think of Addie. I rubbed a hand over Ellie the Elephant in the front seat with me. I'd promised my kindhearted daughter I'd bring it today in case I was sad. I'd told Ivy and Jake I didn't want her to have to be here—this was too depressing for a child to have to deal with. Addie was lightness and good; I didn't want her tainted by any of the negativity that was her grandparents even if this set had never met her and now never would.

"You ready?" Jules asked, popping her head in the open window of my vehicle. I'd parked us a bit away from the graveside, knowing I'd need to get my thoughts in order by myself rather than sitting right there as we waited for the time to begin. Jules had offered to go over and make sure everything was set with Mary and Fred, who'd insisted on being here for me as well. Once we were close to time, she said she'd come back for me. The gratitude I had for them all was overflowing.

I nodded and decided to leave the windows down for the spring breeze to continue to fill the car while we were gone. As I stepped out of the vehicle, Jules held out a hand to me and I took it. I looked her over, not sure if she'd had a fitted long-sleeved black T-shirt dress with her or bought it somehow during the week, but it was perfect for her. I couldn't imagine Jules in the superficial world of my parents and loved that she was who she was, even in this.

Taking a deep breath, we started walking through the headstones toward the blue tent set up over the chairs. My heart pounded the closer we got. I had zero desire to do this and, if not for Jules and Mary, I don't know that I could. I felt untethered, alone, but Jules's hand in mine reminded me I wasn't.

Even so, to know that the only family I had left in the world was Addie was a sobering thought. My parents had both been only children. My stomach turned, and I wished like hell I could be surrounded by loved ones on a day like this rather than the superficial asses who would be here to kiss up to my parents even in death. The day couldn't be over quick enough.

We got closer to the columbarium where the urns would be stored, and the folks gathered came into view. I froze. I looked from the backs of the crowd to Jules, who was waiting patiently beside me, then back to the waiting group. Before I could say anything, Addie's voice rang out over the cemetery.

"Daddddyyyyyyy," she called, racing toward me, her arms outstretched as her neon-pink tutu flowed out around her black leggings. Her blond hair had an assortment of rainbow clips in it, and her navy shirt had a rainbow and flowers decorating the front. I let go of Jules's hand so that I could lean down and grab her when she made her flying leap.

"Hey, pumpkin." Tears sprang to my eyes as I held her close—just the weight of her in my arms settled my heart and centered me.

She put both her hands on my cheeks and pushed them together to make the "fish lips" that she loved. She gave me a smacking kiss and then appraised me with a serious expression. "Did Ellie help you?"

Oh, my heart. This child had it. "Yes, baby. Thanks for sending her with me. She's taken good care of me this week and is waiting for me in the car."

"Addie."

I looked over to see Ivy waving and calling our daughter back, I'm sure wanting to make sure she wasn't in the way. I let Addie down to run back to her mom and looked to Jules with confusion.

"I thought Ivy and I decided Addie was too young for this."

Jules smiled. "You decided that because you didn't want to put anyone out. Ivy disagreed and I had to side with her."

I looked over the crowd. Addie's presence had surprised me, but if I'd stopped to think about it, I should have predicted it. What really had shaken me, besides the strong sense of the rightness of Addie being here, was who else had shown up.

Ivy's parents were there, talking to Ivy and Addie with zero warmth, but for them it was more than they usually did. There were a few folks from my dad's firm. But that was only a small handful of the gathering. The rest of the crowd was filled with people from Highland Falls. Jesus, there were Jake, Ivy, and Addie, of course. But also in attendance were Max and Emma, Sully and Maggie, Drew and Kate, Logan and Allyson, Levi and Maeve, Lou and Verdell, and even more that I couldn't see their faces, but they were all talking in groups.

I looked to Jules, speechless and powerless to stop the tears that were now spilling down my cheeks. "What... I mean... Why are they here? How did they know?"

Jules wrapped her arms around me and rose up on her toes to speak into my ear. "Your family wanted to be here."

I looked at her in confusion. "You mean Addie?"

She squeezed my waist and met my eyes. "No, I mean the family you've made." She gestured to the Highland Falls friends in front of us.

Yep, that did it. I was not going to survive this. I let the tears continue to flow as Jules led me through the throng to the front row of chairs. I felt hands squeeze my shoulders as we passed the folks from Highland Falls. Finally I reached our spot.

Mary and Fred were there, as I'd asked them to be. Mary gave me a tight hug, Fred a quick handshake. Jules and I sat, and before I could nod at the minister to begin, Addie came forward to climb onto my lap. Wrapping my right arm around her waist, left hand threaded with Jules's, I gave him the signal.

Several hours later, I weaved through my parents living room, looking for Ivy. I'd passed a collection of the women from Highland Falls all gathered near food in the dining room and thought I'd find her there, but no. Jules had said she thought she'd seen her on her phone on the deck, so that was my current direction. Jules and Addie had been curled up on the couch in the living room, though it was looking far less formal than anytime I'd been here before.

The first hour after the service had been what I'd feared —stuffy and pretentious people from my parents' life coming to give their condolences with comments about how maybe I'd look for more appropriate work now that I'd have the cushion of my parents' money to relocate or some bullshit such as that. Luckily, Jules had stayed glued to my side and steered every conversation in another direction, usually getting the jackasses to talk about themselves, which was their preference anyway.

Now? It was only friends from Highland Falls left along with some of the staff. Shoes were kicked off, people were lounging around and talking. Someone had brought a speaker, and music was playing. Addie's art supplies were spread out over a ridiculously pricey coffee table, which had she been alive, would have given my mother a heart attack.

Glancing through the windows overlooking the deck and lake, I saw Ivy leaning against the rail and talking on her cell. Before I could move out there to catch her, Mary put a hand on my arm.

"Not so fast, Noah," she said, her eyes twinkling up at me.

I turned and pulled her into a hug. I hadn't had the chance to do that after getting back here and seeing how perfectly she'd set up the dining room. "Mary, I can't thank you enough for today. Well, actually, for everything this week. I would have been lost without you, and I'm so glad you and Jules convinced me to have food here after the service. I hadn't known about any of this." I waved a hand to encompass all our guests.

Mary leaned back and gave me a secret smile. "You might not have known about these folks coming, but your Ms. Jules did, so she let me know and we planned accordingly."

Of course Jules had known. I shook my head, mentally cataloging all the ways to show her my gratitude later.

"I'm just glad I got to meet your Addie and all the rest of your Highland Falls family," Mary said. "You have been blessed."

I looked around the living room into the kitchen, noting all the folks who had given up their Friday to drive up here and support me. Lou was at the dining room table, holding court with some of the staff and many of the women who'd driven up today, telling some story or another. To my horror, based on her gyrations, I think the story involved the all-male revue Jules had mentioned when this hellish week began. I looked over to see Verdell watching his wife, an indulgent smile on his face.

Looking back to Mary, I was torn between laughing and crying, overwhelmed with the gratitude for the family I hadn't even realized I had, including her and Fred. "You're right, Mary. I am so lucky."

"Heck yeah you are." Ivy walked up behind me and leaned in to steal Mary from my arms. "Mary, your food is as delicious as always."

"And you are as beautiful now as the girl you were way back when," Mary said, pulling Ivy to her in a tight squeeze. "I'm so glad to see you."

"You need to come down to Highland Falls—we'll pull you right into an amazing community," Ivy said. "Madison is beautiful and all, but I think you'd love our small town."

"Oh, Fred is pretty settled," Mary said, nodding at her husband, who had found a spot on the wall with Verdell. "But maybe for a visit this fall?"

"Count on it," Ivy said.

Mary stepped back, squeezed my arm again, then headed off to check the food and see what needed to be replenished.

"So," Ivy began.

"So," I echoed. "Last time we talked two days ago, I was going to see you all—including our daughter—when I got back."

"Oops?" Ivy shrugged with a wide smile. "Noah, there was zero chance that I was leaving you, even with Jules by your side, to deal with our parents' cronies on your own."

"You talked with your mom and dad."

"A bit," she said, which spoke volumes. "I talked to Jules, and we decided just to let everyone know what was going on and when the services were. The people who are here chose to come on their own, no pressure from either of us. And that doesn't even cover those friends who wanted to come but couldn't on short notice or the ones who stayed back to watch everyone's kids." She looked around the space and then came right in front of me, putting her hands on my shoulders. "You are loved, Noah. Just as you are. And because our friends wouldn't have the first idea how *not* to show it, you get to see how much you matter. For that, I'm grateful."

I swallowed, not sure at first what to say as I just looked around at all the folks here. Coming back to Ivy, I spoke the words that were weighing me down. "Are you ever surprised that we found this?"

She tilted her head as she looked at me. "Tell me what you mean."

I took a deep breath, getting my thoughts in order. "We're from here, and the people we grew up around valued status, money, connections—what you could do for them." I took another deep breath, warmth filling me up as I thought of all that I'd gained from this group. "And these people here? They'd do anything for us, expecting nothing in return." I wiped at my eyes. "They don't know what I'm inheriting from my parents, but it wouldn't matter one bit to them anyway."

"No, it won't," Ivy agreed.

I'd texted her after I met with Barry, expressing my shock. She hadn't been surprised in the slightest, immediately echoing Barry's thoughts about them caring about appearances even in death.

I looked at her, my oldest friend. "I'm so glad you found Highland Falls."

She laughed. "Well, thank my Nana."

I looked up at the ceiling and thought of her hilarious grandmother, so different than her mother you would never suspect they had been related. I knew Ivy missed her a whole lot, but it was thanks to her grandmother that she had the bookstore and the building it housed. "Thanks, Lorelai the first," I called.

"Now," Ivy said, pulling my attention back to her. "Shall we talk about what's going on with you and Jules and how much I am here for it?"

Chapter 21

Being Human

J*ules*

I'd been sitting in the same position for far too long. The drive back down to Highland Falls was close to four hours, and I'd been writing for nearly every minute of the trip so far.

I couldn't speak for Noah, but I'd been moving more slowly than anticipated when we woke up due to a minor hangover. I'd be shocked if Noah hadn't been struggling with the same, though he didn't mention it at all. Did I expect to have too much to drink after a funeral? Nope, I sure didn't. But that's the way the day unfolded, and I chose to roll with it.

While exploring his parents' home, the guys had discovered Noah's dad's collection of bourbon. To me, bourbon was up there with most types of hard alcohol—things I'd rather not drink. The guys? Well, it was like Christmas morning for kids. They'd been rather enthusiastic when they'd seen bourbon bottles with little horse stoppers and ones that were named after someone in the military—a general? Colonel? Whatever it was, they'd descended on it like folks in the desert at a watering hole and, as a result, had polished off more than a bottle or two. Thankfully, the Highland Falls crew had either crashed at Noah's parents' place or had a designated driver to head back down in the evening, so everyone was able to raise a glass without worry.

Before Mary and Fred retired to their own home for the evening, Mary left pizza for the remaining folks celebrating, likely hoping the crust would help soak up the liquor.

While my downfall hadn't been bourbon, I had fallen victim to Ivy's newfound love of peach sangria. She'd given Mary the recipe, and the woman had whipped up a batch for Ivy, Kate, and me to have with our pizza since none of us were leaving that night. It was delish and went down far too easy. Mental note, I was absolutely giving this beverage to Collette in my new book. I just knew she'd be a fan.

At any rate, Ivy, Kate, and I had all disappeared upstairs with Addie at her bedtime. It had been a long day, and I'd been falling asleep while sitting up. Noah, Jake, and Drew had been still going strong. Turned out the speaker someone had brought out earlier was Drew's, and they were taking turns picking favorite artists and then listening to an album while they debated the best song from each.

We'd woken to a fabulous breakfast spread prepared by Mary. Everyone else had hit the road before us as we'd gone over some final to-dos with Mary regarding the estate and plans to wrap it up. While Noah's parents had left each staff member a year's salary, Mary was still a paid employee while she functioned in Noah's absence for all the final estate items. Barry had drawn up some agreement that allowed that to happen—she was essentially Noah's go-between so he could escape the toxicity that was his childhood home until the estate was closed.

We'd left her and Fred a couple of hours ago with hugs

and promises to see each other soon. Her goodbye to Noah was teary, and once again, I thanked the higher power that put her in his life.

I looked out the car windows, and while we were on a divided highway, the traffic was light and there was nothing around as far as I could see. "Where are we?" I asked, mentally shaking off Julian and Collette's misunderstanding on the pages of my novel.

"Just north of Bloomington-Normal. We've got just over an hour left," Noah said, keeping his eyes on the road.

I rubbed a hand over my face, still struggling with feeling like I'd fallen down on the job. What kind of company was I? I'd disappeared into my book rather than remembering that the man had buried his parents yesterday. And yes, they had a horrible relationship, but I absolutely believed the past week had left its mark.

Better to address it than leave it as an unsaid, right? That's why my characters were struggling in my book, and we didn't need to suffer the same fate.

Communicate, Jules.

I sucked it up and voiced my feelings. "I'm sorry. I have been a terrible road-trip companion. Do you want me to drive? To run the tunes?"

Noah shot me a smile that made me think all was right with the world and I was, as per usual, overreacting. Comes with the territory of living in your head.

"Tunes?" he said, the word laced with amusement.

"Um, that's a word people use, right?"

His grin grew. "Yes, it is a word people use. It just sounded adorable coming from you."

"Phew." I sat back in my seat, wondering when we'd see signs of the city. "Sometimes when I'm writing, I type something I think is a word and the program underlines it that it's misspelled. Then I go online to try to figure it out, and turns out, I've had it wrong my whole life. It can really mess with your head."

Noah chuckled. "Yep, adorable." He paused, turning the music down so that we could comfortably talk over it. "And I enjoy driving—it's almost meditative, so don't give it another thought. If anything, I'm glad you got some writing done." He glanced my way. "Do you need to stop? Food? Coffee? Restroom?"

"I won't say no to coffee." Frankly, I was a fan of more caffeine at any time. "And if it's okay, let's go in to get it. Stretching my legs for a minute would be great."

Noah glanced at the GPS before answering. "We're about ten minutes from the north side of Normal. I think there's a Starbucks over there. That work?"

I nodded, wondering again if I was doing enough. I couldn't imagine losing my parents, much less both, but how did you balance that with having gone essentially no-contact with them for most of the past eight years?

"So." Noah caught my attention and took me to a completely different topic. "Did I see your aunt Lou acting out her experience on stage from Sunday night? We never really talked about that what with everything that happened."

I groaned, slinking down in my seat. "Oh my God, let's never speak about it again. I'm working to try to get the image out of my mind."

"It might take hypnosis."

"You think you're funny, but I'd consider it."

Flashes of Lou gyrating on some man while he held her up and Verdell laughed were at the forefront of my brain. Jesus. I mean, objectively I could look at it and think mental high five to Lou for being as free as she was, hopping up on that stage and having fun with it, age be damned. And I would agree with that sentiment *if I hadn't had to see it*. That was the tricky part—the vision was burned into my retinas.

Looking at Noah, I saw he was absolutely holding back some laughter. "Imagine Mary on that stage," I said, deciding he might need a taste of his own medicine.

"Eww," he replied as he gave me a horrified look.

"Exactly. Be grateful Mary and Fred live up here, because if they were in Highland Falls, I'm sure Lou would have the two of them over for cards and then sweep them into her crew."

"God no. We'd never have any peace." He glanced my way. "Maggie said she has video of the night—other than Lou—if you wanted to catch up on what you missed."

I snorted. "Yeah, I heard. Apparently she and Maeve both went on the stage at one point. I think Kristine from Nomad Yoga was up there when I left. I can't remember everyone." I shrugged, considering how I was feeling about it. "I'm not a prude..."

Noah laughed again. "Your books are testament to that."

"Hey." I flicked his arm. "They aren't erotica."

"Well, they aren't closed-door romances either," Noah pointed out.

"Look at you, using romance terms. Well done. Next thing we know, you'll be talking about third act breakups," I said, rather impressed despite my commentary.

Noah flipped on his blinker to take the exit and glanced my way as he navigated us to the Starbucks parking lot. "I absolutely know what that is referring to in a romance book. When you told me you wrote them, I downloaded your series but also read a few articles about the overall plot structure and unwritten rules of the romance genre."

I sat up straight and looked over at the man while he pulled into a parking spot and turned off the car. "I'm sorry, what?"

He looked at me and tilted his head like he was trying to figure me out when it should have been the reverse. "Did you look me up on social media when we met?"

Topic change much? "Uh, yes. Doesn't everyone?"

He nodded. "I did the same. When you learned what I'd done in Africa, I'm assuming through the women in town or Lou, did you look up the company I work for?"

I began to get a little uncomfortable. Did he think I was internet stalking him? I mean, I'd been curious. "Well, yeah."

"Why?"

Yep, now I was feeling embarrassed. "I wanted to know more about you."

Noah reached out for my hand, I think sensing I was a little uncomfortable. "I get that. And I was doing the same. When you're interested in someone, or least this is how I feel, I want to know more about the things they're fascinated by. You write romance, and I knew very little about the genre other than some folks disparage it because they're sexist—"

"You knew that already?"

His wide smile brought me no small amount of comfort, and I was worried I'd lose myself in the deep blue pools of his eyes. Another mental writing note, use that description in the book.

Noah continued, oblivious to my inner dialogue. "Ivy is my best friend from childhood, remember? She actually sent me a romance to read before I knew anything about yours."

I began to bounce in my seat; I loved talking books. "Ohhhh, what one?"

Noah pulled out his phone, opening what I could see was a reading tracker app. He scrolled for a few minutes, then looked up. "*Jana Goes Wild* by Farah Heron."

I grabbed his phone and saw the cover opened. "May I? Thanks," I said as I scrolled to read the description. "Yes," I said, without looking up. "I read this one, but it was a few years back. I wonder if Ivy sent it to you because it was set in Africa. Was this before or after she got with Jake?"

"Why?" He was watching me with some amusement as I took over the man's phone.

"Well, if it was before, as you might remember from reading it, the main characters have a kid together—unintended—at the beginning of the book. Then they break up and the book flashes forward five years or so; then they go on this destination wedding together and decide they're perfect for each other." I looked up and met his gaze. "Do you think she was trying to send you a message?"

Noah looked at me for a few seconds before bursting, and I do mean *bursting,* into laughter. "You think—" Laughter. "I mean—" More laughter. "Are you trying to say—" You get the picture. I was marginally concerned that the man was either going to expire from lack of oxygen or pee his pants.

I put his phone in the cup holder and sat back with my arms crossed, waiting.

His laughter slowed as he wiped his eyes and took a deep breath. "I'm sorry," he said, still fighting back a chuckle.

"I really don't see what's so funny," I said, feeling a tad embarrassed, though I had nothing to be embarrassed about.

"Sorry, sorry." Noah was almost back to normal. "I

just..." He took a stuttering breath, the laughter threatening to come back. "The thought Ivy would be trying to suggest anything is laughable."

"Why?" I asked, truly puzzled. The two of them were together for some amount of time, right? It wasn't a completely foreign concept.

"Ahh." He sat back and looked from some random point out the windshield. "I don't how to best explain this. You know Ivy and I've been friends since we were young."

I nodded.

"We got together at the end of college. I think it was more about comfort than attraction."

"That. Explain what you mean about that." My heart was beating harder than was normal for a conversation while seated.

He shrugged. "I'm no therapist—"

"Though you could benefit from seeing one," I suggested again. It had become a running joke laced with truth.

"So you've said. For the two of us to grow up without much in the way of love from the people who were supposed to give a damn about us without question, I think we clung to each other for comfort. Usually that came in the form of friendship, but one night when we were both tipsy, we decided to see if there was more. Then we continued that way for a year, never facing up to the fact that we were attracted to each other as friends, not romantic partners. It was comfortable and even more so because there was an expiration date of when I was heading to Africa."

"And then came Addie."

He nodded. "And then came Addie. It was at that point we needed to figure our shit out. Ivy immediately said she wanted to keep the baby, and I was fine with that. She told me I needed to still go overseas like I planned, that our child wasn't going to live their life having held me back."

He looked down at his lap and paused. I waited a few beats before reaching over to hold his hand. Somehow it felt necessary. He gave me a reassuring squeeze.

"I will always regret that I didn't have more to do with Addie's early life."

"But—"

He held up a hand. "I know there's a ton of counterarguments and trust me, I've looked at them all. I'm just telling you that regardless of everything, I'll never get that time back."

I thought about that. The choices we make define us, good and bad. And, I supposed, this could fall into that category. "Would you change the decision if you could go back?"

Noah looked at me, his eyes narrowing as he seemed to really think for a moment. After a minute or so, he said, "I've never really thought about that. Would I choose not to go to Africa?"

I nodded.

He rubbed his free hand over his face. "Hmm... I think I'd still go. I can't imagine who I'd be if I hadn't lived there for five years. I mean, that really shaped who I am."

I gave him a knowing look.

"I hear you. I think what I would change would be to make it a priority to come back more frequently, to have known ahead of time when Ivy would go into labor so I could get back in time, to FaceTime more..."

"Can I say something?"

"Sure."

"What I hear you saying is that you needed to go to Africa. Yes, you missed out on some memories, but when the tipping point came where the need to be with your family outweighed the good you were doing in Africa, you made the necessary changes. You're human, Noah. We mess up, and if we're a decent person, we learn from our mistakes. The best parents are far from perfect."

He leaned his head against the headrest while watching me. "Do you realize we've only known each other for two weeks?"

I mirrored his pose and smiled. "Are you saying you're sick of me and we've spent too much time together?"

"I think you know I'm not. Feels like you've been in my life for so much longer."

"Ditto."

"So when we get back to Highland Falls, want to come over for dinner?"

I grinned at him. "Absolutely. You're not getting rid of me that easy."

He leaned forward, placed a kiss on my nose, and then headed out of the vehicle as he talked to me over his shoulder. "I'm counting on that. Now let's get some coffee. I hear it helps with hangovers."

"Hey!" I said, climbing out of the car and looking his way. "I resemble that remark, or I did this morning. I'm doing better now and am shocked you weren't struggling yourself this morning."

He opened the door for me and shot me a wink. "Never said I wasn't."

Well, at least I wasn't alone.

Chapter 22

Pitfalls of Parenting

Noah

I pulled up the shared drive at my place and glanced over at Jules once I'd parked. She was out cold. Her laptop was open on her lap and tilted to the side where it met the door. Her black leggings let me check out her curves easily, and her baggy top wouldn't be listed on my favorite things except it dropped off one shoulder, highlighting her sports bra or tank below, I wasn't sure, but I'd be happy to find out.

I fought brushing a tendril of her hair behind her ear because she was zonked out and I didn't want to startle her. I wouldn't mention it to her, but her mouth had dropped open while she slept and her head was back against the headrest. You'd think she was the one who'd stayed up late last night instead of me, though I didn't think her sleep was the most restful, she'd tossed and turned a lot. I fucking loved that I knew that, which both frightened and excited me.

I leaned over and squeezed her arm. "Wake up, Sleeping Beauty."

She blinked slowly a few times, then rolled her head to the side and looked at me. "Was I sleeping with my mouth open?" she whispered.

Well, she asked, and I was not one to lie. I nodded, which only served to make her drop her head back and groan as she covered her face.

"Oh no, that's so unattractive." Then she sat up straight and looked at me with more than a little horror on her face. "Was I... snoring?" she whispered the last word.

I fought back a laugh. She was so damn adorable. "Umm, can I plead the fifth?"

"Oh. My. Goddess. That's mortifying." Her head went back again, and her hands covered her face once more. Her muffled voice was just audible when I heard her horrified "Jesus, did I drool?" followed by a quick patting of her mouth and lower face before letting out a quiet *phew* when she found it dry.

I leaned over and attempted to pull her hands down before she could continue her spiral. "Hey, Jules."

She started shaking her head and speaking to the ceiling. "No, no. I'm not looking at you. You're not going to try to convince me that I look fine when everyone knows how ridiculous people look with their mouth wide open as they sleep. Get out of here with those magical blue eyes. I'm just crawling home and will never be seen again." She made a shooing motion, eyes still firmly locked on the ceiling. "You can go in your house now. I'll disappear through the back-yard after you're gone."

Did I want to laugh at her ridiculousness? Yes. But did I think she believed what she was saying? Also yes. The notion that Jules thought I found her unattractive even for the hottest of minutes was ludicrous.

I ran a finger up her thigh as I began. "Jules, you are

absolutely the sexiest person I've ever had the pleasure of watching sleep."

She peeked at me with an impressive side-eye. "That sounds a bit creepy."

I laughed. She was loosening up again. Time to hit her with some more honesty. "Be that as it may, it also happens to be the truth. Sleeping or not. Mouth wide open or not. Snoring or not. You are gorgeous, and I'd love nothing more than to take you up to my bedroom right now and show you how attracted I am to you."

She sat all the way up and looked at me with a wide smile, all embarrassment melted away. "I volunteer as tribute." She raised three fingers in salute.

"Okay, Katniss." I leaned forward and brushed my mouth against hers. "Let's head in."

She gave me a promising grin full of sass as she proceeded to give me shit. "So I get to see more of your place than the front room. Tell me, is it a true single-dad version of a bachelor pad?" She arched a brow. "Or, fess up, is your television the size of a small vehicle? Do you have more than condiments in your fridge?"

"Does your writing brain always seek out this much detail when there is an easy way to find your answers?" I turned to get out of the car, choosing not to answer this woman, whom I was growing more attracted to by the minute. Her mind fascinated me. "I guess you'll have to find out."

Jules laughed. "Yeah, I guess my mind is constantly spinning a narrative. I think surroundings tell their own story... Well, and..."

I glanced over to see a flush across her cheeks. "And..."

She wrinkled her adorable nose, which was dotted with a few freckles here and there. "And I'm a bit nosy?" She shrugged as I pulled our bags from the back, then we headed to the back door.

"Would you be Lou's niece if you weren't?" I pointed out.

"Truth. And my mom's no slouch."

Hmm. Jules and I had only touched on her relationships with her parents. I wondered about them. I knew Lou was her mom's older sister, but what was her relationship like with her mom and dad? All I had really been told was that she hadn't shared she was a writer with them yet, they were flighty, her mom was dramatic, and they lived in an RV. Did they get along and she'd just neglected to share more in fear it would make me feel worse about my relationship with my own? I felt like whatever we had blossoming between us had been a lot about me because of the circumstances, but I wanted to be there for Jules too. I just needed to figure out how to do that because I sure as fuck wasn't a relationship expert.

Jules was behind me as I unlocked the door. I ushered her in and pulled the door shut, wondering if it was a bit too much just to have sex right inside the front door. I thought I had enough willpower to get us to the bedroom, but in all honesty, I might not. We'd only had sex once, and I felt like we had lots of time to make up for.

I had just begun to set our bags down while telling myself to be patient and at least let her see the rooms on the first floor before attacking her, but then the familiar sound of small footsteps coming from the direction of the kitchen caught my attention. Looking up, I saw Addie in all her rainbow-colored-clothes glory headed my way at a trot, her pink tutu billowing out as she moved.

"Surprise, Daddy!" My daughter hit me with a leap. Luckily, I was able to quickly get my brain around what was happening and dropped our bags to catch her on the fly.

"Addie," I gasped as I fixed up my grip and moved to stand. At the sight of Ivy coming down the hall, I quickly adjusted my expectations. I looked to the woman who was responsible for my current train of thought, which had just been derailed. "Sorry," I mouthed toward her.

Jules gave a wicked smile like she knew how much I was being tugged in two opposite directions here. Did I want to go upstairs with her and have a fabulous afternoon between the sheets? Hell, yeah. Did I also relish any time I got with my daughter, *especially* when I wasn't expecting it? Absolutely. Pitfalls of parenting—things don't always work out according to your plans.

"This is a surprise, peanut," I said as I squeezed Addie to me for a tight hug, then let her down.

"Momma said we had to come over and stock you up. I asked if I could stay, but she said we'll see." Addie's face indicated her displeasure at that answer.

"Why the frown?" I asked as my mind tried to figure out several things at once.

"We'll see means no," Addie said, her face scrunched up to show her thoughts on that.

I laughed at that because she was likely right on the money there, at least typically. I glanced over at Ivy, who was leaning against the wall and watching the scene unfold.

"Stock me up?" I repeated to her.

She shrugged. "You mentioned your fridge was bare. Thought I'd take care of that so it was one thing less for you to have to do when you got back down here." She raised her eyebrows and tipped her head toward Jules. "Figured you might have more important things on your mind."

I glanced at Jules and... Yep. She was flushed, but she

was also smiling at Ivy. It was a shared look between them that I didn't understand but also didn't need to. Ignoring that, I turned back to Ivy. "Thanks for the stock up—you really didn't have to do that. Now..." I nodded to Addie. "What's this frown about *we'll see?*"

Ivy shook her head in clear amusement at our daughter. "You know Ads has a highlighted calendar of the month with different colors for which house she's at. She was confused because she should have been with you starting yesterday and wasn't getting why we moved Switch Day to Monday."

"Switch Day?" Jules murmured with a confused look.

"When Addie makes the move from one of our houses to the other," I answered.

Addie's adorable face looked up at us with a look of determination. "I know because of the sad day with Daddy's parents I stayed with Mommy and Daddy Two, but you're home." She stared at me with a look I could only describe as WTF.

Glancing at Ivy, I shrugged. She and Jake hadn't shared their weekend plans with Addie when we were in Madison because time is fuzzy to kids and she would have lost her mind.

Ivy apparently decided now was the time because she spilled some of the plans. "Addie, we have you staying with us this weekend because tonight Steph and Theo are coming and..."

That was all Ivy got out before Addie started bouncing up and down with shining eyes. "Emily and Jennie are coming!" Her screech could rattle the glass in the windows.

I looked to Jules, who was covering her mouth, and it looked like she was attempting not to laugh. I began to explain. "Steph is Drew and Jake's sister. Theo is her husband, and Emily and Jennie are—"

"My cousins!" Addie interrupted with another yell.

Jules's eyes danced with merriment. "So this is why you didn't give her a heads-up. Got it."

Ivy nodded and laughed. "Yep, it's pretty obvious now, right?" She shook her head, then glanced to our girl, who was positively vibrating with excitement. "Addie, can you go count how many peaches we brought your dad? And check to see what other fruits he has."

Addie immediately calmed down as her eyes sparkled and she rubbed her hands together like she was a mastermind. "Is this a job?"

"Sure is."

Addie turned to Jules. "If I show Momma I'm real responsible with jobs, I can get a cat like Malley."

Jules tilted her head, and then recognition dawned. "You mean O'Malley? My cat?"

Addie nodded. "That's what I said." Then she looked to me. "Time me. I'm superfast."

"Not too fast," Ivy cautioned. "You don't want to forget anything."

Addie gave that some thought and then slowly nodded. "Okay, but I still want to be timed."

I pulled my phone out and opened the app. "No problem. I'll time you."

With that, she took off. Ivy immediately joined Jules and me and said, "Okay, so for the party tomorrow—"

"Party?" Jules asked.

"Sorry," I said, realizing that Ivy had sent our kid on an errand so we could have a quick talk. "I haven't gotten you up to speed with everything that happened, but we're having a small party for Addie's birthday tomorrow."

"We were going to postpone with Noah's parents pass-ing, but it all worked out and we're still on track," Ivy whispered.

"And it's a surprise?" Jules asked as we heard Addie's counting from the kitchen in the background.

"Out of necessity. She'd never sleep," Ivy explained.

"Ahh."

"So do you think she could hang out here for a couple of hours? Until dinner?" Ivy asked with a wince. "I mean, you two likely had some adult fun planned, but—"

"Of course she can," Jules interrupted as she spoke for me. With that, my heart swelled. I couldn't care less that she'd answered instead of letting me, what made my day was that she put time with my daughter as the priority.

Ivy's relief was evident. "Oh. Thanks, you two. Lorelai is doing so much better, but Jake has her in the sling while he's trying to sneakily get everything ready for tomorrow and also preparing for Steph and crew to stay at our place tonight. I'm just a bit worried we're not going to get it all done." She glanced toward the kitchen. "You all are welcome to come for dinner too, or you can just do the brunch tomorrow..." Ivy bit her lip like maybe she had said too much. She hadn't, but we hadn't talked yet.

I looked to Jules. "I hadn't asked you yet because this week has been a blur, but clearly I'd love you to come to this brunch shindig tomorrow."

Jules looked unsure. "If it's a family thing, I get it. I don't need to come."

"We want you there," I said, looking to Ivy to back me up.

"Absolutely. I can't always handle the crazy Spencer clan without reinforcements. And I have no words for

Margot—she's Steph, Jake, and Drew's mom. She's someone you need to experience without explanation. Just... brace."

Jules laughed. "Good or bad?"

I shook my head, thinking of the force of nature that was Margot Spencer. "Good, absolutely, but a presence to be reckoned with."

"Ten peaches and then some strawberries, blueberries, and bananas," Addie called out.

"Any grapes?" Ivy called while shaking her head no to us to indicate she hadn't brought any.

"Maybe?" Addie called.

"Can you check?" Ivy replied.

"Is that another job?" Addie asked.

"Part of the same one," Ivy said.

"Okay." The sound of Addie opening the refrigerator got us back in gear.

"Addie can absolutely stay. What time do you want me to walk her back over," I asked.

"Five," Ivy answered promptly.

"And we're set on her gift?" I asked.

"She's going to flip," Ivy answered.

"Oh no, I don't have a gift," Jules murmured.

"No grapes!" Addie sang, slamming the fridge.

Ivy reached over, squeezing Jules's arm. "Noah will fill you in, but we go very sparse on gifts. Ads is already blessed beyond measure, so your presence can be your gift. It really is a birthday party disguised as an opportunity to have brunch. And going back to your earlier worry, in Highland Falls our friends are our family so no worries, you belong at this party."

As she finished that comment, which made Jules's eyes shiny with unshed tears, Addie skipped down the hall and stopped in front of us with her hands on her hips. "Time?"

I held up my phone. "Five minutes, seven seconds."

She did one of her favorite shimmies. "I can't wait to have a cat."

"Don't get ahead of yourself, missy." Ivy gave Addie a perfect mom look.

"What will Chief say?" I asked, highly entertained by this entire situation. I loved our determined daughter and hoped she never lost her gives-zero-fucks personality.

She put her hands on her little hips. "Chief likes friends too."

I nodded like that made sense, and I supposed it did.

Ivy bent down to look Addie in the eye. "So… your dad wondered if you'd want to stay here for a few hours and then come back to our house."

Addie looked from Ivy to me, clearly torn. "Will Emily and Jennie get there before me?"

I put my hand over my heart. "You want to see your cousins more than me?"

"Of course not!" Addie said, her voice indignant.

"I'm kidding, peanut." I smoothed down her ponytail. "No, sweetheart, you won't miss any time with your cousins."

Addie relaxed. "I like spending time with you too, Daddy. It's just I don't see them much."

I bopped her on the nose. "Then we will make sure you get there in time."

Addie looked at all of us. "So I get to spend time here *and* have cousin time tonight?" Her voice betrayed her excitement.

Jules spoke up. "I could go get O'Malley and bring him over here too if that's okay." She looked my way, and I nodded as I braced for what I knew was coming.

"Best. Day. Ever!" Addie exclaimed, her arms shooting up as she spun around.

Ivy laughed. "And with that, I'll leave you all to it. See you in a couple of hours."

Chapter 23

Spilling Secrets

J*ules*

I lay on the jewel-colored sofa in Noah's living room, not sure if I even had the energy to lift my head.

"You okay, kitten?"

Noah's voice came from somewhere above, but opening my eyes seemed like too much to ask of my body, so I just kept them closed and replied with what I could. "Mm-hmm."

His laughter might irritate me if I could muster enough spirit to tell him what I really thought. Instead, I continued to enjoy his couch, and surely at some point I'd have the verve to get up and head home. Or maybe stay here and head upstairs because I really liked our earlier plans, which had been derailed. But could I even make it up the staircase? And if that was possible, would I need to convince Noah to do all the work? I wasn't opposed to being a pillow princess and all, but this early in a relationship, was it even something I could ask for? Lord knows I didn't want him to think he *always* needed to do the work.

"Earth to Jules," he called, tracing a finger over my cheek. "You okay, babe? What can I get you?"

I fought my nature to blush considering where my mind had been. In my head, Lou replied *the gutter* to that comment with a cackle. I was clearly delusional.

"Coffee," I said, then thought what else would help. "Or maybe a Diet Coke. Ohh, from McDonald's because they're the best. Or how much caffeine is in chocolate? Should I start drinking energy drinks? Are they terrible for you?"

Good grief, what had gotten into me? I had no energy but was now rambling about drinks and thinking of what my aunt would say. Was I slaphappy? No, but I was torn between staying on this couch for the foreseeable future and raiding his kitchen. The first whispers of hunger and a desire for something to drink were starting to make their presence known and warring with the urge to jump his bones. Decisions, decisions.

"So what took it out of you?" Noah's voice was closer and made my busy mind calm down. I felt the couch move with his weight as he sat near me, lifting my upper body so he could slide below and let my head rest in his lap. Then he tugged my hair tie out and began running his fingers through my hair. That did it. No more cares about soda, food, sex, or relatives. I'd pay good money for someone to do this on the regular; I was never moving again.

"Hmmmm." My slight moan was more in pleasure but also a little in response to a question that I'd already forgotten.

Noah didn't seem bothered by my nonanswer. "Was it the sangria that has you down for the count, kitten? A less-than-ideal night of sleep? Or the fact that you and Addie squeezed a full day of activities into a span just shy of three hours?"

I raised a finger and pointed to the ceiling at that last one. Indeed, that had been the one to send me over the edge —not that I'd change a thing. I mean, I did start the day with a slight hangover. But that could have been overcome. It was the fort building *and* the homemade cookie making *and* the doll playing *and* the O'Malley grooming *and* the art creating *and*—last but not least—the nonstop dance party. And let's not forget the insanity of a speed round of hide-and-seek.

I had no idea what the step count on my Apple Watch was for the day, but I surely had surpassed anything that would have been expected for a normal Saturday. And while I was exhausted, I was also happy. I hadn't laughed like I did in... Well, I couldn't remember the last time. Since I was a kid?

Noah grabbed my raised finger and squeezed it. "Addie had such a great time this afternoon, and it was all thanks to you."

My eyes were still closed as I enjoyed his hand on mine, his other hand still toying with my hair. This was the best. Still, I should likely dig deep and participate in this conversation. Goddess forbid the man stop what he was doing. "I had fun too."

"You were pretty clear about that," he said, his voice heavy with amusement.

"Please keep up what you're doing with my hair," I whispered, hating to ask but willing to do so to keep it going.

Noah's hand stilled—damn it, I shouldn't have drawn attention to it. But then: "Want me to brush your hair?"

Holy smokes. Yes. Absolutely. Be chill, Jules. "Umm, that would be great?"

He squeezed my shoulder, oblivious to my mental cheerleader losing her darn mind. "Hold tight. Where's your hairbrush?"

I did the mentally taxing work to remember what bag I had here. Heck, my full name would be a big ask right now. At the same time, I wanted to sink into this couch—one that was a style I never for a moment would have assumed Noah would own—and never leave. I was exhausted and at peace at the same time. Couple that with being a little horny, and my mind was not surprisingly a bit of a hot mess. "Front pocket, I think."

He was gone and back in minutes, resuming his spot and... Sweet goddess above, he was brushing my hair. "I didn't mean to leave so much of the responsibility of Addie to you this afternoon," he said as he gently detangled my hair.

Noah had gotten a call from the company he hired to prepare his parents' estate for auction shortly after Ivy left. He'd just gotten that handled only to then field calls from the real estate agent, then Mary, then someone from his office in Springfield, and finally someone who was handling his parents' financial portfolio. I felt bad for the guy—he clearly was trying to get off the phone to be with us, only to get waylaid time and time again.

I cracked an eye and looked up to see him staring down at me. "I know that all evidence points to the contrary right now, but I loved the entire afternoon."

He tapped my nose. "You sure about that?"

"Addie is awesome." It was the only answer needed honestly.

Judging by the movement near my feet, O'Malley was joining us on the couch because of course I had followed through and brought him over to hang out with Ms. Addie.

I did not have a cat who was aloof and removed from humans. O'Malley was the lowest-maintenance cat ever. If I was out of town, he was happy on his own as long as someone took care of the basic daily needs. But if people were around, he wanted to cuddle. And it felt like... Yep, there he was, walking around to lie on my belly. My own personal weighted blanket.

Noah was still on his mission to make my hair the smoothest it had ever been, and I wasn't complaining.

"Addie is amazing," he said in reply to my earlier sentiment. "*And* I do appreciate all you did today."

"You contributed when you could." Truly, I loved how he was in the mix with Addie. He'd been ridiculous creative when we played dolls, doing accents for different voices. It was next level. I was already adding to my mental notes for future books. I'd never written a single dad before, but Noah was inspiring so many ideas for my writing—both the current novel and future stories. It made me itch to get back to my computer.

To cover my need to moan as he worked to unknot my hair, I focused on my surroundings. "This couch is interesting," I murmured randomly as I rubbed the fabric and, quite possibly, a little moan might have escaped at the end. Sue me. People paid top dollar for head massages, and I was getting this one for free and by a guy who was sexy as hell.

He chuckled. "You surprised by my jewel-colored couch and pillows?"

"Not what I expected," I mumbled as I rolled my head to the right so he could get some brushing done at the nape of my neck.

"Ivy's," he replied as he lifted my head in one hand and ran the brush all the way from the bottom of my head up.

"Ahhh." I couldn't help it. Then I refocused. "Ivy's?"

"This house, some of the furniture."

"Ah, the couch is Ivy's." I gave a small nod so as to not

disrupt the brushing. This couch fit Ivy. Noah? Not so much.

"Mm-hmm," he replied. "I started the conversation about moving here right as she and Jake got together. They moved in together and I took over her place because Addie already knew it and it was only a few blocks from Jake's." He put the brush down and buried both hands in my hair as he began rubbing my head in a circular motion with the tips of his fingers. Jesus. This could be his job.

"Makes sense," I replied as I felt my whole body relax. The exhaustion was abating as the peaceful feeling filled me up.

"Can I ask you a question?" he said as he rolled my head to one side and continued to use his goddess-given talent.

"Sure."

"Why accounting?" His voice was quiet, but the question made my eyes open, only to look up and see him looking down at me.

I wanted to reply and just say something like I was good with numbers or there were lots of jobs available in the field. Both of which were true. However, if we were headed where I wanted, I needed to share myself with this man, which required being vulnerable and spilling my secrets, such as they were. And in all honesty, I hadn't done a whole lot of that so far while he had no choice with everything that had happened over the past week.

Attempting to dig deep and find some courage, I kept my gaze locked on his. "My parents are really great people."

He nodded but didn't say anything. Maybe he sensed that I needed to get this out.

"They aren't the most organized."

He nodded again.

"Their love is big—for each other, for me. I've never doubted that. What I did worry about as a kid was if they remembered to pay the electric bills or if they'd budgeted for groceries that week, much less remembered to go get them."

He gave my shoulder a squeeze, almost like he was urging me to continue. Since he kept on toying with my hair, I did.

"They live big and love with their whole selves, but the small minutia of daily life... not always great with that stuff." I thought of what that might sound like and quickly reassured him. "We always had a roof over our head and something to eat, but it might be cereal and eaten in the dark until they could get ahold of the power company to send in a payment." I swallowed. "I was luckier than many."

"Hey." Noah rubbed a finger over my jaw. "Don't discount your experiences. I bet that was scary as a kid."

I shrugged. "Not sure if all kids would find it scary, but if you really like stability... Yeah."

"And accounting is pretty stable," he said, putting the pieces together.

I nodded, watching as he looked off, lost in thought for a moment before he met my eyes again.

"So you had love and not a lot of stability, while I had stability and no love." He shook his head and gave me a soft smile. "We're quite the pair." He paused, then met my eyes. "I think I'm also understanding how you ended up coming to Madison with me this week."

I wasn't sure what to make of that. "I mean, you needed someone with you..."

He nodded. "But not a lot of people would do that for someone they just met."

I flushed. "Verdell and Ivy said it was a good idea."

He bent to kiss my forehead. "It *was* a good idea."

I squirmed. "I just really didn't like the idea of you alone."

"And I appreciate that. I think you also care about people with your whole self *and* want them to feel secure. Kitten, you got the best of your parents and yourself. I'm just a benefactor." He brushed my hair back over my head.

"I know. I was far luckier than you growing up," I said, embarrassed that I had even brought it up when he had really struggled to get his parents to value him for who he was and now they were gone.

Noah bopped my nose again. "Kitten, you're not getting that this isn't a contest. We can both wish things were different. And you've already said you love your parents—"

"I do."

He gave me an understanding look. "I know. You're still allowed to wish things were different. Doesn't mean they're bad people."

I sighed. "They're not bad; they're sweet. And now, in retirement, they're living their best life." I smiled, remembering I'd told him about their life in the RV, but I didn't think I'd mentioned the side gig. "You should follow their social media account; it brings them in a stupid amount of money each month."

Noah paused his massage, darn it, to pull out his phone. "What is it?"

I told him, and he thumbed it in and then showed me an account to see if he had the right one. I nodded, and he immediately hit Follow and began scrolling through pictures.

"They have over three hundred thousand followers," he murmured.

Yep, they sure did.

"Retired Road Warriors has a nice ring to it," he said, a smile in his voice.

"I mean, at least they can't forget to pay the power bill when they don't have a home," I pointed out.

"They've been all over," Noah said as he flipped through their recent pics up in the western part of the country. "Wait, this is you?" He flashed the phone toward me.

I looked up and saw a pic we had taken when my parents came to visit a few months ago. It was the visit that had freaked Mom out and made her pull Lou in and beg me to make some changes. Objectively, even looking at the image now, I could see how tired I had been.

"Yeah," I said, wondering what Noah saw.

"Babe." His expression was soft. "You look exhausted."

I nodded.

"Work? Writing?"

"Both." I took a breath. "That's why I moved. My work-life balance in Chicago was terrible. Mom and Dad visited, and Mom flipped out when they saw me, insisting I uproot my life and move down here to find some peace. The firm I worked for didn't care at all about what working for hours on end did to you as long as you got done what they needed you to do."

"So you're saying it was the opposite of working for Sue?" he said with a grin.

Sue's belief on balance had become a running joke between Noah and me this week. When I tried to work too much from Madison, she'd sent me texts and told me to go outside and touch grass—her way of telling me to get my priorities straight. As she'd said repeatedly, she hadn't originally planned on having an extra employee during tax season. Any hours I clocked were bonus help that they could use to ease everyone's load, but none of it should be done at the expense of my well-being.

"Yeah. I don't think Sue and my former boss would necessarily see eye to eye."

"And that's a good thing." Noah leaned down and pressed a kiss to my mouth. "I'm so glad you moved here for whatever the reason was. And I'm glad you've found some balance in doing so. Looks like your mom was right."

"Hush, you. Don't put that out into the universe. Somehow she will hear you and come to gloat." I shook my head as I pushed up to sit next to him, adjusting until I could sit cross-legged on the couch. O'Malley gave me a look for daring to disrupt him and took off to explore the house.

"Ivy would be proud—first you've adopted her belief in the goddess above, and now you're talking about what we're putting out into the universe?"

"I mean, she's a wise woman," I said with a smile.

"If you end up collecting moon water, I will know you two are spending too much time together," he replied with amusement in his eyes.

"Moon water?" I had never heard of such a thing. Just then a rumble came from my stomach. I wanted to be mortified, but that was secondary to wanting to find some food.

"Want something to eat?"

"Well, about twenty minutes ago I would have said no, I really wanted to find your bedroom."

He waggled his eyebrows at me as he leaned forward.

I pushed his chest back. "Uh-uh," I said. "That time has to wait because now my body has decided it has energy once again but is famished."

He nodded, looking a little smug. "It was the head massage that got you back on track."

"Sure, let's go with that. As long as I get some food, I'm good with whatever you want to claim."

Noah stood up, held a hand out to me, and then pulled me off the couch. Before we could move toward the kitchen, he stepped up so that our chests were flush together. "Jules?"

"Hmm," I said, mesmerized as always by his gorgeous blue eyes.

"Thanks for sharing today."

I wanted to melt in his gaze. "You bet."

"Also..." He looked at me like he was waiting for something.

"What?"

"We got derailed with all the chaos of this week. But we need to talk more about your writing life, right?"

Oof. I crashed my head into his chest. "What about it?" I said, though it was muffled.

I could hear his laugh and feel the vibrations against my forehead but didn't want to lift to look at him.

"Well, there's the little matter that only two people know that you write."

"Um-hmm."

"Which is fine if that's what you want, but you've indicated you're ready to change that."

I nodded against his chest.

"And you mentioned you might want to find a way to make writing your full-time gig," he went on.

Ughhhhhhhhhh. My stomach hurt thinking about it. "Health insurance," I answered because really, wasn't it *the* answer?

"Yeah, I'm understanding that a bit more now, Ms. Stability."

"Retirement. Consistent salary."

"Yep, loud and clear," he replied. Then he squeezed my ass. Yum. More. "But also, didn't you say your second book is next month's book club pick?"

Oh hell. It was. I looked up. "I might have lost my appetite again."

Chapter 24

Connecting

Noah

Jules and I studied my fully stocked fridge, which had been a barren desert of food just days ago when I'd headed north. I'd planned on grocery shopping this week, but it looked like I could skip that now.

After some debate, we settled on making something low-key for dinner. I sent off a text to Ivy and Jake in thanks for the gift of grocery shopping while Jules discovered a loaf of homemade sourdough from a local baker that they'd left. With that we decided egg sandwiches would hit the spot.

There was no other way to describe it. Being with Jules was easy—here, at my parents' place, driving in the car, cooking, hanging out, entertaining my daughter. She was no bullshit, as some of the guys would say—what you saw was what you got. And, most importantly, she didn't play games. It might be hard for her to voice some of her thoughts, but that wasn't because she was purposefully holding back, and frankly that was refreshing from the stories I'd heard. It was why Ivy and I had worked for as long as we did when really our chemistry was more friends than something romantic.

Both of us were authentically ourselves, for better or for worse, and that was all I had time for in my life.

Jules synced her phone with my speakers, and we took turns playing albums we loved to see what each other's reactions were to our favorite artists. I loved watching her let loose, dancing around my kitchen. I learned she hadn't met a Taylor Swift era that she didn't love. I thought the artist was a good songwriter, but my favorites tended to be more like the Killers, or Kings of Leon. We both also loved some older stuff, but it was fun just to be surprised as to what came on next.

After a few hours of our own private game of guess the song or artist, the kitchen was cleaned up, our bellies were full, and Jules was laughing as she held up her phone.

"One more, one more." She shot me a mischievous look and then hit Play, placing her phone down and leaning back against the counter while she watched me, waiting for the song to begin.

"I feel like this is some sort of test."

"Might be," she said with a shrug. "Have to know you recognize good music."

"That should already be established," I said. However, I was willing to give the song a fair evaluation. I stood still, eyes trained to the floor, and waited to see what she had for me. The humming caught my attention first. Then clapping joined with a few instruments. As the voice started, my eyes shot to hers. "Hozier?"

She nodded. "Song title?"

A few more beats in and I had it. "'Work Song.'" I stepped to her and slid my arms around her waist, pulling her to me. "Great song, great artist. Did I pass?"

"Debatable. This is on the playlist for my current book. Actually, I think it's been on the playlists for all of them so far." She looked up at me with a bright smile. "It's weird to talk about my hobby with anyone."

"Weird good?"

"Absolutely."

I pulled her in to do somewhat of a slow dance as we stood together in the kitchen. As I listened to the song, I also soaked in the feeling of Jules in my arms. If I wanted to be like one of her heroes once they'd fallen, I could expound on the rightness of this moment. In truth, I was falling far faster than I was ready for, but that was a problem for later. "Pretty romantic song if you can get past the whole death part."

"Do you think he's really dead, or is it just a metaphor for hard work?" she asked while we swayed together.

"I mean, he's talking about his love for her allows him to crawl home to her from his grave," I mused. "Maybe I'm being too literal?"

"It's romantic." She sighed. "I want that."

I stilled. "How so?"

I felt Jules stiffen, maybe not realizing she'd said that last part aloud. "Well..." She let that just hang there, likely debating what to say.

"Speak up, Jules." My heart was beating so strong there was no way she couldn't feel it through my chest.

Jules cleared her throat, then looked up with a new determination in her eyes. "It's what I write about, Noah. And now that I know you've been reading my books, I'm guessing you know that. I write heroes who fall first, who will do anything for their heroine."

I hadn't looked at her books like that, but now that she mentioned it, I could see it. And this song fell right into that theme. However... Fuck.

"I'm a dad, Jules. Not that I've always been a good one."

I braced, not entirely sure what I was saying but feeling like it didn't fit what she wanted.

She gave me a sad smile. That wasn't a good sign, was it? "Noah, you *are* a good dad. You are now, and you were back then. You need to be kinder to yourself."

Okay. Not terrible. "I'll work on it, but still—"

She held up a hand. "I know what you meant. And I don't think putting Addie first means I'm last. I mean, we're just starting out here after all. That being said, I don't think it would be great parenting to say the woman you've known for less than a month should become more important than your child."

Valid point.

"And while I'm stating what I think is important..." Jules looked uncertain, but she kept going. "And jumping to a lighter topic, though not one easy for me to talk about necessarily, I think a healthy sex life is vitally important."

"You have my attention," I said, my voice coming out deeper than usual as I watched this beautiful woman speak up when I knew it made her uncomfortable to do so.

"And our first time together was only two days ago, but it feels like it has been far longer than that." She looked up at me imploringly.

Oh yeah. I knew what she was insinuating here. Did I want to push her to say everything that was on her mind, or did I want to throw her over my shoulder and hightail it to my bedroom? Both options had merit, though I was leaning toward the latter, and Lord knew my cock was on board with that option as well.

Decision made, I was helping her get to the point so we could get horizontal. The woman had already brought up the subject—she didn't need to do all the work here.

"I think I've got it, Jules. You're saying we should make

sure the first time wasn't a fluke?" I asked, giving her a wide smile to let her know I had zero concern that it had been a fluke.

She looked at me in relief as she nodded.

Damn, I was ready for a repeat. Just kissing the woman got me hard. Our chemistry had been great, in my opinion, because even though we hadn't known each other long, we were absolutely getting there. Knowing her, caring about her, made everything hotter. Add to that the experiences we'd been through together, which had accelerated our bond. Damn. I was on board to head upstairs now.

Songs from Hozier had been playing randomly since we started talking, and now "Too Sweet" was coming out over the speaker. Jules slid her hand under my T-shirt, running her fingers up my chest as she looked at me from under her lashes.

"So Noah," she said as she rose up on her toes to press a kiss to my neck. "How should we go about finding out if our first time was a fluke?" She sank back down and gave me an innocent smile, though the thoughts it inspired were far from pure.

Option two it was. Let's go.

"Put this in your books, Jules," I murmured to her as I bent to get her stomach on my shoulder, and up she went.

"Noah!" She smacked my ass from her upside-down position as I headed toward the stairs, pausing by the front door to lock it as I went.

"Now, kitten," I said as I adjusted her to have a better hold while telling myself this was a little over the top. "I don't think you write BDSM books, correct?" I laughed as I headed up to my bedroom and swatted her butt in response. "Do you really want to explore spanking?"

"What?" She sounded aghast, which was also fun. I could just imagine her expression.

We reached my room, and I lowered her to her feet. Her hair was framing her face, which was a bit rosy from the brief time upside down. In other words, she was gorgeous as usual.

"I'm not into BDSM," she said, and I had a feeling her red face wasn't only to do with her ride on my shoulder.

"I was kidding."

"I mean, an occasional swat on the ass like that..." Now she looked even more embarrassed, which would be fun to explore later.

"I've got you, kitten." I kept my eyes locked on hers and grabbed the hem of my shirt before pulling it over and off, dropping it on the floor. Jules watched it fall, then mirrored my actions with the removal of both her baggy top and the tank that was below.

What followed was a speedy round of follow the leader. I removed my pants; her leggings went. Socks were next, until we stood in front of each other in our underwear, my boxer briefs making it all too apparent what I thought of this situation as my cock strained to get out.

"Well, Mr. Lawson, I think you're happy to see me," Jules said, stepping forward and tentatively reaching out to cup my cock.

"Oh no, Ms. Jules," I said, grabbing her hand and moving it to my chest. "If you get ahold of me, it will be all she wrote, and as we know, your heroines always come first."

"Does it count if I've almost gotten there three times since we started the conversation downstairs?"

"Nope." I moved toward her, then reached around and quickly unclasped her bra before tossing it over my shoulder. "Shed those," I said with a nod at her lacy pink underwear, and I kicked mine down and to the floor somewhere behind me while she did the same.

I stepped toward Jules while she stepped back, almost as if the woman was tugging on an invisible rope to pull me into her grasp. I was a willing participant, that was for certain. Eventually she was at my bed and sank onto it, and I stood to take her in, spread out before me. She was a vision. Her hair had tumbled out of the pile on top of her head and fanned out all over the pillow. She watched me with a heated expression that promised more.

I moved to kneel at the floor and tug her to the edge, but she spoke up. "Uh-uh, buster."

I looked at her with confusion. "Babe, I need you to come. Let me get you there."

"And I need the same," she said. "And right now I need to do that with you, not me by myself." She rolled over and knelt at the headboard, holding on to it while she turned to look at me over her shoulder. "Come on, sexy. Get your ass over here."

I grabbed a condom from my side table and slid it on before I crawled up the bed. She'd placed some pillows below her knees to even our heights out while I got in position. I came up behind her, her back to my chest while she tilted her head to the side and turned to capture my lips. I lost myself in her kisses while she ground her ass back in contact with my dick. Jesus. This woman was my fantasies personified.

"Slow down." I placed a hand on her hip. "This could be over all too soon."

Jules arched a brow at me over her shoulder to tell me that I needed to get with the program. I slid my hand over her lower belly to what she'd hilariously called her happy place, then moved past her clit and checked to see how ready she was for me. A finger into her canal and she began arching into my palm, which pretty much told me everything I needed to know.

"Ready?" I asked, straightening up and notching my cock at her entrance.

Her reply was to push back into me. Holy fuck. I guess that was her way of telling me she was.

The angle when kneeling against the headboard was new, but it gave both of us the opportunity for hands to roam. And Jules floored me when she knocked mine off their path to her happy place and started touching herself in what was clearly a familiar rhythm that brought her to the brink in moments if the flutter of her canal against me was anything to go by. I quickly began kissing her neck right at the nape and ran a hand up to tweak one of her nipples. That did it.

Jules arched back, a long, low moan coming out as she kept her hand moving through her orgasm. I fought coming as well, wanting to give her the chance to ride out her pleasure to the end. I knew we were there when she placed her hands to the headboard to brace herself and angled her torso forward. She looked at me over her shoulder before taking a breath and sending me a wink.

"Your turn," she said breathlessly.

I slid my hands to her hips and pistoned in and out, chasing my climax until it was right there. With a final thrust, my entire body was flooded with endorphins, and I draped my chest over her back, dropping my forehead to her shoulder to catch my breath.

We remained in that position for several breaths until Jules broke the silence.

"Noah?" she whispered.

"Jules."

"I don't think the first time was a fluke," she said.

I wrapped my arms around her torso and laughed, sliding us down the bed to lay on our slides. I was rapidly softening, so I knew I couldn't stay like this for long. But for the moment? Yes please.

"I think you're right, kitten. Our chemistry is unlike anyone I've been with."

"So..." She hesitated but then made the decision to say it. "What are we going to do about it?"

I kissed the top of her shoulder. "I think we keep doing what we're doing and see what this is like when not dealing with major life events."

She nodded. "So keep connecting..."

I moved my hips forward. "I definitely like connecting with you."

She reached back to slap my torso, such that she could. "That way, sure, but also..."

I kissed her temple this time. "Yes, also outside the bedroom. For example, like at my daughter's birthday party tomorrow. You still in?"

"Yes?" Frankly, she didn't sound completely convinced, but I'd take it.

I slid out, took care of the condom, and came right back, but this time lying face-to-face. "How can I reassure you?"

"I don't think you can." She met my gaze. "I'm a little scared of Jake's mom."

I laughed. "I mean, she's harmless in that there isn't a mean bone in her body, just a big personality." I thought for a minute. "She'll love you."

She nodded. "Can I make something to bring?"

I thought of all the brunches I'd been to at Ivy's place.

"Well, the amount of food that will already be there is ridiculous, but you're welcome to if you want."

She nestled into my space, resting her head on my arm. "Thanks."

I lifted my head in surprise, but she was already growing heavy in sleep and not looking at me. "For what, kitten?"

"For accepting me as I am and constantly reassuring me." Her sleepy voice grabbed my heart and squeezed.

"Always," I whispered, kissing her head and following her into dreamland.

Chapter 25

Who Doesn't Love a Brunch

Jules

Noah and I were headed up the walk to Jake and Ivy's place, a dessert carrier in his hands. I'd insisted on making something and, upon looking at the groceries Ivy had stocked, I realized I had all the makings of a peach-and-blueberry cake. Of course, it would be better when the fruit was all in season, but it would still be delicious now. Bonus points, it gave me something else to obsess over while we sat around this morning.

I knew these weren't Noah's parents. Hell—now I would never meet them, not that he would have even wanted me to. But somehow it felt like Jake's parents were stand-ins for the parental figures that Noah, and in many ways Ivy, lacked. I wanted to make a good impression. I felt certain my joggers and lightweight long-sleeved tee weren't dressy enough, but Noah explained that all the Spencer siblings were big fans of a casual and leisurely brunch. If I dressed up, I would be out of place, thus I went with it.

As we got to the sidewalk that curved up to the back

door, Noah tugged on my hand and I came to a stop in front of him.

"You sure you want to do this?" he asked.

"Of course. Who doesn't love a brunch?" I said, momentarily uncertain if that was his way of hinting he'd rather go alone. "Do you still want me here?"

He shook his head and placed a hand under my chin, tilting my face up and pressing the sweetest of kisses to my lips. Moving back just a breath, he whispered, "I'd really like you by my side. I just don't want you to do anything you're not comfortable with."

"I'm good. Promise."

In response, Noah leaned down for another kiss. We fell into it and I silently ranked it against all our kisses so far. How was every one of them better than the last and far and away superior to any I'd had before? I was continuing to enjoy this one when I heard some whistling coming from the house.

We pulled back, and I looked beyond Noah to see Jake, Ivy, Drew, Kate, and two new folks I was assuming were Steph and Theo on the porch.

Drew looked to us, then to his siblings and in-laws. "This feels like a whole lot of déjà vu, am I right?"

They all laughed at what seemed like an inside joke. Noah grabbed my hand, squeezed it in a quick gesture of comfort, and we headed up the walk.

"Welcome." Ivy stepped forward and gave me a hug. "I'm so glad you came."

"Jules." Jake stepped up and pulled me in a hug after Ivy, then pulled back and pointed at the two people to his side. "This is my *much older* sister Steph and her long-suffering husband Theo."

Steph smacked him on the back of the head, then gave

me a wide smile. "Welcome to the circus that is a Spencer family brunch. Hope you're hungry."

Theo reached out and shook my hand. "We can always use some more non-Spencer blood around here."

"It's that bad?" I asked, mainly joking. Mainly.

"It's something," he replied, clear in his tone that while he was serious, he was also fond of this crew.

"Daddy," Addie cried, coming out on the porch, positively vibrating.

"Which one of us?" Noah asked, looking from himself to Jake.

"She used to call them Daddy One and Two, which made it a bit easier to tell the difference. Now she often drops the number, which is fine except when you want to know who she's talking about," Steph stage-whispered all that to me.

"Both of you," Addie said to the audience. "I need you to come in since everyone is here. We can have *donuts*, and Emily, Jennie, and I have been waiting *forever*."

"Or five minutes," Ivy said from behind her hand.

"We're coming." Jake began ushering us all in.

We walked through Jake and Ivy's back door, which took you straight into their kitchen. There was a large island running the length that was positively groaning under the amount of food spread out, which was truly positively shocking in quantity.

A couple that was clearly the Spencer parents stood at the stove and were arguing about how many pancakes they were making.

Addie and two other girls were now standing by the donut boxes, debating which ones they would choose.

A chocolate lab was lying on a dog bed in front of a

window, his tail thwapping the floor in a clear indication of his joy at being surrounded by this crowd.

This was a lot to take in.

Ivy called from her spot, "Jules, do you want a mimosa or coffee?"

I looked to Noah with big eyes. They really were serious about their level of brunch. "Um, I'll take a mimosa."

She looked to Kate and Steph. "Refills?"

The ladies cheered, and Mrs. Spencer looked up from her conversation at the pancake station. "Ahh, new recruits." She was my size but had a presence when she came around the island to meet me. "I'm Margot," she said as she pulled me to her. "Hope you're a hugger, because I am." She stepped back and pointed to her husband. "That's Sam. He can't be bothered while he's making pancakes."

Sam waved in introduction. "Plain, blueberry, or chocolate chip?"

"Any," Noah replied.

Sam nodded and got back to work.

"So." Margot leaned against the counter, giving me an assessing glance. "Did Noah mention that I was pretty rough on him when we met?"

Noah shook his head, looking toward the ceiling before accepting a coffee mug from Drew with a thanks. I took the proffered champagne glass from Ivy and looked back to Margot. While it was true that everyone, including Sam, was in casual wear, Margot's look was far more upscale than an outfit from Athleta or the like. She had on loose linen pants and a T-shirt, but it was accessorized with a chunky beaded necklace, orange Birkenstock sandals, and thick turquoise glasses. I wanted to grow up to be her.

"Why's that?" I asked to her comment.

Margot shrugged, seemingly unrepentant regarding her

previous treatment of Noah. "I didn't think he was good enough for Addie and Ivy."

I stood up straight, ready to give her a piece of my mind while I heard Steph to my right murmur *interesting* to Kate. Whatever. "Why would you think that? He's an exceptional human. Addie is lucky to have him as her dad."

My heart rate was up as I worried a tad about offending the woman I'd just met, but I'd rather do that than let her comment go. Who knew I could go from nervous to pissed in a matter of seconds?

"Oh dear," Margot murmured. "I didn't mean to offend. Noah knows how much we care about him now."

"Easy, kitten." Noah came up to my side. "Claws in—Margot was just looking out for her family."

I spun toward him. "You were not the bad guy here, Noah, and shouldn't have been treated as such."

He gave me a look of such gratitude that my knees threatened to buckle from the weight of it. "Jules," he murmured.

"She's right," Ivy said, coming to my side. "And I wish I had spoken up more in defense of you, Noah."

He looked in surprise from Ivy to me, a crinkle forming between his brows. "Margot was really fine."

"I was cold," Margot said, giving him a haughty look now like no one should dare question her. "And I'm sorry for it. You're a great dad, and it wasn't my business why you weren't around as much when Addie was a babe. You were there when you could be."

"Not enough," Noah said as he watched Addie with a look of sadness.

She was playing with her cousins, laughter abounding. Addie grabbed Chief, and the three girls took off out the back door with the pup to race around the fenced-in yard.

"Ugh!" Ivy growled out the word, drawing attention back to our circle. "Noah Michael Lawson, I'm going to whip your ass if we must have this conversation again. You *are* a great dad. You are now, you were then, and you need to get the hell over yourself about the fact that you were in Africa, trying to make a better world for kids who have so much less than your daughter. Do you know what kind of role model you are to her? Do you understand that you are the reason she wants to volunteer at the animal shelter because she learned from you that when you see a need, you can fill it with your own hard work and not just platitudes like most of us do?" Ivy was breathing heavily, her hands on her hips. "Do I seriously need to remind you of all this *again?*" She threw her hands up in the air like she couldn't even believe she was having to say that.

Silence filled the kitchen. I glanced around and saw that every adult was focused on our group. Noah was looking at his feet, not meeting Ivy's gaze as he processed her words. I didn't know Ivy super well, but from what I knew of her, this was totally out of character. She was typically relaxed. I'd classify her somewhere in the world of hippies or boho chic, but definitely chill. Right then she was anything but.

"Ivy cussed," Steph said at my side.

"Twice," Kate said from just beyond Steph.

Apparently I wasn't the only one noticing the out-of-character behavior.

Noah looked up, focusing on Ivy. "I appreciate the kind words, but—"

"This 'but' is going to piss me off, isn't it?" Ivy looked fierce.

Noah was undeterred. "But you have said it yourself, you and Addie struggled to make ends meet when she was first born. That's why you're so cautious with money even now."

Ivy looked to the ceiling and visibly counted to ten. Looking back at Noah, she took a step toward him and gave him a lighthearted slap on the temple. "Noah Lawson, you might drive me crazy today. Yes, we struggled, but if you remember, you wanted to help us financially at the time and what did I do?"

"Ow," he replied, rubbing his head, but I could see the lightness in his eyes. He was pushing her buttons, and the fact that he was teasing her gave me some relief. "You said no."

Ivy threw both hands out again. "Exactly! Maybe if we're questioning anyone's parenting choices here, we should look at mine because I might have been a smidge stubborn."

"Might?" Jake piped up from over by his dad.

"That's enough from the peanut gallery," Ivy shot back.

"Love you, babe," Jake said with a wink in her direction.

Ivy rolled her eyes, then looked at Noah. "I'm not going to hijack this entire brunch, but Noah, you and I are going to have to revisit this if you're still carrying around guilt. And I'll leave you with this final comment, then I need a donut." She gestured at the giant windows overlooking the backyard and pointed at Addie, who was spinning in circles while Chief barked. "That little girl knows exactly how loved she is—she's never questioned it. She has so many people who adore her just as she is, and you and I both know that's not the case for everyone. She has always known you loved her—always has, always will."

Noah was clearly struggling to accept what Ivy was saying, but she held up a hand. "Noah, we know what it's like to grow up without the love of our parents. Addie has never felt that, even when you weren't with us. So, my dear friend, you need to get past this." She looked to all of us, then grabbed a donut out of the box. "Now I need to nurse Ms. Lorelai. I'll be back." With that, she exited the kitchen, followed by Jake, who had the baby in a sling.

"Well, Bookstore does tend to say it like it is." Drew shrugged.

I looked to Kate in confusion. She leaned over. "Drew calls Ivy Bookstore. It's their thing."

Margot stepped up to Noah and reached a hand up to pat his face, her multitude of bangle bracelets sliding down her arm. "Noah dear, I hope you listened to Ivy, though how anyone would have missed that, I'm not certain. What I should have seen immediately instead of rushing to judgment is that you are a positively excellent father. Addie is blessed to have you."

"Thanks," Noah said in a low voice. "And this got a little crazy today. I never thought you treated me badly."

"She could have been kinder," Drew said in a serious tone but with a shit-eating grin.

"Hush, you," Margot said, giving his stomach a backhanded slap, her bracelets clinking.

"Dad, Mom is abusing me," Drew whined with a wide smile.

"I'm sure you deserved it," Sam said from his place at the stove, the pile of pancakes growing to astronomical size.

Margot returned to Noah. "Ignoring my youngest—I'm not sure where we went wrong with him—but Noah, you need to find a way to forgive yourself. Life is short—no need to hold on to guilt that isn't earned."

"Thanks, Margot," Noah said, then stepped closer to her but faced Sam as well. "And also, unrelated, but I didn't get a chance to thank you both for the flowers you sent to the service for my parents. I truly appreciated it."

Margot patted his arm again. "It was the least we could do. I'm so sorry we couldn't make it to support you, but Ivy said the Highland Falls crew was headed up."

"Yep, had to have his back in case his parents' friends were as big of assholes as they were. Or is it bad to speak ill of the dead?" Drew looked lost in thought while this time Kate gave him a light slap.

"What?" Drew glanced from Kate to Noah. "Weren't they?"

Kate dropped her face in her hand with a groan.

"Mom, seriously, did you drop him as a baby?" Steph said from her spot by her dad as she wiped down the counter.

"Only once," Sam said.

"Dad." Drew shook his head with a disapproving look. "Not cool."

"It's fine," Noah replied. "They weren't the greatest, I can say that, but they are no longer here, so I'm trying not to think about it too much."

Margot tapped Noah's arm. "Not that I'm your mother, and Lord knows I'm not trying to tell you what to do—"

"Bullshit." Drew coughed into his fist.

Margot leaned over to slap the back of Drew's head before turning back to Noah. Drew rubbed a hand over it and looked at his mom with laughter in his eyes. He clearly loved egging her on.

"As I was saying, take this advice for what it's worth. The loss of your parents, regardless of your relationship with them, is a big one. Allow yourself the time you need to grieve. And know that Sam and I are here for you in any way we can be." She patted Noah's cheeks. "You hear me?"

Noah gave her a warm smile. "I hear you, Margot. And thanks."

Margot pulled him in for a hug as Sam spoke up from the stove. "Pancakes are ready."

I scanned the island. Three types of pancakes, coffee cake, my cake, scones, muffins, egg casserole, bacon, fruit, donuts, and toast. Good Lord. Was a bus of people coming to join us?

"Are we ready to eat?" Ivy came back in; Lorelai was in a sling on her chest. She had a blanket tossed over her shoulder as well. "Avert your eyes if any bit of breast offends. I need some food, and the babe is taking a bit longer than necessary."

Could I add Ivy to my people I wanted to become? I really appreciated her "tell it like it is" vibe. It was one that I certainly didn't possess, but maybe my current heroine could borrow some of that while I worked on myself.

Steph was rummaging in her bag but looked over to Ivy. "Want me to fix you a plate?"

"Nah, Jake is headed in. He went out the other door to corral the girls."

Sam piped up as Drew snagged a piece of bacon. "You all can go ahead and start. We have a few more guests joining us any minute."

Ivy looked up from her spot where she'd sunk onto a stool at the island, her arm cradling Lorelai as she nursed. "Who else is coming, not that it matters. Clearly we're not low on food."

"Just some friends from town," Margot replied as she poured herself another mug of coffee.

"Oh." Steph pulled a book out of her bag. At first I couldn't see the cover, but when she turned, I immediately wanted to vomit as I recognized my second book. "Didn't you say this is next month's read? I already told Mom she's bringing me on FaceTime to the club meeting since she'll be in town for it. I absolutely devoured this one. How many books are there in this Sleepy Valley series again?"

Margot immediately piped up with an answer. I looked from Steph to Margot in horror, realizing this meant Margot had also read my book. Then Kate and Ivy began to add to the conversation. My gaze found Noah, who was watching me with concern. All these women had read my books. Holy bejesus.

"Sorry, I need to use the restroom," I murmured, fleeing the kitchen and praying I could find one to hide in. What I would do after that, I had no idea.

Chapter 26

The Shit Hits the Fan

Noah

I knocked on the door to the bathroom. "Jules? You okay?" I'd vacillated between checking on her and giving her space, but she'd been in there for five minutes and it was clear to everyone in the kitchen that something was going on. I didn't know if I should make excuses and say she wasn't feeling great or if she was going to want to stay, so hovering outside the restroom was where I'd found myself.

The door cracked open and Jules peered out, her brown eyes so watery that it was abundantly clear some major tears had been shed.

"I'm so embarrassed, Noah. I can head out a side door or something and get out of your hair so you can all enjoy your brunch." Her voice wavered as she tried to pull herself together.

"Can I come in?" I asked quietly, ignoring her comment about leaving.

Jules stepped back to let me into the bathroom, which truly wasn't meant for two.

Once we were both inside the half bath, I leaned against the sink. Taking in the woman standing in front of me, my heart broke for her. She hadn't done anything wrong beyond caring far too much what people thought—or more to the point, caring that she didn't alter the perception of her in the minds of the people she loved. I ran my hands up and down her arms to try to help her relax. She looked miserable.

"Okay, let's talk about this. You're in tears because..."

"I'm a moron?" Jules threw up her hands. "I know, I know. This is insanity." She exhaled in clear frustration. "I just need to tell my friends and family that I write romance. It shouldn't be a big deal." She wrapped her arms around her waist like she was trying to hold herself together. "But Noah, what if they disapprove? What if they think it's wrong in some way?" Her breath started coming in short, quick huffs, so I mirrored for her, taking a cleansing breath and breathing it out slowly. I was grateful I'd started attending a few of Kate's yoga classes with Drew because some of her lessons were coming in handy right now. Slowly Jules began to follow my lead.

"Okay, kitten." I grabbed her hand, feeling the need for a connection. "If you want my opinion, and I'm giving it whether you do or not"—I shot her a wink to lighten the mood—"I think the time has come and maybe this was the universe's way of telling you that. Certainly that's what Ivy would say."

She nodded, looking like she was hanging on my every word so she wouldn't lose it.

"I'll say this about your main concern—remember, these people have already read your books and shared that they loved them. And not one part of me believes they will be anything but excited for you." I squeezed her hand and gave her a soft smile, thrilled when she sent me a small one back. "I truly don't think you have anything to worry about except them losing their damn minds with excitement that you are one of the authors they love."

Jules visibly relaxed as I spoke, like she was processing what I was saying and was starting to believe it. "You really think that, don't you?"

I looked her straight in the eye. "One hundred percent."

Jules looked down at the floor while she took a few deep breaths in, then out. She had some type of internal conversation with herself before she lifted her head. "Okay, let's do this."

I quickly leaned forward to press a kiss to her lips before whispering against her lips, "You've got this, baby, and I am so proud of you."

Jules leaned her forehead against mine, closed her eyes, and took a moment. I kept my gaze on her as she opened them to look back at me. The connection I felt to the woman was unreal and shouldn't be true after only a matter of weeks. Regardless, it was there. Jules stepped back and gave me a nod to tell me she had this. I was so damn proud of her.

She headed out of the bathroom to the kitchen, hand in hand with me. She walked with determination back into the space where the shit had hit the fan for her, but the rest of the room had been left with questions.

Looking around, I saw that everyone was still pretty much where we'd left them. Most folks were enjoying a drink or a donut—especially Addie and her cousins. The Spencer clan was doing what they did best, enjoying time with each other as they gave one another shit for a variety of topics. Sam, Jake, and Drew were having what looked like a somewhat heated debate about what Jake should buy next: a smoker, a Blackstone, or a Green Egg. Not shockingly, they all had strong opinions.

Margot, Ivy, and Kate were being entertained by the three girls, who were eating donuts while telling a story about the Little People they believed, thanks to bedtime stories from their parents, lived in the basement of their houses.

I'd only known the Spencer family for just over a year, and my heart warmed with affection for them. They knew something had upset Jules. They weren't making a big deal about it, and I knew if asked they'd say it hadn't impacted their brunch at all but gave them time to catch up before eating. They'd waited for us because of course they did. It was just who they were, through and through. I was so damn grateful for every one of them.

"Hey, all, I have an announcement," Jules said, and the room immediately fell silent.

Steph and Ivy looked at each other with eyebrows raised. I had a feeling they thought this announcement would be about our relationship; boy, were they in for a surprise.

Jules stepped over to Steph and pointed at her book sitting on the counter. "May I?"

Steph looked confused but handed over her book from the Sleepy Valley series. "Sure."

Steph looked to Kate, and they both shrugged.

Jules turned around in front of the back door, a gorgeous April morning visible in the windows behind her. She took a deep breath and quickly looked to me. I nodded, trying to silently send her my support. She had this, and once this secret was free, I knew she'd feel so much less burdened. She'd still have to tell her family and the rest of the book club, but we could make that happen once she was ready.

Jules seemed to focus on Margot, which, I guessed made sense. The woman did command a room. She was also front and center, sitting at the island.

"Several years ago, in response to some stressful times at work, I took up writing fiction as a hobby." She bit her lip and looked down at the book in her hand, then back up at all of us.

I met her eyes again, willing her on.

She cleared her throat and stood up straight, gaining some strength. "Originally I thought my writing was just for me. For fun, you know, when the stress of work at my firm became too much." She looked around, almost imploring everyone to understand. And because they could feel that desire pouring off her even though they were still confused, everyone nodded.

Ivy was sitting just to my side as she nursed Lorelai. I glanced over at her to see her head tilt as she looked from Jules to the book, back to Jules, and then her head spun to me.

"Noah?" she whispered.

And I knew she'd put two and two together.

I nodded in Jules's direction. "Let her finish," I said in a hushed tone.

Ivy's eyes were like saucers, but she looked back to Jules.

"I'll cut to the chase, but I'm happy to answer any questions you have," Jules was saying. "This hobby became a secret kind of by accident. I didn't know how to finally tell people because when it started and only existed on my computer, why would I mention it? But then, once my stories got out into the world, it seemed to get bigger all at once. And now I'm tired of worrying about what people will think about it, so I'm starting with telling all of you." She looked to me and then gave me a shy smile. "Well, Noah already knows." Then she held up the book and spoke with a wide smile on her face like she was owning her truth. "I'm the author of this book, Jules Jenkins."

Margot and Kate cheered and rushed Jules to pull her into a group hug.

Ivy slapped my arm and said, "I knew it!"

The guys and the kids all whooped and clapped, though I'm not sure that any of them realized what a big deal this was.

Then I realized the back door was open behind Jules. From behind the swaying hug in front of us, I heard Lou's voice ring out. "I'm sorry, what did you just say, Jules?"

Jules's eyes widened as she stepped back from Kate and Margot to spin around.

All of us could then see Lou and Verdell in the doorway, looking puzzled. But then two more people stepped out from behind them. Jules made a shocked noise. "Mom? Dad? What are you doing here?"

Oh shit.

Chapter 27

The Bombs Explode

Jules

Shit. Shit. Shitty shit, shit. My parents, *my mom and dad*, were standing in Ivy and Jake's kitchen. What world was I living in? Sure, Lou and Verdell were surprising, but at least they lived in Highland Falls. The two of them showing up for brunch wasn't completely out of the realm of possibility. But my parents?

My brain whirled as I contemplated where in the States I'd thought they were currently traveling, and I realized that with everything in the past week with Noah's family crisis, I hadn't even considered their location or paid much attention to their social media.

Not that any of that knowledge was making the current reality any better.

Could one get whiplash from an extreme about-face of emotions? Asking for a friend. Moments ago, I had just told the Spencer family about my books. They'd reacted better than I could have imagined. I'd felt pure joy and somewhat of a lightness inside, having shared this big of a secret with at least a few people close to me. That lasted what, mere seconds? And now?

Now?

Now I was just standing there, staring dumbfounded at my family. I heard murmurings behind me and somehow knew the Spencers were gathering their food and heading somewhere... The dining room? No idea—I hadn't exactly had a tour yet.

They were giving us privacy because of course they were. I'd invaded their family brunch, made them wait while I had my meltdown, dropped a literary bomb on them, celebrated, and now was having a family moment in their kitchen. I'm sure I would be invited back again next weekend.

Mental note, this would be great fodder for a character once I got over the little t trauma I was having here.

As I spiraled and wrapped my mind around the fact that not only were my family members standing in front of me but they'd also heard me announce I was an author, I felt an arm wrap around my waist. I immediately knew it was Noah standing beside me because of course he was, the giant green flag of a man. Too bad his parents were no longer residing on this earth so that I could tell them that despite their best efforts, the man would stand alongside me to dismantle the patriarchy. That he was the type of guy who would shout from the rooftops to celebrate my accomplishments long before he'd ever do the same for his own. That he was good, down deep into his core, and couldn't care less about their money or their world. It had to be the strangest "get to know you" few weeks of all time, but I'd take it all over again to feel the support that was emanating out of him right now.

"You've got this," he whispered, his arm squeezing me,

and I nodded in response just before hearing my mom start up.

"Jules Marie Maxwell." Her voice was a borderline screech.

Did I mention my mom was a fan of theatrics?

"Brace," I whispered to Noah.

He gave me a knowing smile that indicated he remembered, at least.

"Hi, Mom." I waved like a dork. "Dad." Normally I'd give them both a big hug. Same with my aunt and uncle. Right that minute though, I was waiting for the bomb to explode and choosing to give them all some space.

"What do you mean, *you're an author?*" My mom's arms were waving in the air in her attempt to plead to the universe to make this make sense. Her light brown hair had more grays than she liked, so she was likely headed to her fountain of youth soon to get that fixed. I enjoyed the fact that she was still playing with fashion, a new interest of hers, with some baggy cuffed jeans and a flowy top. At least she looked good while she lost it for a few minutes because we'd reached screeching levels now.

"Frannie." My dad's calm and cool voice worked to do its normal magic on my mom. I had a sinking feeling it was not the day—we were going to need more than Dad being chill. He was looking at her over the top of his glasses. He looked casual, as he always did. The only hair on his head was a bit of a scruff on his face because he hadn't shaved for a day or two.

"Jim," my mom said, volume not decreasing in the slightest. The Spencers hadn't needed to leave the room because as long as they were within two blocks, they'd hear the whole conversation. Or at least Mom's side of it. "Did you not hear our child? She said she's an author and she had not informed her own flesh and blood." She turned to Lou. "Did you know?"

"Sure didn't," Lou said, though I was grateful to see she didn't look upset. If anything, it looked like she was enjoying the show.

"I'm so hurt. Where did I go wrong? Why didn't you trust us?" My mom was approaching wailing levels now and making my guilt deepen. She clutched her chest like I had physically wounded her. If she could have placed a fainting couch in the kitchen, she would have been down for the count. All for show, but still.

"Frannie." My dad's voice was now at level two, the warning level he used when my mom didn't respond to his calm one. Hopefully that would be enough.

"I know, I know, I know." Mom's hands were flying as she now moved around a kitchen that I don't even know if she realized wasn't hers. She was fully in her element, like she was back in their days of community theater. They'd given it up to travel the country, but Mom got her dramatics in when she could. Sure enough, her tears started, right on time. Big crocodile ones down her cheeks. "It's just, why didn't you tell us?" She turned to me, and I knew she was finally ready for me to speak.

Don't get me wrong. My mom wasn't a bad person, not at all. I knew to the very fiber of my core that my parents loved me. But my mom was a true extrovert and felt her feelings deeply. She lived her life loud and, at times, a bit haphazardly. I simply didn't. I appreciated her for being her, but to say we didn't always look at the world the same way would be a severe understatement. And maybe that was part of what had held me back from telling them.

Actually, as that popped in my mind, some realizations were hitting me hard and fast.

"Mom, Dad." I looked to their left. "Lou, Verdell, I'm not sure what to say."

My dad nodded to my side. "How about we start with introductions?"

Oof. I'd told my parents the bare-bones version of who Noah was over the past few weeks, especially when I'd left Highland Falls to go up to Madison, so they'd known where I was but they hadn't met.

"So sorry," I said, and Noah squeezed my side to tell me he understood. "Hey, guys, this is Noah Lawson. Noah, this is my mom Frannie. My dad Jim. And you know Lou and Verdell."

My dad stepped forward with a hand out to shake Noah's. "So sorry to hear about your parents, Noah, but it's nice to meet you."

"Thank you, sir," Noah said. "And same."

"Jim," my dad replied.

Noah nodded. "Jim."

Dad stepped to the side and gave me a hug. "Hey, sweetheart."

I melted into his familiar embrace as I slid my arms under his lightweight vest and was enveloped in the scent that brought me home. "Hey, Dad."

Mom came flying over, switching to caretaking mode. "Oh, Noah dear." She pulled him to her chest and rocked him back and forth forcefully, which was comical considering she was all of five foot three and Noah dwarfed her at almost a foot taller. Of course, I was shorter than my mom, but I also wasn't attempting to rock the man.

My mom was still hugging him. "I was so sorry to hear about your parents. If we hadn't been all the way in the southwest, we could have made it back in time to be with you."

Noah had some muffled response that was inaudible, but I smiled. It would do him some good to get my mom's hugs for a bit. And it gave me some time to decide how to respond.

"Now Jules," my mom said, stepping back, her tone indicating that she meant business.

Okay, maybe that had been wishful thinking.

"Mom."

She moved over and picked up Steph's copy of my book. Looking at the cover, she ran her finger over my name, or my pen name, then looked at me with confusion evident on her face. "I've read your books. They're good. I mean, *really good*. Why on earth wouldn't you have told me, or told us, you wrote them?"

Lou stepped up next to Mom. "I've read the first and second one, Jules, and I agree with your mom. They're wonderful books."

Noah was back by my side because of course he was. He stood like a silent sentry while I got my thoughts together. Frankly, when I thought about it for a moment, I was tired. Tired of keeping this to myself, tired of keeping it all in.

"Honestly? At first it was just a fun hobby. I started four years ago, and I wasn't going to publish them. But work was stressful, and this was my way to relax and write the world I wished I lived in." My heart ached when I thought of that girl because as tired as my mom thought I was months ago when she had me upend my life and move down here, if she'd seen me a few years ago, she would have lost her damn mind. I had not been in a good place and, as Lin-Manuel Miranda's Hamilton said, I was able to write my way out.

"And then?" My mom prodded me, knowing there was more.

I shrugged. "Then I ending up publishing for fun. The books came out fast, and I had four written before I knew what to do with them. I didn't tell anyone because I figured maybe two or three people might read them and then I'd be done. It was still just something for me, although my friend up in Chicago, Kylie, did know eventually, but we didn't talk about it much."

My mom nodded, shocking to anyone who knew her. She stayed quiet and let me finish.

"And then book three went viral on social media when an influencer shared it. People went wild for it and went back and read all three that were out. It became a lot, and I didn't know how to go back in time and tell people about it now that it was out there."

I felt the familiar sinking feeling I always did about that time. People thought going viral was fun, but I wondered how many women who actually had would recommend it. My readers were fabulous. But other people online scared and saddened me. I'd learned to avoid comments like the plague. As the goddess Taylor Swift said, our energy was expensive and not everyone deserved it. I was learning that lesson, but it had taken me some time to get there.

"You didn't want me to ruin it for you." My mom's voice held a lot of sadness.

"It wasn't just that, Mom," I started to say.

"But that was part of it. I know how I can be." She stepped forward and grabbed my hand to give it a squeeze before she stepped back with a shrug. "I would have been so excited for you—I'd want to tell the world and see how you were running ads, what your social media campaign was, if you were doing a blog tour—" She held up her hands in a "what are you going to do" gesture. "Sorry, sweetness, it's the only way I know how to be."

"Full steam ahead, gas pedal on the floor, one hundred percent of the time." Dad stepped up and put his arm around her, kissing the top of her head. "But babe." He nodded to Lou and Verdell at his side. "We would have tried to reel her in."

I raised my eyebrows and looked at Aunt Lou.

Verdell chuckled. "Well, your dad and I would have tried."

Lou elbowed him in the stomach and winked at me. "Jules, we're dang proud of you, whether or not we knew about it from the beginning. And I'm here to say you write some *steamy scenes*. Why, Verdell benefited from those, didn't you dear?"

I slapped my hands over my ears like a child. "Lou! This is another reason you didn't know before."

Lou cackled.

My dad looked to the ceiling like he was begging for patience from above. My mom stepped over to her sister and linked their arms together before facing me. "We won't talk about my thoughts on those scenes, though the fact that I'd already read all of them tells you something." She winked at me.

I groaned.

"Now." Lou looked at me with a serious and determined expression, which didn't really fit her. "How did this impact your stress before you moved down here? Is this what caused the Chicago meltdown?"

"Well, I think you and Mom were right—moving down here was a good idea for me for a multitude of reasons, though I didn't see it then." I looked to Noah, and he nodded, telling me to keep going. I stepped from him to Mom and Lou, leading them to the kitchen table so we could sit together for a moment. "Working for that firm was a lot..."

"Those bastards. They didn't appreciate you." My mom positively growled. Mama bear was here—watch out. She hadn't even latched on to the notion that she was right. Amazing.

"Want me to spread rumors about them online?" Lou asked. "I'd be happy to, and so would my friends."

I shook my head. She was such a menace, but she was ours. "No, Lou. Let's not send your senior citizen friends into online forums to cause havoc. That's already happening enough in this world."

Noah laughed behind us. I turned and saw him standing at the island with my dad and Verdell as they piled food onto plates. Jesus, the Spencers. I needed to wrap this up.

"Anyway, yes, my job was a lot. I was experiencing writer's block this winter because writing when you know lots of people are reading your books is interesting. I'd seen some negative reviews. And mostly I've realized I was lonely. My closest friend was Kylie, but she has a full life beyond me, and I couldn't ask her to spend all her time at my side—that's ridiculously needy. The rest of the people in my life were just acquaintances; I've heard nothing from them since moving." I sighed. "Trying to do it all was getting exhausting, so you were right—the move was necessary and good for me." I watched my mom, waiting for her to say "I told you so." But as she often did, she surprised me.

Looking at my book that was on the table, she said, "Aren't you selling a lot of copies of these? I have several friends who recommended them to me."

"Yes," I replied, not seeing where she was going with this.

She tilted her head and looked at me. "Why are you still working? I know authors don't make a lot per book, but if you have the numbers of readers I think you are, can't that replace your accounting salary, or at least most of it?"

My heart beat harder as we hit the topic that I'd been struggling with. "I can replace it, but I wouldn't want to disappoint Sue—she took a risk with me." I immediately held up a hand as Lou started to interrupt me. "And I like the security of a salary and health insurance." Then I gave a nod to Lou, telling her she could speak now.

"Work part-time," Lou said simply.

"What?"

She shrugged. "Work part-time. You still help give Sue some wiggle room with hours that work for you. And I know you don't know all the folks who work there well yet, but there are many that only work there part-time. Some just work during tax season, but several are part-time all year because that's what they prefer. They pay into the health insurance that Sue provides for full-time workers. She also pays part of it for her part-time folks. Her belief is that if she creates a position that meets your needs, you're happier and do better work."

My mind was whirling. I could have a stable salary, albeit half of what I was used to, but something I could count on, and it could cushion the up-and-down nature of publishing plus give me more time to write. I could have health insurance. Could it be so easy? "Do you think she'd be interested in that kind of arrangement?"

"I can almost guarantee it, but you also have an ace up your sleeve," Lou said with a knowing smile.

"What?"

Her smile widened. "Sue is a huge fan of the romance author Jules Jenkins."

"What?" My voice was far too loud for this space.

Lou laughed a huge belly laugh. "Yep, she's who recommended your first book to the book club and she is also a member. Didn't you see her at the all-male revue the other night?"

I held up my hand. "We don't speak of that night ever."

My mom looked to Lou with a knowing look. "Tell me later?"

"Absolutely."

"So we're good?" Mom asked.

"We're good," I said. "I'm sorry I didn't tell you all sooner."

Mom got up and came around the table, pulling me into her arms. "We know now, baby girl. And we are so proud of you."

"Let's eat," said Lou, rubbing her hands together as she surveyed the buffet of goodness.

Ivy poked her head in the kitchen. "Are you all done?"

I laughed. "Yes, sorry you all had to vacate and I've hijacked the day. We need to celebrate the birthday girl and open some presents."

Ivy shook her head. "No worries about that. Addie is happy with any party with donuts, and we make the birthday-party idea low-key so she doesn't become a monster about it. There isn't even a cake, just some gifts to open in a few. However... can we now talk about you doing a signing at the bookstore? Because Jules, my friend, I have plans for you, girl."

Noah came up behind me and whispered in my ear, "I think it's your turn to brace."

I gave him a huge smile. Ivy could make the plans she wanted; I didn't care. People knew now about my writing, they were all happy for me, and I felt free.

Chapter 28

Darkest of Days

Noah

I sat in front of my computer, impatiently checking the time as I waited for the video call to start. My boss had said we needed to do a quick meeting today because she wanted to run something by me. I'd rearranged my day, and I was hoping to get this over with quickly so I could run some errands before I picked up Addie from school.

I thought of Jules and wondered if I could see her tonight. She'd been scarce this week because her parents were staying at her place and Addie was at mine. We still found the time to talk via text, but I knew we needed to see each other face-to-face, or at least I did. After being together for a week straight, time apart like this felt like too much distance.

We'd agreed we were trying something, but it felt like we hadn't had a conversation we needed to. We were on the same page, right? I'd texted this morning to see how long her parents were going to be in town and if they all wanted to come to my place to have dinner with us, but I hadn't heard back from her, which was unusual. I glanced at my phone, but still no reply.

I was just picking it up to send her another message when my monitor showed the call starting, so I put my phone to the side. Karen's face came on the screen as I made sure my mic and video were all set. I was taken aback by her appearance. She had shadows under her eyes and looked strung out, not at all like herself.

"Hey, Karen, you okay?"

We'd worked closely together for years, and I'd never seen her like this. She was typically unflappable and always put together.

Karen sighed, exhaustion visible even through the screen. "Noah, I'm cutting to the chase because we share a distaste for bullshit."

"To be fair, I don't believe anyone enjoys the taste." I tried to joke, but I could see it fell flat, which only increased my concern.

"We've lost major funding."

"Wait, what?" We had multiple streams of funding to avoid any catastrophes. I'd had some meetings earlier in the month to deal with a few issues, but I thought they'd been resolved.

"The grants we were able to secure in the past have been reallocated due to the current federal climate. We haven't had as many donations this year, and costs across the board have all gone up."

She shared her screen, and I looked at the numbers she was referring to. This was bleak.

"What are you saying?" My heart was jackhammering in my chest. I had a damn good feeling I knew what was coming.

"Noah, I'm sorry. I've been looking at these numbers for

the better part of a month. You have a ton of seniority in the company, so you're not out a job, but the only positions currently open are on location in Africa." Karen looked like she might vomit.

I wanted to join her.

Africa. I loved the place, but I knew it wasn't where I belonged anymore. Addie had just turned six. Last night I'd lain in her room under the large castle canopy we'd gotten her for her birthday to go over her bed. She had a matching one at Jake and Ivy's place. She'd told me her bedtime stories as I lay beside her and cataloged all the ways she had changed already in the past eighteen months of seeing her daily.

I couldn't leave her again, but what was I going to do?

"Karen, when do you need to know my answer?" I asked, figuring that was the fastest way off this call.

"I can give you a week," she said. "Noah, for what it's worth, I'm so damn sorry. Maybe in a year or so we'd be able to get you back in the States, but with the fluctuations in funding, it's too precarious right now."

"Not your fault. Thanks for looking out for me." With a wave, I signed off and dropped my head to my desk.

I sat there for a few moments, feeling sorry for myself. I had worked for this company for eight years. What else did I know beyond this world? Maybe I could find a job locally. Or I could give whatever funds we could access from my inheritance as a donation, but I didn't know how quickly I could get my hands on anything. And, frankly, would that fix the fact I needed to stay local? How long would it fund my position? Would the company even want to funnel the money to ensure I could still stay stateside? Maybe they already had more pressing needs.

In the future with the estate settled, I wouldn't need to

work full-time, but that wasn't helpful now. Also, I knew bone-deep I'd need something fulfilling work-wise to be happy. Most people wouldn't understand that, but after a lifetime of watching people in my parents' sphere live off inheritances, that wasn't for me.

My stomach churned with unanswered questions, and I found myself getting up and heading out my back door and to Jules's house before I even really put it together. I needed to see her; I had before the call and now it was imperative.

I reached her back door and was surprised to find it locked. I rang the bell once, but nothing. I knocked.

"Jules?" I called. I rang the bell again. *Please be here, please be here.*

The door swung open, and in it stood a tall dark-haired woman I didn't recognize. She had long hair piled on top of her head and more freckles on her face than I had seen on most adults.

"Who are you?" I asked.

She batted her eyes at me. "Your fantasies come to life. Who are you, gorgeous?"

I shook my head, so confused. What the hell was happening? "Where's Jules?"

The woman looked at me with an assessing glance. "Went with her dad to get more moving boxes." She gestured behind her, and I saw boxes stacked in front of Jules's favorite kitchen nook. "Want me to pass on a message?"

I blinked, willing everything to make sense. Nope, still didn't. I stepped away and then turned and jogged back to my house as I heard the door shut behind me. Moving boxes? Her house was being packed up? Not replying to my messages? What was going on here?

Thirty minutes later, after pacing my house and trying

to call Jules no less than ten times, I still had no answers. I'd taken off to pick up Addie with my stomach in knots, taking the scenic route to her school to try to get my mind right. Now not only was I unsure about my job, but a relationship I'd decided to pursue looked like it was going to crash and burn and I didn't understand why.

My mind raced, thinking about showing up at Jules's house to find that she was moving and I hadn't known. Was I not enough for her? Was Highland Falls not what she'd expected? Or now that her family knew about her writing career, was she less fearful of diving into life as a best-selling author? I'm sure she figured out she could do better than a single dad in a small town who didn't have his shit together in the slightest.

Yep, I was all up in my feelings. Seeing Addie would help me put everything in perspective and was exactly what I needed. I pulled up to Addie's school only to find I was running late. There were only a few kids still on the playground, and most of them appeared to be playing on the equipment while their parents watched from the sides.

I got out of my car, checking the time. Yep, fifteen minutes late. I was so preoccupied that I had my head up my ass and had missed pickup. Shit. I scanned the kids, but where was Addie? I jogged to the school and saw Addie's teacher standing by the door, talking to the principal. I knew them both, so I headed in that direction.

"Ms. Tracy, so sorry to interrupt, but I'm late to pickup and I don't see Addie." I was breathless at that point. The run hadn't been hard, but everything else about the past hour sure had been.

Addie's teacher turned toward me and gave me a reassuring smile. "Oh hey, Mr. Lawson. No worries—Addie's grandfather picked up today. Sorry, he thought you knew."

I looked at her in confusion for a moment. Clearly she wasn't referring to my dad, and I'd fall over in shock if Ivy's dad ever lowered himself to pick up his grandchild from school.

"Which grandfather," I asked for confirmation, though I had a good guess. Really, the only one that would make sense.

Ms. Tracy double-checked her clipboard. "Sam Spencer. That's okay, right? He's on the approved pickup list."

I nodded, not wanting her to worry because Sam was welcome to pick up Addie, I just usually knew if he was. "Yeah, I must have just gotten some wires crossed."

She nodded. "I'm sure it's hard to keep track of schedules at times. For what it's worth, I think you all do a fabulous job of co-parenting. Addie is a lucky girl to have so many people around her that care about her."

Ouch. Shot to the heart. I nodded and waved as I headed back to my car where my phone was. As soon as I got in, I started it up and dialed Sam's number. No answer. I tried Margot and bingo, she answered in one.

"Afternoon, Noah. Isn't it a beautiful day?"

"Hey Margot. I'm somehow screwing up all over the place today. Did Sam pick up Addie?" My heart was thundering in my chest, thought logic was telling me that everything was fine.

"Yes, he picked her up to have their goodbye tea party. We're heading home in a few hours, but we'll be down again in a few weeks." Then she paused. "Oh no, didn't Ivy message you?"

I exhaled for the first time in an hour, though there was plenty to still stress about. "Ah, no, she must have gotten sidetracked. No problem."

Margot was quiet for a moment, which was always dangerous. "Noah, you don't sound great. Come on over to Jake and Ivy's. I'll make you a snack or Sam can make you a drink."

"No, I don't want to intrude on your time with the grandkids."

"Noah." Her voice had the don't-fuck-with-me tone she got at times. "Get your ass over here."

"Yes, ma'am," I replied because there was no arguing with Margot Spencer. The woman had raised Jake and Drew. Steph too, but I'd heard stories about the Spencer boys. Margot might be small, but she was mighty, and if she were Catholic, she'd likely qualify for sainthood. I hung up and headed that way.

Just before pulling up in the drive, my phone rang. I looked at it eagerly, hoping it was Jules. Nope, Ivy.

"Hey, Ivy," I said as I answered.

"Noah, I'm so sorry. I meant to call you and tell you Sam was going to grab Addie and bring her to you for dinner, but I got waylaid by a shipment, a sick employee, and a leak in our bathroom at the store. I'm so sorry! Did you go to the school? I am the worst. I owe you a case of beer from the Homestead. Or Jake and I can have you over for dinner every night next week. Sorry, sorry, sorry. Do you forgive me?" The woman gasped for air because that entire moment of verbal diarrhea sounded like it came out in one breath.

Despite my afternoon, she still made me smile like she had been doing since we were young. "Ivy, you're fine. I figured it out. Margot ordered me to come over, and I just pulled up to your place."

She was immediately on alert. "Why did she order you to come over?"

"No idea. Heading in to find out."

"Noah, are you okay?"

"Totally fine. See you soon."

"Okay, if you're sure. Frankly, better you than me, my friend. And for what it's worth, I really am sorry."

"Promise we're good."

I started to hang up, but then she spoke again. "Hey, Noah?"

"Yeah?"

"I'm so glad you live in Highland Falls. Even when I screw up, it's pretty great co-parenting with you."

I looked at the phone. What the fuck, universe? Are we just wanting to kick a man when he's down today or what?

Shaking my head, I refocused. "Thanks, Ivy. Back at you. Now I need to go see what your mother-in-law wants."

"All right. Talk soon." She hung up, and I swung out of the car and headed to the house.

When I hit the back porch, I saw Margot in the kitchen, clearly waiting for me. Super. I walked in and put on a smile, hoping I could do one of those fake-it-till-you-make-it moments and then hit the road. "Hey Margot, how's the tea party? Is Lorelai part of this too?"

Margot gave me a look that said she wasn't buying what I was selling. "Lorelai is with Jake; Addie and Sam are in the living room with tea, snacks, and *Bluey*. And now I'm ready to find out what's going on with you." She pointed to a stool at the counter. "Sit."

I debated trying to bullshit her, but one look at her expression told me that would be for naught. I sat.

Margot bustled around the kitchen for a few minutes before putting a plate of warm chocolate chip cookies and a glass of milk in front of me. I looked from the snack up to her and tilted my head. I mean, I was all for cookies and milk, but I also wasn't six.

"I could give you a beer, but when my boys had a lot on their minds and were struggling with being vulnerable human beings and letting it out so someone else could help them carry their burdens, this did the trick." She gave me an expression that said she dared me to stay silent.

I thought about it for a few beats, but then I was done. I wasn't done with the events of the day; I was done carrying it all for thirty years, mostly on my own. I could count on one hand the amount of times my parents had asked me to share my troubles with them, and I didn't even have to think about it. Zero times. Didn't even need a finger or a thumb.

I'd learned early you got through it all on your own. Mary was there for me in the ways she could be, and without her, who knows how I would have made it. But Mary could only do so much because Lord knew if my parents had seen her showing that she cared about me, they would have told her I needed to toughen up and the real world didn't care about my feelings.

So today, in Jake and Ivy's kitchen, I laid them all down. All of it. With tears welling up, I told Margot about everything: the fact that as much as I had already given up on my parents, it hurt to know that I would never have the chance for them to change; my call from work and the decision I had ahead of me; my fear that I wasn't enough as a dad; my concern that I'd missed out on a chance at a relationship with Jules and didn't know what I'd done but was worried that I hadn't been enough.

It all came out. Sitting at the counter, I didn't feel like a thirty-year-old man but the small boy who had been begging his parents to give a damn about him and had them turn their backs time and time again until he had to find somewhere else to pour his love into the world so that he wouldn't turn out just like them.

Margot rushed around the counter and wrapped me in her embrace. I sank into it, feeling the love she poured out as she held me and rocked me back and forth, not telling me it would be okay but just allowing me to feel. It was like a dam had been holding back all these emotions, and now they were free and they just needed to be let out. Every exhale felt like another boulder off my chest.

I heard the door open and close behind me, and I assumed it was Ivy, likely concerned about our call from earlier. As I took another deep breath, Margot stepped back and a new pair of arms came around me. I opened my eyes and saw Jules, my Jules. I shook my head, feeling like I'd somehow imagined her. I looked from her to Margot, who raised her hand before I could say a word.

"Noah, you beautiful boy, I think you and Jules need to head to your house and talk. We've got Addie. Jake and Ivy can keep her tonight, and you can work out what you need to, but listen to me when I tell you a few things. One, some people aren't meant to be parents." My heart thumped, but then she continued. "Get that look off your face, son. You are the best dad there is. Addie is blessed beyond measure. How you came from the two robots that were your parents from what you said, from what Ivy has told me, is a miracle that we should all thank God for."

"Or goddess." Jules spoke up. "Also Mary—Noah had Mary."

Margot nodded. "Yes, I think we all have a lot to thank Mary for. So it isn't on you who your parents were. And because you are the caring individual that you are, of course you grieve for what might have been. That also speaks volumes to your nature. Two, jobs are jobs. You can support your passion without giving it your lifeblood. Three"—she nodded toward Jules—"communication is critical. Always. Don't leave things left unsaid, and always talk before jumping to conclusions. That's how Sam and I have survived all these years. Grand gestures are for the romance books Jules writes. The real love stories are built on small moments and being heard, over and over, until eternity."

She stepped forward and kissed my cheek and then looked to Jules. "Remember this for your books, Jules Maxwell Jenkins, the truth is that we all just want to be known by the ones we care about. That's all, but it's everything. Now, you two, head on out of here. I have a tea party to attend."

With that she swanned out of the kitchen to join Sam and Addie. I debated following her if only to see Addie, but I'd seen her this morning, and if I felt like it, I could come back for dinner. Margot was right—I'd jumped to a lot of conclusions with Jules and there was so much I hadn't said. It was time to remedy that even if I didn't love her answers.

"What's going on, Noah?" Jules wiped moisture from my cheeks. "I got home from the hardware store, and Kylie told me someone had come over looking for me but hadn't left their name. She described you and the direction you'd headed when you left, and I assumed it was you. Then I saw that my phone was dead and plugged it in to see a ton of missed calls and a few texts. Before I could call you back, Ivy called and said you were here and sounded like something might be up, so I came right away."

I exhaled. More boulders fell. Jesus. What a day. But this didn't need to happen here. "Want to go for a walk?"

She tilted her head, trying to read my face. "Your car is here."

"It's fine. I need to walk."

She nodded and stepped back, allowing me to get up. Linking her hand with mine, she headed for the door. Then she paused, spun around, let go, and moved back to the counter to grab two of Margot's cookies. She handed me one. "Okay, let's go."

I laughed, and out we went, eating the goodness that was a chocolate chip cookie fresh from the oven.

I steered us in the direction of our houses, and we headed down the quiet afternoon streets of Highland Falls. Brilliant blue late-April sky above was dotted with a few clouds. The trees were budding, and I could see just the beginning of the tulips coming up. Addie would be ecstatic. I didn't walk far before I started talking.

"It's been the darkest of days."

"I can see that."

I let out a long, measured breath and then spilled out my concerns. I told her about the work call. About the worry in the back of my mind that I wasn't enough for her. That I was concerned we hadn't talked enough about what we wanted. That I'd come over and thought she was moving. I told her all of it. I figured if I had this shot, I was going for broke. Finally, in front of a mini park on a side street, I tugged her hand over and sat down on a bench in front of what would be a gorgeous bed of landscaping in just a few months. Right then it just held the promise of what was to come, much like I hoped we did.

"Jules, I don't know what your future holds. I'm not sure why you're packing up your house, and I don't know where you're going. I don't know what my job will be in a few weeks, but I know my place is here with Addie. I can't leave. If you need to, I won't hold you back. But I hope you will consider a long-distance relationship because what I realized today while running around this town like a crazy person was that while I thought the job would be the worst thing that could happen to me today, what was ten times harder was coming to the deep understanding that I love two women—one is six and one is sitting in front of me. And I might be pulled in two directions if they aren't in the same place, but somehow I deeply want to make this work. I haven't felt a lot of love in my life, but that's what was buoying me during a horrible week last week. I'm not a fool, and I'm sorry that sometimes I act like one. I know it's fast and you don't have to feel the same yet, but I love you and I need you to know it."

The final boulders fell, and I could breathe freely.

Chapter 29

Feeling That Way

Jules

"...I love you and I need you to know it."

As Noah finished a romance monologue that I wished I could have my heroes say, he looked at peace. My heart broke for him because what I'd seen when I walked into Jake and Ivy's was just that, heartbreaking. As flighty as my parents were, I thought of all the times over the years that I'd come to them for advice, to dry my tears, just to be held. Noah hadn't had that, not even anything close. And today, he'd found some comfort in Margot. I was grateful he had that, but I wanted so much more for him. I wanted to be that. I wanted him to get that from my parents, from Lou and Verdell. I wanted him to feel love coming from every direction and have an endless supply of support, anywhere he could turn.

"Jules?"

I looked up and realized I'd gotten lost in my head again.

"Sorry, sorry, I was just thinking of how much I love you

and what I want for you in this world," I said, still thinking of the best way to support him.

"I'm sorry, did you just say you love me too?"

I looked at him in confusion. "Yes, of course. I thought that was established."

He gave me a brilliant smile. "For a romance writer, you don't feel like you need a long-winded speech?"

I laughed. "I mean, I thought in yours you mentioned you felt my love supporting you all week."

"True, true. But you can love someone like a friend, care about them. And I love you like that but more."

I got up to sit on his lap.

"Oh my, Ms. Maxwell, is this appropriate?"

"Hush. It is for this." I put my palms on either side of his face. "Noah Michael Lawson, I love you. Frankly, you are all my romance heroes come to life. I think I fell a little in love with you when I saw you walk into the Homestead the first time. I know I did when I saw you holding Addie's hand. When I saw you with her, it was there. Watching you with Mary and realizing how deeply your soul craved love. I felt it when we were in the kitchen, when I slept by your side in the dark, in the silence of our everyday life, on the car ride back to Highland Falls, in all the little things you do for me. The way you treat me told me you cared too. Watching you sleep, waking up next to you, I knew I was in love with you. I just didn't want to scare you by telling you, which I now know was just stupid." I pressed a kiss to his lips.

Noah dropped his head to my chest and wrapped his arms around my waist. I had mine around his shoulders and we just sat together, breathing.

Then he leaned back and looked at me. "So why are you moving?"

I looked at him in confusion, then thought of my house. "Oh, because the boxes?"

He nodded.

"Oh, you sweet man. We are the ultimate miscommunication storyline of one of my books. My dad was checking my rental out. The foundation in the front room is shot. I called my landlord this morning, and fortunately she knows of a mason who has time in his schedule to do some work next week. I'm clearing out that room because they're jacking the house up to fix the foundation and I just figured if it got dusty or anything, it would be easier."

He dropped his head to my chest again. "Not moving."

I kissed the top of his head. "Not moving."

"And that was Kylie?"

"Yep. Did she hit on you?"

"A bit."

I snorted. "She wasn't serious, just who she is."

He didn't lift his head, just nodded his understanding. "Is she staying?"

"For the weekend. I figured she could have my bed." I waited for him to put the pieces together.

He lifted his head. "And you will stay..."

I shrugged. "In yours? If you're okay with that when Addie is over."

Noah leaned his head up and pressed a kiss to my mouth. "I'm very okay with it when Addie is over, but I think she can stay with Jake and Ivy tonight. Maybe a big dinner for all of us—including Addie, the Spencers, your parents and Kylie—at the Homestead? And then you and I can celebrate finally getting our communication down at home in my bed?"

I traced a finger along his jaw. "Sounds good, but we

could also do a little pre-celebration in your bed oh, I don't know, say in ten minutes or so if we walk fast."

Noah held me tight as he rose, and I slid down his body and then stood in front of him. "I think we can make it closer to seven if we run." He grabbed my hand and tugged me to get started as I laughed.

Forty-five minutes later, I was running my fingers over his abs and tracing his cock, which was spent. It twitched, and I looked up to him with a grin.

He snorted. "I can go again, but you'll have to give me at least ten minutes. I'm not twenty anymore."

"Poor baby." I was lying on my side, my head propped up on my hand as I took in the naked glory that was Noah. He had ruined me for writing sex scenes because nothing on paper would compare to the connection I felt with him. After he'd shared some of his fears, it was even better. Who knew?

"So, what do you want to do for a job?" I traced my hands over his chest simply because I could.

He put his hands behind his head and looked from me to the ceiling. I loved that he was on board with being a feast for my eyes right now. "I don't know. I want to still do something that gives back. I thought about using my inheritance to shore up the funds, but that doesn't seem right."

I ran a finger over a nipple, then over one side of his chest. I loved the feeling of his wiry chest hair over his muscles. There was a contrast that I struggled to figure out how to describe. Even so, there was something nagging in the back of my mind. "Using your inheritance to donate to worthy causes is admirable, but funding your job seems like a short-term solution. You could benefit lots of organizations instead of just one if you plan it out."

He nodded. "That sounds good. I also have been

thinking I originally went to Africa because it was something I heard about when I was young and I wanted to do something to put good in this world that was counter to the negativity my parents were pouring into it. But I don't have to go to Africa to do good, I'm just not sure where to start."

I sat up stark naked and didn't even care. "That's it!"

He looked up at me and slid a hand up my belly to rest on one breast. "This is lovely."

I slapped his hand. "Not the time, babe. I just remembered what was nagging me."

He squeezed my breast because of course he did. "I am happy to nag you. I think I'm almost ready to go again if that helps."

I scooted back and put a hand out to stop him from following me. "Stay there, sir. You're going to want to hear this."

He rolled to his side and leaned his head on his hand. "Fine, fine, say your piece, kitten."

"I met a woman named Cristin at work this week. She's a friend of Sue's and heads up some multicounty nonprofit that links donors with needs in this area. They fund everything from educational initiatives to community-engagement ideas to scholarships, micro grants, and so much more. She was saying they've grown so much in the past few years that she was drafting up a new leadership position for their group. After she left, Sue said she was beyond impressed with everything they were doing." I sat, my mind spinning on what that could mean for Noah. "You could apply for that job, and if that doesn't work out, there's the University of Illinois. I'm sure they'd have something in their foundation. Heck, there are so many local opportunities if you don't have to be worried about a huge salary, which you wouldn't."

Noah pulled himself up to sitting and faced me. "Can I touch you now?"

I shrugged. "I suppose."

He reached out and pulled me to him as I clambered to straddle his lap and wrap my arms around his shoulders.

"Thanks for caring about me," he whispered before kissing me.

I fell into our kiss, never tiring of the way we could move from light pecks to a kiss that felt like being devoured. I was so hungry for this man. It was soon and I cared not at all; he was it for me. I wanted to be by his side as he figured out a new job. I wanted to be with him as he continued to deal with the impact his parents had on his life. I couldn't wait to see Mary again and celebrate who she had been—and still was—in his life. The idea of watching him raise Addie from the sassy and spunky six-year-old she was into the woman she would become sounded like perfection. And the notion that we might have our own kids one day... Well, there weren't words to describe how that filled me up.

I pulled back for just a moment. "Hey, Noah?"

He pressed his lips to mine and then drew away. "Hey, Jules."

I moved to his ear and whispered, "I'm so glad I moved here."

He turned to look at me with a beautiful smile. "Me too." And then he flipped me on my back and proceeded to show me how much once again.

Two hours later, we walked into the Homestead hand in hand. The place was hopping for a Thursday night. We weaved through tables to get to the section of low tables and couches in the bar area where I could already see our crew gathered. But more than that, as I looked at some high tables around the area, I saw my parents, the Spencers, Lou and Verdell. Sue was with Lou, and I waved at her. She and I had a great talk earlier in the week, and she had been on board with me working part-time after I signed all her books and had a half-hour conversation about my plans for the series. Far from being annoyed about it, I informed her she'd just become one of my beta readers when she remembered details I hadn't. She was thrilled.

As we finally reached our friends, I smiled. Kylie was right in the mix, sitting between Maggie and Maeve, Kristine from the yoga studio across from them. While I didn't know everyone super well yet, I knew that would be a dangerous group. Addie was stretched out on the floor with her coloring supplies and a ton of little farm animals set up in some type of scene. She looked over to Noah and me and blew us a kiss before getting back to work.

"So I hear we have a famous author in the mix." Maeve spoke up.

Kylie held up her hands. "It wasn't me."

Ivy raised a hand. "It was me. I already have some posters I'm putting up in the shop. Hope that's okay."

"Absolutely." I loved how this group of people were in each other's lives. I'd never had anything like this, but I was there for it.

"Do we need to go to another male revue in the name of research?" Kristine asked, a smirk on her face. "I'm happy to do so."

"Me too," Maeve said as Levi shook his head.

"I'm good with not going again," I said to the boos of some of the ladies, some nods from others.

"I'm going to grab us a drink," Noah said, but before he could get away, Drew and Kate walked up with another guy who seemed to fit right into the Highland Falls model—tall, scruffy, and gorgeous.

Drew spoke up. "Hey guys, do you remember James? He was here last year for a week or so and we worked together in the hotshots in Colorado. James, our crew." He gestured at all of us. "Guys, James."

I watched the table and noted that Kylie was giving me an expression. I tilted my head to ask what was up and she nodded at Kristine, who got up and stormed out. I watched her go, but then Drew's friend noted the same thing and took off after her. Kylie and I exchanged a glance, and I looked to Noah.

"I have no idea, kitten, but we're staying out of it."

"Noah, think of this as research..."

He laughed and pulled me to him. "I love you."

"Love you too." I kissed him. "Now I'll take one of those rosé ciders if they have it."

"On it." He took off, and I looked around the space. So many people I cared about: my family, new friends, my boss, Addie, Noah. They knew who I was, no secrets, no changing to be like other people to fit in. They liked me for me and didn't expect me to be anyone different. I'd found my own real-life romance story, and it was better than anything I could have written.

Was it love? It was feeling that way and even more. It was forever.

Epilogue

Six Months Later

Noah

I walked into my house to the noise of chaos, which I loved. My work for the foundation could often be done from home, though today I'd met with some colleagues at the Sanctuary Café where we brainstormed goals for the next year in terms of fundraising and the kinds of grants we wanted to branch out to. I felt like I was making a difference locally, and it was far more rewarding than I had ever anticipated.

In an added bonus, the money my parents left me was more than I could comprehend, but there was enough that I could give to many worthwhile organizations in big ways while still holding on to enough to make our lives comfortable. Addie was set, as was Lorelai because that was her sister. Any kids that Jules and I had would be too. And retirement would not be a concern, whenever that came about. It was the peace of mind I didn't know I needed, that my parents certainly hadn't had as a goal, but I appreciated it nonetheless.

And while I knew Jules hadn't planned on it, with her

upbringing I knew it gave her some solace as well. Not that it mattered—she was one of the hardest workers I knew. She had followed the suggestion of Lou and was working for Sue part-time while writing. She could easily write full-time, but she liked the variety that working for Sue brought to her life, and she said their clients gave her endless story inspiration. She also insisted on paying for her own insurance through Sue, though I'd be happy to do it. One monthly expense that had been eliminated, however, was her rent.

Jules had moved into my place three months ago. To her surprise, Kylie had fallen in love with Highland Falls and had come down to work for Sue as well. It was early in our relationship to live together some might say, but I'd have been happy to have her with me from day one. In fact, any nights we had been apart had been ones where I slept like shit. Just the mere presence of her in my bed brought me relaxation. It was like how I slept better when Addie was at our house. Not that Jake and Ivy weren't perfectly safe and their place also her home, it was just that life felt "right" when she was here. Same for Jules. She was it for me and I was for her. We just knew.

"Hey, big guy," I said to O'Malley, who was lounging on the couch. He'd somehow piled the pillows up in his version of a nest and was curled up in a ball. "They hanging out in the kitchen?"

The cat gave me a look that if he could speak would say "duh." I ran my hand down his back anyway and was greeted with a loud purr. He was my first cat, and I had to say I didn't know if there was another one like him out there. We'd talked about getting a puppy as well, Addie was campaigning hard, but for now O'Malley was enough.

Moving through the dining room, I paid attention to the sounds coming from the kitchen. Clearly Addie and Jules were making dinner. I heard music coming from the speakers we had in there. Addie had always been a big fan of Fleetwood Mac, though I missed when she'd mispronounce their name. Her new favorite came from their rerelease of an old album. "Crying in the Night" was one of her favorites, and as I stood just beyond the door where she couldn't see me, I worked to commit her sweet voice to memory as she sang about things that she couldn't yet comprehend.

"When am I going to see your mama and daddy again, Jules?" she said.

I heard Jules at the oven, shutting the door. "Hmm, that's a great question. I think they're currently driving through the northeast part of the country to see the leaves turn colors in the fall, and then they plan on heading back this way. Do you want to look at the pictures they posted on their account on my iPad?"

"Maybe after dinner." I had a feeling that Addie was twirling or something because her voice was a little breathless.

"Hey, Jules, why doesn't O'Malley like a dance party?" she asked, making me smile. She strongly believed Chief, Jake and Ivy's lab, did. I think Chief would beg to differ, though he sure did love her.

"O'Malley is a lazybones," Jules said, and I could hear the smile in her voice. "He loves lounging with you when you're reading though."

"Hey, Jules?" Addie asked again. Bless her six-year-old heart. The girl had a lot of questions.

"Yeah, peanut," Jules said, turning off the sink.

"When can I call you Mommy like I call Jake Daddy? I think it's cool to have two Daddies."

Jules was silent, I'm sure as she tried to process what

would be the right answer. What I knew was that my kid had just given me the moment I was looking for. I stepped over to the buffet in the dining room and slid the drawer open quietly, pulling out the ring box I had put in there weeks ago. I knew I wanted to marry Jules. We had already talked about it. But in the past six months we'd moved in together, I'd started a new job, she'd finished a book and edited it, and today she'd released it into the world. Our friends had wanted to have a release party. She explained that she just wanted to be home today, but this weekend we'd gather and celebrate.

And it looked like we could celebrate more than the release of her fifth book.

I stepped into the kitchen where Addie was facing me and Jules was kneeling in front of her, saying something. It was derailed because Addie let out a shriek.

"Daddy!"

I caught her as she ran around Jules and gave me an exuberant hug.

"Hey, peanut." I gave her a smacking kiss. "Can you go grab the special picture you made for Jules that we put in the living room?"

Addie squirmed for me to let her run free. "On it," she shouted, right hand up in the air as she charged off.

One of the things Margot had told me was the hardest about kids was that you missed the lasts. You remembered their first steps, first words, first experiences. But the last time they called you Daddy instead of Dad. The last time they wanted to hold your hand as they walked into school. The last time they greeted you as if they hadn't seen you in weeks instead of a few hours. Those were missed because you didn't know they were lasts until later. Once Margot told me that, I began trying to soak it all in even more.

In case it wasn't obvious, Margot had appointed herself my surrogate mom. She was fighting for that title with Lou, Frannie, and Mary. Much like Addie felt about Jake and me as her dads, I was happy to report there was room for all my surrogate parents, and I felt their love deep in my soul. It was healing.

"Noah." Jules was up and coming my way. She gave me a kiss, and her eyes twinkled. "Your daughter is a chatterbox tonight."

"Is that any different than usual?" I gave her a wry smile.

She shook her head. "Nope."

"How is release day going?" I moved around her to pour myself a glass of water, hoping she wouldn't notice my shaking hands. I knew she'd say yes, but part of me felt like no moment would be perfect enough for this woman. I didn't want to screw it up.

"Great so far. And thanks for the flowers, though you didn't need to do that."

"Got it," Addie said when she returned. The drawing was rolled up, string tied around it like a little diploma.

"Why don't you give that to Jules, peanut." I said, my heart hammering.

Jules gave me a curious look.

"Here you go," Addie said in a singsong voice.

"Thanks, babe." Jules gave her a hug in return and slid the string off and unrolled it. She bent down by Addie and let her lean against her chest while she surrounded her with her arms, the drawing unfurled in front of them. "Tell me about your picture."

Addie studied it and pointed to each person and the word above them on the picture. "There's Momma, Daddy Two, baby Lorelai, and Chief. Then over here there's Daddy, you, O'Malley, and me in the middle of everyone."

Jules looked up at me with watery eyes, then back to Addie. "What's written above my drawing, sweetheart?"

"Momma Two. I mean, I don't call Jake Daddy Two anymore, just when I draw sometimes it helps. I thought I could do that for you too, which is why I asked." Addie was shimmying, which meant she was feeling happy.

"And what's it say at the top, Ads," I prodded.

"My family."

Then I saw a tear make its way over Jules's cheek and knew I was up. They were already kneeling, so I joined them, coming to my knees in front of them both.

"Jules, this wasn't how I planned your release day to go, but I know an opening when I see it. And to be honest, I've been ready for this for a while." I pulled the box out of my pocket and opened it.

"Ooohhh, pretty," Addie said, running her finger over the ring set with an opal and pink spinel.

"I'm guessing most of your heroes don't propose with a six-year-old in attendance, but it seems pretty on par for us, so I'm going for it." I slid the ring out of the box and held it out to her. "Jules, I'd like nothing more than to make you Addie's second mom, but most importantly, my wife. I love you for everything you are and everything you stand for. Will you do me the greatest honor of becoming my wife?"

Addie had clocked what was happening, and her precious little face was frozen in an *o* while she made her surprised expression, compliments of reruns of the movie *Home Alone*.

Jules laughed when she realized what Addie was doing and pulled me to the two of them, making Addie sandwich herself between the two of us. "You bet your butt I will," she said before she pressed her mouth to mine in a quick kiss.

Pulling back after a moment, I slid the ring on her finger. "I heard you comment about this one at Melinda's shop, so I called and had them hold it for me. It's not your traditional engagement ring—"

"No, it's perfect and I love it," she said, holding up her hand.

"Dance party!" Addie shouted, squirming out from between us. We stood up and joined Addie in dancing around the kitchen. O'Malley even came in and wound his way through our legs. Our home was filled with love, light, and laughter. And it was perfect. Against all odds, I'd found what I'd been looking for.

Acknowledgments

Since I began writing romance books, I wanted a heroine to be a romance author. Because of who Noah is and where his story needed to go, I couldn't focus as much on Jules and her writing as I originally intended, but I absolutely gave her insecurities that I've had. I only wish to have a book go crazy on social media like she experienced.

That being said, writing is scary. Sending your creation out into the world knowing and expecting it to be judged is a bizarre feeling because the world you have created is just so much of you, or at least mine are.

The only way I've been able to do this has been to have the best support network in the world. Romance authors like Kate Canterbary, Sara Whitney, and Skye Malone have answered countless questions for me since I began this journey. A small but loyal group of folks make up my ARC team and send me the best messages for each book. Friends, family, colleagues, and community members—including the Hartfield Book Company—cheerlead each novel as it gets released. Kind readers who have found this series send me messages that fill me with joy. My new crew of students pestered me the first weeks of school this year, reminding me I needed to finish. And my husband remains my most loyal of beta readers, reading each chapter as I write it and giving immediate feedback.

It takes a village and I know how lucky I am to have this one, just as Jules is blessed to have hers.

Thank you.
xo,
Kat

About the Author

Kat Ryan is a middle school teacher by day and a budding romance author in the free time she steals for herself. She loves to write about small towns, found families, strong women, and cinnamon roll heroes that love them. She's a sucker for a HEA and more than a bit of steam in the stories she writes.

Kat lives in the Midwest with her husband and her two sons where she consumes a steady diet of coffee, chocolate, and romance books. And while her students and sons plan to never read the books she writes, her husband has and continues to cheer her on.

Want more from Noah and Jules? Subscribe to Kat's newsletter on her website, https://katryanwrites.com. All "extras" for each of Kat's book are linked in the newsletter that comes out every month.

Also by Kat Ryan